This book is entirely a work of fiction. The names, characters, and incidents portrayed in it are the work of the author's imagination. Any resemblance to actual persons, living or dead, events or localities is entirely coincidental.

www.onetruekev.co.uk

This paperback edition 2024

Copyright © Kev Neylon 2002, 2003, 2016, 2024

Kev Neylon asserts the moral right to be identified as the author of this work

A catalogue record for this book is available from the British Library

ISBN: 978-1-7385396-0-4

All rights reserved. No part of this publication may be reproduced, stored in a retrieval system, or transmitted, in any form or by any means, electronic, mechanical, photocopying, recording, or otherwise, without the prior permission of the author.

For Helen

Thank you for all your encouragement and support

And For Ann-Marie

Without you constantly asking where the next instalment was, this would have never been written.

Chapter 1

He was having that recurring dream for what felt like the thousandth time, as was the case every other time; he was strapped to a white padded table, with bright white light flooding the room he was in.

There were others in the room with him; they were similarly strapped to tables to his right-hand side, as far as he could tell there were at least another five people he could see. He couldn't be sure how many there were, or how far away they were, the brightness of the light in the room made the judgement of size and shape of the room virtually impossible, and although he could guess that they were on tables the same as the one he was on, he couldn't make out the tables, it looked like the other people in the room were hovering in the air.

There was nothing that he could make out to his left-hand side except bright whiteness. There didn't appear to be any single source for the light, it just seemed to explode out of every surface. It was painfully bright, meaning he spent most of the time with his eyes tightly shut, trying to keep the light out of his head. Stopping the brightness invading his brain like millions of tiny daggers, stabbing persistently away into his consciousness.

He briefly opened his eyes and one of his masked captors was stood over him, looking intently at him, seemingly impervious to the bright light that had been driving him insane. It was a man as far as he could tell, stood there in a white lab coat, and a white surgical mask, and what appeared to be a little white skull cap, much like the one that the pope would wear when in full dress robes.

The man had a large needle in his hand, from which he took the protective cap, and pressed gently on the plunger until a little liquid dribbled out of the end of the needle. Then without warning or ceremony, the needle was plunged deep into his upper thigh.

As normal at this point in the dream he woke up, resisting the temptation to open his eyes, always suspicious that when he did, he would find that the room he was in would be bathed in that bright unforgiving light, and he would be living that dream again.

He hadn't had the dream for a few weeks now; it had come to him less and less often nowadays, not like the times when it had been an almost nightly experience. Considering the amount he had had to drink the night before, he was surprised that he had been dreaming at all, let alone this one.

The dream always seemed so real, but his memories played tricks on him when he thought about it. Part of him told him that it was something that had happened to him several years before, and he seemed sure that it had, yet another part of his psyche was telling him that the repeated dreams were making him think that he was remembering a real event.

Chapter 2

He woke suddenly, shaken from his slumber by something deep in his consciousness, covered in sweat, and slightly disorientated, as was often the case after this dream. It was dark, a lot darker than expected, and he took a few seconds to remember that he was in a hotel room. The blackout blinds were drawn, and not a single ray of light could be seen peeping through.

He instinctively looked at his watch, only to realise as he moved his arm that it wasn't in the normal place on his wrist. Even if it had still been on his wrist, he doubted that he'd have been able to see it in the darkness. He couldn't remember taking it off before getting into bed, though that may have had more to do with the number of drinks he'd had the previous night, before getting into his bed.

He slowly dragged himself to a sitting position and after feeling where the edge of the bed was, swung his legs round to put his feet on the floor. As he edged along the side of the bed towards the foot of it, he could see some light filtering through from the corridor under the door into his room.

He reached over to switch on a light, and after a few seconds fumbling around, managed to switch on a light, finding the one that shone directly into his eyes, pretty much blinding himself. He shuddered at the memory of the dream it triggered as he closed his eyes, letting them settle for a few seconds, before moving his head away from the light and re-opening them, and looking around the room. He initially searched for his watch on the various surfaces around the room, but with no immediate success, he stood up, and walked gingerly to the bathroom, turning on another searing light, and then stood blinking at his reflection.

As normal, the hair and five o'clock shadow were in the exact same style, nothing ever seemed to change there, and he was happy to see there were no unidentified drinking injuries on his reflection, then again, he didn't expect to see anything untoward, his outward appearance never seemed to change no matter what had happened.

His watch was sat by the side of the sink, face down, with some remnants of toothpaste on. He'd obviously taken it off before brushing his teeth when he'd got back to the room, and not been particularly careful with the brush strokes, little white splatters were all around the sink, and on the mirror in front of him.

It would also appear he'd taken a shower, a used towel on the floor, and small puddles of water were the tell-tale signs. He had been on automatic pilot when he'd gotten in, and was just thankful that he'd not slipped, or broken something whilst showering.

He picked the watch up and turned it over to check the time. It told him it was just before seven, he'd asked for a quarter past alarm call, so he was slightly ahead of the game for a change. He quickly jumped in the shower to wash the sheen of sweat he'd woken up with off himself, and to try and bring him round to the land of the living. He turned the temperature down as far as he could, and within a few seconds blasts of cold water were coming through. He endured the icy water for as long as he could, and then turned the water off.

He picked up a fresh towel, and began to dry himself off, and he thought about having a shave. His early morning brain obviously not up to speed yet as he remembered how pointless that would be anyway, and the fact he didn't have carry a razor with him anymore. Five years down the line and he still hadn't shaken off the automatic thought to shave after a shower.

He walked over to the windows and opened the blinds; the room brightened a bit with the hint of daylight, but not as much as he hoped. It would seem that the British weather still left a lot to be desired, even in what was supposed to be their summertime. Rain ran down the outside of the window, and the flat roofs of the surrounding buildings were covered in several small puddles.

He stood looking out of the window, admiring the different, and sometimes contrasting styles of buildings that he could see. London was amazing like that, as he looked round, he could probably see buildings that had been built in six or seven different centuries, seemingly happily co-existing together. He may have stood there a while longer, but was interrupted by the alarm call, and he moved away from the window and picked the phone up, heard the automatic robotic voice message, and put the receiver back down.

He looked properly around the room for the first time that morning, and besides his watch, everything else was exactly where he'd expect it to be in the room, he hadn't taken much out of his case, and he'd piled up his clothes from the previous evening neatly on the chair in the corner of the room. His pre-prepared clothes were hanging up, ready to go, and he wandered over, took them off the hanger and got dressed.

He took the lift down to the basement of the hotel to the restaurant where breakfast was served. It was a relative success, a decent buffet choice, he hadn't eaten the healthiest options, but at least he hadn't spilt any of it on himself, always a bonus when already dressed. He got hot and cold drinks inside him, and felt a whole lot better when leaving to go back up to his room.

He did another check round every drawer, wardrobe, cupboard, and even under the bed in the room to make sure he had everything that he'd arrived with, and wheeled his case out of his room and down to reception.

He checked out, and was glad to find he'd not randomly ordered any food or drink when he had got back to the hotel the night before, and that there was nothing else to pay on his bill. He headed out of the hotel, and across the square, and then down into the Underground station next to the hotel, to do the journey out to the airport.

He had been over to London so much recently, he'd acquired an Oyster card for travel around the city, and public transport was pretty good, although it was carnage during their rush hour. He realised that it was going to be smack bang in the middle of rush hour as he made his way through the ticket barriers, fighting with them to get his case through behind him, and made his way down to the platform.

As he turned from the bottom of the stairs and stepped onto the platform, the train was on the platform and its doors slid shut and it started to move off, he wasn't surprised, and it didn't really matter, he always missed the damn Tube by seconds, it didn't matter what time of day or when he was going, whenever he arrived the doors were always shutting. It seemed to him that it was the same with all public transport anywhere around the world; it was almost as if the driver could sense him nearing the doors and therefore knew it was time to go, leaving him behind.

He had first noticed that five years ago, just after his strange experience, and it had started to make him feel a bit paranoid, however his sense of paranoia had reduced over the years, as his previous belief that it was part of a global conspiracy to drive him to distraction was just crazy thinking. As if transport operators all over the world had nothing better to do than to make their transport leave as he arrived.

And anyway, the good thing today was that he had plenty of time to get to Heathrow and on the line he had chosen, the Tube was frequent, and once on a train he wouldn't have to change, if he could get a seat, he could relax all the way to the end of the line and the waiting airport.

Chapter 3

As the Tube he had just missed pulled out of the station, he saw her again, sat there staring into space, oblivious to him as always. In the five years since he had initially met her, he had seen her on a lot of occasions, maybe thirty times in all, always in a different city, and always on public transport that was just pulling off, leaving him behind.

She never seemed to change either, hair and make-up always immaculate, and it was always the same style, length, and colours. He wondered whether he was imagining it, as it seemed she hadn't aged either.

Then again, if he thought about it, he hadn't changed in the same period either, his hair was always the same, it hadn't needed cutting since that first meeting, though he welcomed the fact that he no longer needed to shave.

At first it had freaked him out big-time, he had tried to style it, only to find it back the original style the following morning. He'd even had it all shaved off, but it was back to its current length and style when he woke the next morning. He had learnt to live with it, thinking that at least it was a non-descript hairstyle, and not some god-forsaken style nightmare such as pink streaks or a dodgy weave in dreads.

As for the rest of him, it didn't seem to matter what he did nothing changed, no matter what he ate or drank, every morning he was exactly the same, almost as if he was living some kind of permanent groundhog day, but with the actual date, and his life moving on. He thought about trying something mental like in the film, as if he was Bill Murray, trying to get a different result upon waking up.

Then he thought back to the woman, and that made him think back to the first time he had seen her.

They had been in some kind of strange white room, the room of his dreams, white as far as the eye could see, with a strange lighting method that threw no shadows, and that didn't appear to have any obvious source, it was almost as if the light was in everything in the room. This has made it difficult to try and estimate how big the room was, as there was no contrast to use to get a judgement of size.

The only things in the room that weren't white were their heads and their hands, the two of theirs and those of another four people that were also visible in the room. Even the white gowns they had on seem to shine with the same bright light as everything else.

He hadn't seen any of the other faces from that room at all in the last five years, but had seen the woman at regular intervals. She was always ahead of him, as if escaping, always the same, from the first time in Kuala Lumpur, just a few days after he found himself awake in his apartment with no recollection of how he got there, through four different continents, in his hometown of Philadelphia, and now here in his latest client's home city of London.

He had spent much time thinking whether it really was the same person, as there was no pattern, to the location, or to the frequency of sightings. It had been three months since the previous sighting, just a short hop away from where he was now, in Manchester.

He'd been a guest of his previous client at a Champions League soccer game, which in itself hadn't been bad, just that it had finished a tie, with no attempt to get a winner on the night, which was a foreign concept to him as an American, and the sports he was used to watching.

He had come out of the game and got to the Exchange Quay tram stop, just as it pulled away, and she was sat right at the back of the tram, appearing to stare right through him. He had tried waving to get her attention, but to no avail, nothing changed in her features, she just continued staring through him as if he wasn't there.

The longest gap had been about a year which had ended with that sighting in Manchester, the shortest gap had been just a single day, between her being in his hometown of Philadelphia one day, and then in San Francisco the very next day.

The shock of that sighting in San Francisco had caused him to come to a grinding halt, as everything seemed to shut down around him, all his senses stopped, and he stood oblivious to everything, rooted to the spot. As his consciousness returned to him, he turned to see the tram was only a couple of hundred yards away from him, and only trundling along.

He had ran like a maniac after the tram, and to his mind having broken the one hundred, two hundred and four hundred meter world records, he caught up with the tram just as it was leaving its next scheduled stop, the good thing being that he could manage to still get on even though it was moving – something that he could have done at the previous stop if he had kept his presence of mind.

The seat that he was sure had only moments before housed the woman was empty, and she was not on the tram, he had jumped off the moving tram, much to the consternation of some of his fellow passengers, and raced back to the stop he'd got on at, but there was no sign of the woman in any direction.

If only he hadn't frozen, he might have been able to speak to her, though there was a large part of his consciousness that wondered whether he had just imagined seeing the woman, and another substantial part of it that wondered whether he had been making the whole thing up all along.

Had he ever met this woman? Did she even exist? Was the bright white room real, or just a very bad dream that recurred to him? He didn't think the answer to any of those questions was no, but he really wanted to speak to this woman to find out for certain.

Chapter 4

The rush of air and noise that greeted the arrival of the next train hit him, and he flashed back to the present. How long had he been stood there motionless with all those thoughts going through his head? It had seemed like an eternity, but looking at his watch indicated only three minutes had gone since he had arrived on the platform. It also indicated he hadn't managed to clean all the toothpaste off it earlier either; and he set about removing the last traces.

He looked down the platform towards the approaching train, and he could see that people were staring at him, and he wondered what he had been doing whilst his mind was elsewhere to attract their attention, it had happened before that he had randomly shouted out, and the rocking side to side incident, but things like that had only happened on a couple of occasions.

He jumped on to the train as the doors opened, and was surprised to find a seat available pretty much directly opposite him. He rushed over and sat down, whilst doing so, noticing an extremely attractive brunette in the seat next to the one he had taken. That was nearly as good a reason to be in that seat as the fact that it was right near the doors as well.

For a reason he couldn't explain, nowadays he always felt the need to be as near to an exit as he possibly could be, almost as if he could make an escape at any moment, though by nature he had always been a rational calm man, recent years had added an edge to him that, although unnoticeable to strangers, had been picked up by those few who knew him reasonably well.

His closest associates - he found it difficult to go the whole enchilada and call people friends, as he had difficulties bringing himself to confide in them - could pinpoint the change in him to roughly five years ago, and had tried to get inside him to help, but who could help, and who would have believed what he had to tell them.

It was probably a good job that he had no surviving family members that he knew of, as to deny that closeness and sharing of feeling to family would have been a lot tougher.

He casually glanced at the woman sat next to him, and realised his initial estimation had been somewhat off the mark. Extremely attractive was somewhat of an understatement; her hair was perfectly coiffured into a bob that allowed her striking features to be accentuated. Well-mascaraed eyelashes outlined the kind of perfectly green eyes that he could easily drown in. The remaining make up was minimal, with just a hint of pink lip gloss, on full, but not pouting lips, and a perfectly formed nose. She was slim, but not one of those horrible stick-like creatures that graced so many a magazine cover, and wore a tailored cream suit, with a knee length skirt that showed shapely legs. Underneath was a smart white blouse that made the image of a perfect businesswoman, though still allowing her full femineity to show through.

As he stared at her reflection in the window opposite his seat, he wished he wasn't such a tongue-tied fool when it came to women. He might have tried to declare his undying love there and then. However, she looked back at him, catching him looking at her, and he reddened visibly and shifted his line of sight away from the reflection, glancing occasionally at the reflection out of the corner of his eye.

She smiled to herself and looked away again, obviously used to drawing admiring glances, and confident enough in herself not to be overly bothered by it, and therefore able to brush it off.

Embarrassed by being caught staring, and his obvious reddening, he decided to look up at the map of the underground that was positioned above the seat opposite him, and tried to concentrate on that, instead of the beauty sat next to him.

Despite the intense concentration he was putting into studying the mass of different coloured overlapping lines to occupy his visual senses, he couldn't help but notice the sweet smell emanating from the woman next to him, and he groaned inwardly.

She was wearing the only brand of perfume that he recognised, and for that matter really liked the smell of. No matter when it was, or where he was, that smell always seemed to invade his consciousness, and it made him stop what he was doing as he tried to figure out just where the smell was coming from.

He didn't need to wonder where it was coming from this time; it was obvious it was coming from right next to him. He needed to resist the temptation to turn round and look directly at the woman, and the other temptation to lean over and start sniffing her, so he closed his eyes and tried to think of something else.

Chapter 5

The thing was that when he smelt that particular smell, he always hoped that he would turn around and find that it came from his fiancée and only real love Keera Fallenfant. She had always worn Eternity, from the very first time they had met, right up to the end, and he smiled at all the times when she wouldn't wear anything else but the perfume.

He drifted away, his memory caught up with visions of Keera, he closed his eyes as tightly as he could and thought back to their time together, remembering everything about her, starting with her smell, the way she looked, the way they had made love, the way she smiled, and the way she had made him smile during their time together.

But that had all changed; the pain had started not long after her twenty-third birthday, just a few months after they had been engaged. At first, she had not really thought about it seriously, and hadn't mentioned it to him, and then as the pain increased, she stopped smiling. She still didn't mention the pain, and he selfishly blamed himself for making her unhappy, not thinking that there might be something wrong with her that didn't involve him.

They started rowing about little things, bickering over the silliest things, her because of the pain she was feeling and him because he didn't understand, and was still hurting from family tragedies, which made him act like a little spoilt immature brat. Then one day, during yet another argument, she let it slip about the pain in her back that was troubling her so much. She told him that it had been hurting for nearly three months, and that it was making her tired and irritable.

He realised what a pain in the arse he had been, and was concerned for her, knowing that it wasn't right to have this pain for this length of time and, although she was reluctant, he persuaded her to go to her doctor. She was in turn referred to an orthopaedic clinic specializing in back pain.

She was diagnosed as having a malignant Vertebral column tumour, which had spread there from some, until then undetected breast cancer.

A course of Chemotherapy was started immediately to try and eradicate the cancer, and was partially successful. The breast cancer was diagnosed as being in full remission, but the pressure on the spinal column caused by that tumour was still causing her great pain, and it was decided to operate to remove the tumour.

She was admitted to hospital, so she could be treated with the correct level of pain medication whilst they waited to get a slot for the operation. The few days spent waiting saw him hardly leaving her room, when she was awake, they spent the time talking about everything they would do when she'd recovered from her operation.

She went down for the operation in the early evening on the Thursday. It was the last time that he saw her alive, his last words to her had been "I love you".

Unfortunately there were complications from the operation caused by her having a previously undiagnosed extremely weak heart, the tumour had been removed successfully, and they were stitching her back up when she had a heart attack on the operating table. Her heart stopped, and after forty-five minutes of fruitless attempts to get it restarted, they had declared her dead.

When the surgeon had found him to tell him the news, he refused to believe them, and eventually had to be restrained and sedated after attacking the surgeon and trashing the private room Keera had been in.

The funeral had come and gone in a blur of some serious drinking, and the insinuations from Keera's family over the length of time to report the back pain being his fault had led to angry scenes at the wake.

He didn't really speak to anyone for months after, a feeling of guilt refusing to leave. His only correspondence being with Trebling software, who he was working for as a freelance computer programmer.

His speciality being the animation of human motion, and he was busy doing the coding for Trebling's blockbuster summer release Sacrilege, a role-playing game involving a priest of all things.

At least being freelance he didn't have to go in as long as he sent in regular updates. He had plenty of time to do just that, as he seemed unable to sleep, sometimes three or four days would go by, and he wouldn't have been anywhere near his bed. He refused to speak to his "friends" and after two months most of them had given up on him. They no longer rang or came to try and visit.

It was during the testing stage for Sacrilege that he had decided that he was going to leave Trebling. Yet even this couldn't clear his mind of everything and his mourning period for Keera continued, even though all he seemed to remember of her now was her pained expression from her last few months.

Chapter 6

He opened his eyes, and wondered how long he had been drifting in his memories. The Tube was now in daylight, and just leaving somewhere called Osterley, and he looked up at the map to find himself only five stops from Heathrow, the journey had gone a lot quicker than expected, probably because he had been drifting in his memories all the way from just after Russell Square, some fifteen or so stops earlier. He looked in the window opposite to see if the woman was still there, but there wasn't a reflection now they were in daylight, so he glanced to his side, and was somewhat surprised to see the woman still there, and still smiling.

Then it hit him like Tyson blow; the woman sat next to him was so obviously a beautiful double of Keera, only one that smiled, and was sat there next to him in the here and now. He closed his eyes again, rubbed them and then reopened them and turned to look at the woman again. It was true, it wasn't just the olfactory sensation of the Eternity and the memory of Keera that it had triggered, the woman looked enough like Keera did that he was surprised that he hadn't noticed it immediately. The features were more outstanding, and the hairstyle different, but the likeness was almost spooky.

She turned and looked at him again, and this time he didn't look away, their eyes locked, and they held each other's gaze for what seemed like an eternity, but what was in reality only a few seconds. He found himself smiling, but was unable to bring himself to speak, dumbstruck at what he was seeing and feeling. The woman's own smiled broadened and a small giggle seemed to tumble out from somewhere within her.

She opened her mouth and started to speak, but from the moment she started to speak, he couldn't be certain of a single thing that she had said, he was vaguely aware that she had called him by his name, which didn't even register as being a surprise, what had stunned him was her voice.

It was as if Keera speaking to him, the Philadelphia accent was there, though somewhat anglicised, but the pitch and tone were the same, almost as if it was a recording. He felt like he was going to suffocate, was he imagining it all, unless he could snap out of his trance and speak, he couldn't be sure.

He felt like he'd fell from a great height into a freezing cold pool of water. All his senses were numb, and yet screaming at him at the same time. He couldn't breathe, he tried but no air came, there was just a moist taste and smell of salt, his lungs felt like they were going to explode.

He tried to look around, but everywhere he turned everything was dark and blurry, he couldn't hear sounds as they were being made, he only heard them as hollow vibrations, all his senses felt the same as if he was underwater, and in danger of drowning. He became vaguely aware of something shaking him.

His senses began to return, and he realised it wasn't something, but someone - the woman was trying to shake him out of his reverie. The smell of her Eternity invaded his nostrils again, and snapped him back to the land of the living. His eyes opened wide, and he could see everything outside of shadow now, and he managed to take that first gasping breath, just as he would have done if he were emerging from beneath the water of a swimming pool, or the sea, after too long underneath.

From the corner of his eye he saw that the Tube was stopped at a station, and as if he had been given an electric shock, he jumped up, grabbed his case and dived from the Tube just as the doors were shutting, amazing himself in the process, both with the speed of movement, and with the fact that he had had the presence of mind to remember his case.

He turned as he heard the woman shout

"Wait!"

But it was too late, the doors had already slid shut, and the Tube was starting its slow build-up of speed as it pulled away towards the next stop. He looked around and found that he was at Hatton Cross, and was surprised to find the Tube had travelled four stops in what seemed no time at all, especially at this end of the line where the stations were further apart.

How long must he have been in a fugue state this time? He found a seat on the platform, and slumped down into it. He needed time to pull himself together before he could continue his journey. In the space of less than forty minutes his mind had descended into the kind of panic and desperation that had previously taken three years and thirty thousand dollars-worth of therapy to remove after the death of Keera, and acknowledging that he had some issues.

It wasn't that he had seen the same mystery woman on the Tube pulling out of the station, before the one he had boarded, that had happened enough times by now for that to be of minor consequence. Yes, he'd love to speak to the woman, and see if she knew any more about that white room, and what had happened during those missing eleven days of his life, but he was certain that it wasn't supposed to be.

There must be a reason why he just kept seeing her, but just missing her, and he was sure that it would become apparent at some stage, but it wasn't worth worrying about now.

He was also sure that it wasn't the Eternity thing, god knows how many times he had smelt it in the years since Keera's death, and although it normally bought about brief thoughts of her, more than often it was gone in seconds, and he just carried on.

For some reason today, it had triggered a drift away that had lasted the best part of half an hour. He wondered whether his subconscious had been well ahead of his senses and realised that the attractive brunette he had sat next to on the Tube was so spookily similar to Keera, that when his olfactory senses kicked in, it triggered a larger flashback the like of which he had never experienced before.

The look-alike had really freaked him out, and he remembered that it was her starting to speak to him, and sounding exactly like Keera had sounded as well, that had triggered such a large sensory shutdown, he vaguely recalled that while he was slipping into his mental paralysis that she had called him by his name.

He wondered how the hell she knew it; he was certain that they had never met before, and although he was becoming a known face in Philadelphia, it wasn't as if he thought he had national, let alone international recognition outside of security circles.

He thought that it must have been the combination of events that had caused him to lose it completely and then bolt from the Tube like a crazy man, which he supposed was what he had been like. As his heartbeat returned to normal, he made a mental note that perhaps he should give his shrink a ring when he got back to Philly.

Chapter 7

He let another three trains pass while he sat at Hatton Cross, as he still had plenty of time to check in, he decided he would get on the next one, he'd given it enough time, as he didn't want the Keera look-alike to be waiting for him as he got off the Tube at Heathrow, nor did he want to still be here too much longer, just in case, if for some reason she came back to look for him.

He got on the next Tube and completed the now short, journey to Heathrow, he gingerly stuck his head out of the carriage door and looked up and down the platform, but there was no one there, and he made his way up to the airport and through the terminal building to the check in.

He was surprised to see just how close to the check-in closing time it had got to be, he felt as if time had rushed by him, as if in some kind of Narnia state. He checked his case in and made his way to the security line.

The queues weren't bad, and he set about putting all his metal items into his jacket, so that he could just put his jacket into one of the plastic trays for scanning. He pushed it towards the conveyor belt, and with just his ticket in his hand, he waited to be called forward through the scanner.

He always worried about going through the scanner, that the beeping would start, and numerous sets of eyes would be drawn to him, and he'd have to get a deeper search. This was despite the fact he knew he had no metal, and there was nothing on him that would set the alarms off.

He held his breath as always as he walked through the scanner and that split second pause as he got through the other side to see if there was any noise. As normal, there wasn't any alarm; he managed to exhale again, before going over to get his jacket from the plastic tray.

He took a couple of minutes to get everything out of his jacket pockets and put them back into their normal places, before making his way through into the vast shopping area, and immediately searched for a departures screen so that he could check where his departure gate was. Typically, when he found a screen, there was a gate showing, and judging by the number showing, it was going to be quite a trek to get there. He got his bearings and set off.

It took him about fifteen minutes to get to the gate, and when he did get there, the plane to Philadelphia International Airport was already boarding, but he knew that as a first-class passenger, he didn't have to rush to fight for a decent seat, as it had been pre-booked. He ambled up to the queue, and waited as the passengers had their tickets scanned and were let through to the plane.

He always booked a central aisle seat in first class, which allowed him to sit next to someone else as opposed to one of the two side window seats, which meant he would be sat by himself. Even though he wasn't the most outgoing person in the world, he liked to try and talk to someone new on the plane, as it took his mind off the flight, allaying some of the nervousness he had about it, even after all the years and flights he had experienced. He hoped that he would get some interesting conversation from his plane neighbour, and that they weren't the kind of person who'd rather not speak to anyone.

He got on to the plane and was pointed in the direction of his seat by one of the stewardesses. He had no hand luggage to stow, everything he wanted for the flight was in one of his pockets, and he liked to keep his jacket on until after the plane had taken off, and everything had settled down.

He found his seat easily and sat straight down, and sorted out his seat belt, adjusting it to fit him, so that it was tight enough to be useful, but not so tight he felt trussed up like a turkey. He turned to his right to see who he was sat next to, and to introduce himself, and his heart almost stopped, he was sat next to his mystery woman. She was busy rooting through a handbag, and as usual didn't even seem to notice he was there. He looked straight ahead, and tried to control his breathing, he couldn't believe that he would get the chance to speak to her after all this time and perhaps get some answers.

This thought was interrupted by someone calling his name from the left of him, in a voice that seemed all too familiar. He turned slowly with a sense of dread, knowing that he would find Keera's look-alike in the seat across the aisle from him.

Even though he knew it, it didn't make the shock any less in seeing it was her, a pain hit him, and a blinding white light filled his head, and he drifted away again.

Chapter 8

They had gone to Keera's family home for Christmas, despite the fact the rest of her immediate family were away for the holidays, they felt that it would be more homely and Christmassy than their flat. They sat in front of the hearth, with the coal effect gas fire roaring - well gently hissing - to keep them warm, as the snow fell heavily outside.

Keera was opening her presents, working her way through the various bits and pieces that she had received from her work colleagues and other friends and family, it was the first such opening of the day as there would be another set of presents when they went over to her aunt's house for Christmas dinner later, and joined up with various other members of her extended family.

The "whose family to visit?" thing had ended earlier in the year with the death of his mother, the last of his living relatives that he knew or spoke to, he had some distant relatives, but he'd never met them, and he had no contact with them. And with her parents away they only had one real invite for Christmas dinner, which they'd accepted to avoid having to cook for themselves.

She looked up and got him to open one of his presents, but he wasn't really that interested in them, the only important gifts would be the ones from Keera anyway, besides it wouldn't take long to open the couple he had. He was much more interested in watching the reactions and delight on Keera's face as she opened her presents.

His main group of friends that he had at that point in his life had a tradition of not buying each other presents, but instead using the money to go out, have a slap-up meal, lots of drinks, then off clubbing, Zanzibar Blue again this year, that was beginning to become a habit. This year they'd carried on to get an early morning breakfast at Jim's Steaks just a bit further down South Broad Street. And it hadn't ended there either, after a chance to freshen up and a change of clothes, they'd all gone on to catch a Flyers game the following afternoon, which had descended into more drinking after the game before getting home and collapsing into bed. On reflection it would have probably been cheaper to buy each other, plus half the population of Philly presents, but it had been a good 36 hours.

Basically he enjoyed watching Keera open her presents, and to watch the expression of joy on her face whenever she opened anything. It didn't matter what it was, everything she opened would draw an excited gasp as if it was the most wondrous item in the world. It wasn't fake emotion either, she genuinely loved anything she received and was always grateful. He knew that she would spend much of the followed afternoon writing out thank you notes with gushing enthusiasm.

She started to open some of the smaller items that he'd bought her, the latest Patricia Cornwell novel, which was yet another one featuring Kay Scarpetta, as he knew that Keera was a fan. He read most of them himself as well, and had enjoyed them, and he'd probably read this one once Keera had finished with it, though it did seem to him that it was getting to the point where Scarpetta was being flogged to the extent of a dead horse.

He'd also got her recent Mariah Carey release. Someone that was not his taste, as he thought her to be a bit of a screaming witch, and totally bonkers to boot, but Keera was a big fan, and he'd found it a bit surprising she hadn't already got it. The obligatory chocolates and toiletries came and went, and then the final small item for opening was a matching scarf and gloves set that he'd seen her admiring in JC Penney's the week before. As she was opening this, he produced the final item from its hiding place, and passed it over to her.

He watched with bated breath, hoping that she would love it; he'd spent his entire generous bonus from Trebling on it. It was a gold, diamond encrusted Cartier watch, with a personalized inscription on it.

She had unwrapped the outer layer of paper, and was then faced with the plain protective layer of cardboard, and then underneath to the plain black box with just the word Cartier engraved in gold leaf on it. She opened the box lid, and her face lit up, and she took the watch out of the box. She placed it around her wrist and secured the clasp in place. It had been measured and altered accordingly by using one of her other watches as a guide, and it fitted perfectly. She beamed at him and came over and hugged him tightly, whispering in his ear.

He felt himself smiling, but he also felt himself shaking. He closed his eyes, and paused for a couple of seconds, then reopened them.

Chapter 9

He woke to see a stewardess in front of him, the plane was in the air, and appeared to be levelled out, it was all just a memory of his last Christmas with Keera, he now remembered where he was and what had caused him to pass out in the first place, he looked from side to side to confirm that he hadn't imagined his neighbours on the plane.

He hadn't been imagining things at all, mystery woman one side, and Keera lookalike the other. He set himself ready to start on the barrage of questions that he had for both women, he needed to decide which one to start asking first. His brief encounter with the Keera lookalike had scrambled his brains this morning already, so he decided to speak to the mystery woman instead, and was about to start as a man, dressed in jeans and t-shirt, knocked into him as he rushed past.

He didn't look like he belonged in first class, although he thought about times when he'd caught planes and didn't look the part, it was a bit harsh to judge solely on appearances. But there was something off about the man, and the fact that he went straight to the door of the cockpit, and was starting to open it rang bells.

And from the corner of his eye in the other gangway strolled another man, again in jeans and t-shirt, just like the first man, and as he turned to look at him, the man took something out of his pocket.

It was some kind of handgun, taken out and brandished so casually, it didn't seem that anyone else had noticed it. He looked towards the cockpit, and the other man was already in there, and in his hand was a handgun of his own as he waved it at the pilots.

What had already been one of the strangest and most disturbing days of his life, looked like it was about to get a damn sight worse, the bleeding plane was being hijacked. He thought to himself that he really should have stayed in bed this morning, having all this as a dream instead.

Considering his rather fragile state of mind today, with the memories of Keera that had been flooding into his mind since seeing her lookalike on the tube, with her knowing who he was, and having spoken his name, alongside seeing the mystery woman, who had been in that strange white room with him, and since then had been forever ahead of him, on departing transport all over the world, he was feeling in a state of mental upheaval. He was surprised that he didn't shut down completely, but he was now alert, and started checking things out.

The man in the aisle to his right was the kind of person for whom the phrase non-descript was made for. In normal light blue denim jeans, and a Fred Perry polo shirt, he was neither exceptionally tall, nor short.

He was of medium build, and as he looked around the cabin there were no distinctive features on his face, his hair was brown and short. In fact he was the kind of person that you would walk past and not give a second glance to, he could be any one of a hundred similar men that you would walk past every day and not know whether you'd seen them before.

The man who had entered the cockpit was virtually the same. Again he had light blue denim jeans on, and a polo shirt, his hair was short, but was slightly darker than his compadre, he was of medium build and height, and had the same kind of non-descript features, again totally unremarkable. In fact they could almost be clones, and he quickly looked at them again, with the thought going through his mind of "do they look like Jango Fett?"

He thought about the non-descript thing for a few moments, and asked himself whether this was a deliberate tactic. After all they would be the kind of people that wouldn't arouse suspicion, they looked like everyday people, and you really wouldn't look at them twice in normal circumstances.

These however weren't normal circumstances and it now seemed that everyone was looking at them more than once, he had a quick look around the cabin, and it seemed that everyone was looking at them and they weren't drawing admiring glances.

From a couple of rows in front of him a woman screamed, well he assumed it was a woman, and at first, he felt some surprise that it had taken so long for a reaction to the situation, but in reality, it probably had been less than thirty seconds, time was just crawling, as if it was trying to wade through treacle.

The first scream, having broken the silence, was quickly followed by further screams from his cabin, and more from back in the standard class cabin, which suggested that there may well be more hijackers back there. That would make sense, and he wondered if the other hijackers were all as non-descript as the two up here.

The screaming rose in pitch and volume as more people joined in, and it went on for what seemed to be an age, but he was sure was only about twenty seconds, before the pilot's voice came somewhat shakily over the plane's speaker system.

"Ladies and Gentlemen, this is your captain speaking, as you may have noticed there are several gentlemen walking around the plane in jeans and polo shirts carrying guns."

There was a tone of disgust in the captain's voice, and he had almost spat out the word gentlemen with as much sarcasm as he could muster in the situation. He continued,

"They insist that no harm will come to anyone on board this plane, as long as their requests are followed. They have asked me to point out to all on board the plane; that they will shoot any passenger or member of crew that tries in any way to interfere with them."

"Furthermore they request that there is a level of peace and quiet on board, excessive noise, such as screaming may make them anxious, and anxious people are more likely to shoot. As for our onward journey, it is with regret that I inform you that the destination of this aircraft is no longer Philadelphia, as expected when you all boarded, but we now have a new destination of Kangerlussuaq. We are now going to Greenland."

"Any passengers with serious medical ailments will be allowed to leave the plane upon landing at Kangerlussuaq, but the rest will remain. Please try to remain calm while we continue with our flight."

The intercom clicked off, and an uneasy peace descended upon all of those on the plane.

Chapter 10

Kangerlussuaq! Why on earth would anyone in their right mind, or for that matter, out of their mind, want to hijack a plane and insist that it lands in Greenland. He couldn't believe it, he knew that in hijack situations some strange locations were requested but this would surely take the biscuit, cake, and the rest of the confectionery section. Which kind of demented lunatic would want to go to Greenland? Had they been hijacked by the polar bear liberation front?

He also had serious doubts that Greenland even had an airport capable of landing a plane of this size, he was sure that they had to get smaller planes into the island, stopping over at Reykjavik to change onto something suitable to land at the airports there. Though as in most places around the world, he thought it was likely there would be an ex-air force base left by some country or other. As he thought on the fact that it may not have an airport of the right size for his plane, he had visions of them coming into land on an ice rink, failing to get good purchase on the ground, and skating off miles into the middle of frozen wastes like a kid trying to stop at the bottom of a hill after a toboggan ride.

With this vision he smiled, he thought it was to himself, but the turning of other people's heads, and the accusing, staring eyes that looked upon him suggested that he had not only smiled, but laughed out loud.

The hijacker in the aisle to his right turned around from the front of the plane, walked down the couple of rows of seats, pointed his gun at him, and asked,

"What do you find so funny?"

The hijacker asked with a perfect English country gentleman's accent, as if the hijacker had received elocution lessons at a top finishing school. He looked at the hijacker and said,

"For me it's been one of those days, there really is only so much freaky shit that can happen to an individual in the course of a single day, before they need a release, and to me, the thought of going sliding across Greenland's frozen wastes in a massive metal tube just seems funny."

The hijacker didn't respond, and just eyed him suspiciously before putting his gun down, and then walking to the cockpit to talk to his compadre. They spoke briefly, and they both turned towards him and the hijacker that had spoken to him pointed him out.

Great he thought to himself, just what he needed, less than five minutes into a hijacking and he had already attracted the attention of the hijackers. The two hijackers spoke for a few more seconds before the hijacker that had questioned him before made his way back out of the cockpit.

The hijacker came back down the plane towards him, this time on his side of the plane, looking directly at him all the time he was doing so. When the hijacker got level with him, he drew his gun and pointed it at him.

"On your feet"

He undid his seatbelt, and got up as slowly as he dared. Once fully upright the hijacker's free arm reached out and grabbed him firmly by the bicep and led him out into the aisle. He was then pushed up the aisle to the cockpit, where he was left face to face with what seemed to be the head honcho of the hijackers.

"Good morning,"

Another perfect English gentleman's voice came out of the head honcho's mouth, they must have all gone to the same finishing school.

"Well it was before some clowns hijacked the plane."

The words were out of his mouth quicker than he had expected. The head hijacker looked less than impressed and hissed a single word at him

"Silence!"

There was a brief pause before the hijacker continued.

"I believe that you expressed to my colleague that you find something about this situation to be amusing. Whatever the reason may be for your amusement is not really a concern of mine."

"What is of concern is that if you manage to find something in this situation amusing, then it would suggest that you are either scared stupid, which it would seem from your response to my colleague, and for that matter your more recent response to me, you are not, or you are not afraid. It is this second possibility that somewhat worries me."

"People who are not afraid are capable of doing unexpected things. When running a precision operation such as the one that I am currently undertaking, I don't like the unexpected, in fact the unexpected makes me decidedly nervous, and when I get nervous, I tend to make rash decisions. Rash decisions can cause lives, and much as I wish the passengers on this plane no harm, as after all they are only victims of circumstance, I will not so much as bat an eyelid if I have to kill any of them."

"Therefore in order to prevent the unexpected, and to keep myself from getting nervous, you are going to be secured in that seat there."

As he finished the sentence, the hijacker gestured to a seat at the front of the first-class area on the left-hand side of the plane, before continuing

"From there I shall be able to keep an eye on you, and being secured to the seat you won't be able to get up to any mischief, and therefore you cannot be of any danger to yourself, or to the rest of the passengers. To begin with I have no intention of gagging you, however if you start shouting your mouth off, then that decision will be under review, and you may find yourself being gagged, probably with one of your own socks."

There was a pause then the hijacker continued,

"Have I made myself clear?"

"Perfectly," came his somewhat muted reply, managing to suppress any flippant response that may be trying to escape his lips.

"Good!"

And the head honcho nodded, with this the sidekick moved the existing passenger out of the seat that had been indicated to the sidekick before, and pushed the obviously scared passenger that had been sat there, down the plane to his seat that he had been removed from. The sidekick came back, and he was pushed into the indicated and recently vacated seat. As if by magic, large amounts of rope appeared. God only knows where it had come from, but no sooner was he in the seat, then there it was. He looked around for a shopkeeper wearing a fez, still smiling to himself.

The sidekick proceeded to go about securing him into the seat. Within a couple of minutes he found each of his forearms secured to the seat's armrests, he found further rope around his chest and upper arms securing his upper body to the back of the seat. His thighs were also bound to the base of the seat. He could move enough so that he wouldn't seize up, but there wasn't anywhere near enough slack for him to consider trying to work loose. It was a very thorough job, and he wasn't going to be able to escape his binds, there again he really wasn't in the frame of mind to try and escape, it wasn't as if he could run and hide on a plane.

He silently cursed his misfortune at his predicament, mainly caused by his sense of humour and inability to filter what was coming out of his mouth, and thought immediately to the bright side; at least he wasn't dead, with the Monty Python boys singing inside his head as he did so. It was just another of those strange situations that he just seemed to manage to get caught up in, without even trying.

He did think that the head honcho had over-reacted to someone laughing, being hogtied into a plane seat for giggling did seem a little heavy handed, the operation they were running must be highly strung if they were so worried about a bit of laughter, perhaps their training only really covered screaming, crying, and whimpering. Of course there was always the possibility that he might do one or all of them later.

He looked across at the head honcho, who now had his back to him, as he leant through the door of the cockpit, he then glanced at the sidekick, who was now moving across to walk down the aisle on the other side of the middle seats, and from observing them, he had the feeling that there was something missing here.

He sat and thought about it for a few moments until it struck him what was missing. Neither of the men was carrying any form of communications device that he could see. It had been some time since the pilot's announcement, and he had not seen or heard any form of message between the first and standard class. Were they that organised that they didn't need to communicate?

He thought about it some more, before giving up on it, it wasn't really his concern, all he had to worry about was staying quiet, and therefore hopefully staying alive, and resisted the urge to start singing falsetto Bee Gees style.

There was one thing that was true in what the head honcho had said to him, he didn't feel afraid in the situation, but he didn't know why. He thought it might be because there was no one waiting for him, and apart from his clients, and a few associates no one would really miss him if he did die, but there were many other things on his mind that were distracting his attention from being scared. There were several things he wanted to find out before he died.

He desperately wanted and needed to talk to the two women who now sat a few rows behind him. He felt sure each of them had things they could tell him that he needed to know, and that would help him make some sense of events that had gone on in his life prior to today. However, as much as he wanted to talk to them it wasn't going to happen in the foreseeable future, so he moved those thoughts to the back of his mind. He closed his eyes and tried to get to sleep, thinking that whilst asleep he couldn't do anything else that had stupid written all over it.

Chapter 11

He was born on a Tuesday night, the twenty-seventh of May nineteen seventy-five in South Philadelphia's Methodist Hospital, the son of a Methodist preacher, and a social worker. He was an only child, and as he later came to find out, he wasn't planned, and certainly wasn't expected, with both his parents being well into their forties.

The contrast between his parents was strange to behold. His father was a very pious man, who believed in a strict puritanical upbringing, and insisted upon a Methodist school education, which somehow never came to being, and still believed that children were to be seen and not heard.

On the other hand his mother was a very warm and open woman, who brought the empathy and consideration required by her job into their home life, and allowed him to talk about anything to her, just not within his father's earshot.

He often wondered what had brought his parents together, with them being such totally different people, with vastly differing tastes and hobbies, and as it seemed to him, very little in common. They were the archetypical chalk and cheese; the perfect example of "opposites attract", yet despite this, they seemed content with each other, as if they balanced each other off. He couldn't remember them ever arguing or even having cross words with each other. He thought there must have been times they did, but if that was the case, they kept both the arguments and any potential ill-will from them away from him.

His father was a preacher at the Tindley Temple United Methodist Church, on South Broad Street. From being born and living in the Church's accommodation, right up until today, he had lived in the same area, even when moving out to live by himself when he went to high school, he lived either on or just off South Broad Street, and even now he rarely went out anywhere else in the city.

From an early age he attended the church's Sunday school, which thankfully wasn't taught by his father, but was instead taught by a sweet little old woman called Mrs Price. As a small child he had a lot of time with sweet old ladies.

Both of his grandfathers had died before he was born, but his grandmothers made up for this by doting on him, much to the obvious disgust of his father, who quite often would accuse them of mollycoddling him. Being older and wiser, as they would say, they wouldn't pay any attention to that, and with great regularity would remind his father that he was their only grandchild and therefore they would spoil him whenever they wanted to.

He started pre-school at The Philadelphia School, a non-sectarian independent school, which although not being a Methodist school, his father had no qualms about sending him to. This was mainly down to the fact that it's reputation, both academically and from a disciplinary point of view was outstanding, and his father couldn't have the same disdain for a non-sectarian school that he showed to any of the non-Methodist, Christian faiths. Most of this was directed at what his father called "The Catholic Devils".

It was in fact this point that was the main – and probably only – cause of tension in their household as he grew up, as his only aunt – his mother's sister – had done the unthinkable many years ago, and had converted to Catholicism and become a nun of all things! The very mention of his aunt would often cause his father to change colour to a deep shade of red, and it would appear that his head was on the verge of blowing up at any point. This would often lead to his father locking himself away to write another fire and brimstone sermon for the next Sunday service, and his colour would return to normal as he delivered it, as the words seemed to act as a pressure relief.

His early schooling set the pattern that seemed to follow for much of his life, in so much that he made acquaintances very easily, and very rarely had cross words with anyone, but by the same token never really had what he would call friends, the ones that you would tell everything, and spend all your time with. In truth it had never bothered him, and he hadn't even considered that this was unusual until he was at high school.

While in second grade his father's mother had died, and he was quite sure that this was the only time he had ever seen his father be emotionally upset. The death of his grandmother didn't really affect him as a child, he was just too young, and didn't understand why he should be upset, and all he knew later was that he missed the kindly old woman.

Meanwhile his schooling was going well. He was above average in most subjects, but it was maths that he excelled at, it all came so naturally to him, he found that numbers were interesting, and would quite happily sit there playing with numbers for hours. At the same time he also loved to read, and was always well ahead of his reading age, he could read novels from an early age, going to his mother with any difficult words, but he preferred to read factual books, and therefore gain knowledge. This marked him out as a strange child amongst his peers, but it didn't lead to the normal animosity that could be expected by children of that age.

He had learnt to ice skate from the age of six, and by the time he was nine it came naturally to him. For some reason it was an activity that both his parents agreed on, his mother on the basis that it was a healthy activity that wasn't competitive.

His father had a slightly different outlook, yes it was a reasonable activity, but by being able to skate well, it would give him a good chance to try out for junior hockey, as hockey was the only non-religious activity his father seemed to have an interest in.

Therefore by the time seventh grade came around he found himself trying out for the school hockey team. Despite being slight in build, and a bit short for his age, his natural skating ability got him on to the team, and he soon learnt how to make the stick an extension of his arm, and played not only at his own grade, but at the grade above as well. Even at that age he felt lucky, academic work came easily, hockey came easily, and although considered strange by a lot of the other kids at school, he wasn't picked on, and was on speaking terms with many of them.

Whilst in the eighth grade his remaining grandmother died, and he could remember feeling sad because of it. He remembered going to the funeral, being dressed all in black, along with everyone else, and above all – not crying, something else that would be the case for the rest of his life.

When he reached the ninth grade, he had to change schools due to the fact that The Philadelphia School only covered up to the end of eighth grade. He ended up going to the Masterman School, and academically the change in school made very little difference, but from a hockey perspective there was a world of difference, with his slight build being more of a disadvantage, especially with the fact that there was only one team for the school, and he was competing for a place with boys up to three years older than himself.

There was also a greater mix of people at the Masterman School, and he still found it impossible to find a true friend, but he also found it more difficult to even make acquaintances, and withdrew into himself somewhat. This wasn't helped when early in the tenth grade his father died. The funeral was a very serious affair, and he was one of the pallbearers, along with some members of his father's congregation.

The next couple of months were not good for him, he got somewhat of an attitude problem, as he withdrew into himself more, and he started to give his mother a really hard time, which was the last thing she needed, but he couldn't see that, being too wrapped up in himself.

They also had to move house, as they could no longer live in the church's designated house, as the new preacher and his family would need to move in. They did however receive a generous death benefit from the church, and used it to move into an apartment only a couple of blocks further along South Broad Street. The new apartment was smaller than the house they had lived in, but there was less of them living there, and his room was of a similar size, he didn't really pay much attention to the rest of the apartment, as long as he could hide away, he was happy enough.

In his final year at Masterman – he had decided that he was going to go elsewhere for high school, his aunt died. If he thought that his father's funeral had been a serious affair, it was nothing compared to the rigmarole of a Roman Catholic funeral. The Latin mass, the incense, the dirge like singing, and with hundreds of nuns in attendance, it seemed like the whole thing went on for days. He was glad to get back home afterwards, feeling like he had just attended a penguin convention.

His mother really withdrew into herself for months after the funeral, and it took him a while to realise that it was because she now only had him as family, and she felt somewhat alone in the world. It hadn't occurred to him that as it stood, they only really had each other. He then realised what an obnoxious little brat he must have been since his father's death, and how difficult he had made it for his mother. He declared to himself that he would stop being as self-centred as he had been, and that he would make an extra effort to reconnect with his mother, and to try and change his outlook on dealing with the other children at school. He shouldn't go through his life by himself.

Chapter 12

He found himself being shaken awake by the head hijacker. He slowly opened his eyes and looked round, and tried to stretch, forgetting that he couldn't as he was bound to his seat. He had no idea how long he had been asleep for this time, and he was not really in the mood to struggle with his binds to try and see what time it was.

The hijacker in a calm, almost friendly voice said,

"So glad that you're awake now, and just in time for lunch as well it would seem, the stewardess will be around with food in a minute. I am somewhat curious though, how you can manage to sleep, when it would appear that most of your fellow passengers seem to be in a state of great agitation? You are the only person that has had to be woken up to be fed."

He looked at the hijacker as if he was stupid as he replied,

"Well, what else am I supposed to do? I'm sat here in a seat by myself, hog-tied to the seat, unable to move more than a couple of inches, with a threat of being gagged if I speak. It's not as if I can get up and do a song and dance routine to help pass the time is it? I might as well go to sleep and slip off to a different reality."

"And speaking of reality, how am I supposed to eat any lunch when I'm trussed up like a turkey? Am I supposed to use magical thought patterns and levitate the food into my mouth? Abracadabra, hocus pocus; I can get the food to my mouth, if I really focus?"

The hijacker let out a hearty laugh before replying,

"I see that the time you've spent sleeping, and being tied up hasn't diminished your sense of humour. My apologies, I hadn't got around to telling you, that if you promise to behave then I will have someone untie one of your arms long enough for you to enjoy your meal. Of course it should go without saying that any funny business on your part shall result in even more rope to bind you, plus a gag, and a blindfold just for the sake of it. But I am going to say it, and ask whether you understand me?"

He thought about the hijacker laughing, pondering the unfairness of it all, the hijacker was free to laugh at will, and got rewarded by being able to wander around the plane unencumbered with a gun in his hand. One small laugh from a passenger and you spent the rest of the flight tied to your seat. The sense of injustice came out in the tone of his response.

"Yes, I understand perfectly well thanks, I just hope that there's nothing that needs an effort to cut up, as that may pose problems with only one free hand."

The humour in the hijacker's voice had gone

"Tell me something; are you awkward by nature, or do you have to practise?"

"I don't believe that I'm awkward, it's just that I tend to think things through a lot, and quite quickly, and don't necessarily worry about what I say to people, or who I say it to."

"Yes, this little quirk in your personality has already been noticed, but I wonder whether there is something else with you. Try as I might, I don't think it would be possible to find anyone else as blasé about the situation that you are in, and there is certainly no-one else on this plane with your disposition. Anyway, I have many other things to do and all of them better than having to talk with you. Just remember, no funny business."

"Ja, mein Fuhrer!"

The little dig stopped the hijacker in his tracks as he went back to the cockpit; he turned and glared, and stood straining to keep himself in check, his gun hand twitching. After a few tense moments, the hijacker turned away once more and carried on to the cockpit, and left him to his own thoughts again. He tried looking around, but found his movements restricted by his bindings, and was unable to twist enough to see anything behind him. He thought about whistling a tune for his own amusement, but for once common-sense won out, and he settled down and waited for lunch to be served. He could do without further aggravating the hijackers.

A couple of minutes later a somewhat worried looking stewardess came round and placed his food in front of him. She didn't make eye contact with him, almost contorting herself to be able to put the tray down in front of him, with her head looking the other way. It would appear he was also person non-gratis to the rest of the normal crew and probably the other passengers as well.

He looked down and instead of finding the expected first-class gourmet meal, he found himself confronted with the standard class meal on a tray, with a yoghurt, a small white bread roll, orange juice, and some as yet unidentified pre heated meal, with its foil still covering the small plastic container. He thought about complaining and asking where his first-class meal that he'd paid for was, but decided again, that under the current circumstances he'd be better off keeping his mouth shut.

The other hijacker that was in the first-class compartment came over and untied his left arm, well untied the forearm enough so he could just about manoeuvre it enough to reach the items on the tray, and then to reach his mouth.

With this he managed to take the foil lid off the meal, to find himself faced with some kind of pasta bake. He struggled with the plastic wrapped cutlery and napkin set, finally using his teeth with his left hand to tear the packet open, slid the fork out of the packet, and started to eat. He had had better food, but it was edible. He finished it reasonably quickly, surprised at how hungry he found himself, and moved on to his bread roll. He tried spreading the butter onto it, but found that the combination of the butter being bullet-proof, the roll being very soft, and only one arm to use made this virtually impossible. He gave up and used the bread to mop up the slop left in the bottom of the plastic container that had housed his pasta. The yoghurt was a "winter fruits" selection, and tasted vaguely of blackberry, and was gone in what seemed to be just seconds. He washed the whole lot down with the miniscule carton of insipid orange juice.

His surprise at how hungry he was led him to look at his watch, which with his left arm untied he could now see, and he was surprised to find that he must have been asleep for almost six hours. It was now late afternoon, and if they had been going straight to Greenland, he would have expected them to be there by now.

The previous night's drinks had obviously caught up with him, but he wondered if he'd been asleep that long, why hadn't they landed already? Greenland was on the usual flight path to America, even with a detour, they should have been there by now. Were they flying around randomly to try and fool whoever would be tracking the flight?

He sat reasonably still pondering this, as he waited, hoping for a stewardess to bring him a choice of coffee or tea, or really anything else to drink.

Despite being a regular visitor to England over the last few years, he had never understood their passion for tea, as it always tasted and smelt as if it shouldn't be an everyday drink, that it would be better suited as some kind of medicine, given out as some kind of punishment. Surely, no one in their right mind would really choose to drink it. You'd need to have something wrong with you to be able to force it down, either no sense of taste, or a very poor sense of smell, the only tea he'd ever wanted was of the Long Island iced variety, though he doubted it was cocktail hour here.

As his mind was wandering, another stewardess came over to his seat and asked him if he wanted coffee. He said yes as quickly as he could before she took it away and whoever was carrying the teapot arrived and tried to pour that instead.

He watched the stewardess pour the coffee into his little white plastic cup. As he watched her, he could see that she was struggling to keep her hand steady as she poured the liquid in to his cup, and realised that she must be under great stress, still doing the normal duties expected of her, under abnormal circumstances.

He looked up and caught her eye, and could immediately see the fear residing in her eyes, and felt as if he could almost read her mind, certain that she was wishing that she was anywhere apart from here, on this plane serving food and drink, while some madmen had control of the plane and everyone on it.

Chapter 13

In fact this was true.

Her name was Andrea Bittern, she had been a stewardess for nearly three years now, mostly doing long haul, because of the places it took her, and the fact it almost always enabled a stopover before heading back home.

She was only on this flight because she was doing a favour for a friend. She was supposed to have been on the British Airways flight to New York instead, but had agreed to a last-minute swap with the friend, as she had desperately wanted a stop-over in New York this week, so that she could meet up with her latest beau before a series of far-east flights that were scheduled in.

Andrea hadn't minded the swap at all. She hadn't managed to get a stop-over in Philadelphia before, and this flight had included a thirty-six-hour stopover, due to the airline scheduling, and the minimum eight-hour rest between flights.

It would appear now; however, that she wouldn't be going to Philadelphia after all, but instead to Greenland, where god only knows what was going to happen. Granted, she hadn't been to Greenland before either, but she had no wish to, and certainly not under these circumstances, plus she didn't think she had the wardrobe for it either, summer dresses probably weren't going to cut it in Arctic climes.

If she survived whatever was going to happen here, she was sure of one thing, if she remained a stewardess – something that was by no means certain – there wasn't a hope in hell that she'd be swapping flights with anyone again in a hurry. This was the first time in three years that she had – unusual in both the company and the industry as a whole – and look at what had happened to her.

She looked at the passenger she was pouring the coffee for, and wondered what on earth had possessed him to talk his way into being tied up in his seat as he was. Although she hadn't screamed out loud, she had internally, and didn't want to speak to anyone, and not in a way to antagonise the hijackers.

There was brief eye-contact with the passenger, and there was nothing to suggest that he was frightened, or even the slightest bit worried about being tied up on a plane, taken over by hijackers, and being diverted to a random country, and an unknown fate.

As long as she wasn't the one tied up, it was no concern of hers what was going through his mind. She finished pouring the coffee into his cup, and moved on to the next passenger. The sooner she could get through the service, the sooner she could take a seat and calm her shaking limbs.

Chapter 14

As the stewardess broke eye contact and moved on to pour coffee for the next passenger on her route, he looked down at his coffee and suddenly felt an urge to take the cup of hot liquid and throw it in the face of one of the hijackers, and try to overpower him. The urge faded as quickly as it had arrived as common sense kicked in.

For a start he wouldn't get very far, while for the main part he was tied to his seat, which would hinder the movement required to action the thought, and secondly, he really wasn't the hero type. He had enough difficulties being responsible for himself, let alone trying to be responsible for everyone else. There would be gunshots, people would get injured or killed, and he really didn't need that on his conscience, plus there was the fact that he could do without being killed as well.

Instead he picked up his cup, and started to drink the coffee. It was hot, but not too hot to drink immediately. He took his coffee black and savoured the bitter taste as he swallowed it greedily in one go.

He wasn't what most people would consider a regular coffee drinker, in fact it was rare for him to drink coffee at all, he much preferred cold drinks, and would normally get his caffeine from something like Pepsi. However when he did have coffee, he enjoyed the strong bitter taste that black coffee had, and thought of it as sacrilege to spoil it by adding either milk or sugar.

Even though he had drunk his coffee almost as soon as he had it in his hand, he had no sooner put his cup down, than a different stewardess appeared by his seat and collected his tray, that now consisted of empty wrappers, and very little else.

The new stewardess, he noted, seemed even more nervous than the previous one, and was again reluctant to even make eye contact with him. It suddenly dawned on him why this was, why should she risk being friendly with what was obviously the most troublesome passenger, who had managed to get himself bound to his seat, within only minutes of the plane being hijacked.

He realised that his position was a strange one, caused by his own strange sense of humour, and his somewhat bizarre ability to laugh at things that no one else would even consider being even slightly amusing. In fact the only person who laughed at anything more inappropriate than he did was probably Dr. Hibbert from the Simpsons, and he was a fictional cartoon character!

Despite himself he found himself laughing gently again to himself, and only stopped chuckling away when he turned to his right to see the big boss man of the hijackers standing to his side, with a look of bemusement on his face.

"Yet again, I find you laughing at nothing in particular; you are indeed a most peculiar chap."

What was a gentle laugh now broke out into a full volume guffaw, as the imagery of the hijacker being the perfect English gentleman invaded his consciousness. Images of him being sat in a gentleman's club, somewhere in Mayfair, London, sipping a Pimm's and lemonade, and saying "Splendid show old chap", rushed into his mind, and he found himself genuinely amused, and unable to prevent himself laughing out loud.

He glanced to his side, and saw that the hijacker however was not so amused, and when he started to speak in a voice dripping ice, he made it clear.

"Have I said something that you find amusing?"
"Yes, as a matter of fact you have."
"Would you like to share your amusement with me?"
"Not really."
"Why not?"
Quickly changing the subject he asked,
"Would you like to share the reason you have decided to hijack this plane with me?"

There was a brief pause from the hijacker as if he was deciding on whether to answer the question or carry on with his own original question, before going with the former.

"Not yet, though you will find out in time, as will everyone on the plane, but only when I decide the time is right."

Once again, his mouth was off and running before the sensible part of his brain had a chance to shut it down.

"Is that time going to be soon, or have I got enough time to have another little sleep after the glorious meal we've just been served?"

The ice in the hijacker's voice dipped a few degrees, as he spat out a response.

"In case you hadn't noticed, I am the hijacker here, and I will be the one around here asking the questions, and you, you there tied to your seat, and at the point of being gagged are a hostage, and as such you are not in a position to be asking me questions, but you will give the answers to my questions."

Just as the ice in the hijacker's voice had become more acute, so did the sarcasm in his own.

"I have been giving you answers, but I can't be held responsible if the answers you get are not to your liking."

The hijacker eyed him warily for a few seconds, his face strained as if he was trying to make a difficult decision, before somewhat surprisingly, breaking into a laugh of his own.

"I think that in different circumstances, I would have liked to have known you as a friend, you have a sharp wit, and an ability to laugh that seems to be missing from most on the run of the mill types that one meets these days. However this still leads me to believe that under the current circumstances you may well be a dangerous man, and therefore I think that your free arm shall be re-bound."

"I'm not sure, we could have been friends, I don't make friends easily, don't really have any, and I'm not sure that I move in the right circles of the English upper classes to be hob-knobbing with the hijacker's finishing school candidates."

"Like I said, in different circumstances. The hijacking happening here isn't a run of the mill affair, as you will find out in due course, and you might have found that away from here, I'm a different person. You may not find me friend material, but you would be an interesting person to be around. Now, it is time for your arm to be reunited with the arm of your seat, and for me to carry on with the managing of this situation."

He waited until the hijacker had turned round before offering his parting shot, in an overly comical upper class English accent.

"Excuse me old boy, but would you mind terribly, telling me what the in-flight movie is, and when it's due to start, but I appeared to have mislaid my flight programme."

The Hijacker stopped, looked over his shoulder briefly, and then rolled his eyes and went into the cockpit shaking his head.

Almost immediately, his happy go lucky compadre arrived at his seat and started on the task of securing his free arm back to the arm of the seat. Whilst being secured he sat there smiling at the underling, which in return got a dirty look, and he was quite sure, a glimmer of hatred in the underling's eyes. Once he was fully secured the underling growled through gritted teeth at him,

"Be thankful that he," Indicating the big boss man, "Is a patient person. If I was in charge, you would have been shot by now and dumped into the cargo holding area, along with the rest of the useless baggage."

Unable to resist he responded,

"You see, that's why he's in charge, if you will the organ grinder. He has the ability to think, whereas, in your case, as the monkey, it would seem that you have only just about mastered the ability of learning how to speak."

The underling raised his gun, and put it to his temple, and for a split second it looked like he would get shot, however, as if realisation had suddenly dawned, the underling lowered the gun, gave him a dirty look, muttered something under his breath, and turned quickly, and stomped off to another part of first class, still muttering darkly.

He wondered just what had got into him. He hadn't recalled any death wish tendencies recently, and yet here he was antagonising hijackers, who as far as he could tell were carrying loaded weapons. He needed to be a bit smarter in what was said, instead of just being a smart arse. The latter was going to get him into more trouble than he already was.

With this final thought on the subject, he closed his eyes and tried to relax. He was surprised to find that this was remarkably easy to do, and within a matter of moments he was fast asleep again.

Chapter 15

He had started at the Abraham Lincoln High School in the fall following his aunt's funeral, and found it a totally different experience to the Masterman School, and due to the recent life events, he had gone to High school with a totally different mindset.

During the summer vacation between changing schools, he had had a sudden spurt of growth, and had bulked out so that he was no longer the slight boy whose frame had been hampering his hockey aspirations over the previous three years. Despite this growth and bulking out, he had decided that he wasn't going to try out for the hockey team anyway; it wasn't really where his future was going to lie, and no matter how much he had wanted it to be when he was younger.

As well as growing physically, he felt he had grown mentally as well, and during the break he had got a job as an office boy for Trebling Software, a small local software company that had only started up the year before. He hadn't had much experience with computers previously, there were a few at Masterman, but he hadn't really used them that much, and certainly not for anything useful. He had spent a fair amount of time in the local arcades playing on the various video game machines, and had been intrigued by how the games were put together. However, if he was honest with himself, he had not really been interested in normal computers, and up to then had never considered wanting to have one.

The time he spent working at Trebling over the summer certainly changed his mind, he saw the way that games were being made for computers, and how they could move away from arcades. As he got round to starting high school, he knew that the world of computers was where his future lay, he wanted to be involved in the creating of new games. He had never previously known what he wanted to do at the end of school, but he certainly did now.

Towards the end of the summer, as the return to high school drew near, he had found himself staying late at Trebling so that he could learn more about computers and what could be done on them. He managed to persuade the owners, and the principal programmers, Dave Dorling, and Andrew Trebilcock, to keep him on a part time basis while he was in high school.

Looking back, they probably didn't need him for as many hours as they gave him to work, but they seemed to like him, and a smart, enthusiastic kid could be an asset to the firm, after all that's what they started out as.

He spent his first few days at Abraham Lincoln High changing his courses and rearranging his timetable, so that he could manage to do computing. Once again, he had found something that he had a natural aptitude for, and found that computing took over from hockey as a spare time activity to partake in.

Dave and Andrew let him have an old monitor and that, along with pieces from wrecked machines and spares, meant he was able to build himself a computer. It may not have been the most powerful machine, or the most aesthetically pleasing in terms of how it was put together, but it was his, and it meant that he could play and experiment as much as he wanted without having to stay late in school or work. To be honest, this might have meant the end of his contact with the outside world, and probably would have done if he hadn't met Keera.

Keera Fallenfant was a senior at Abraham Lincoln High, and he had bumped into her in the refectory, literally, by almost running her over whilst in a rush to grab lunch and get back to the computer lab. He had been mortified and was worried that he had hurt her, but as he helped her up, he could hear her laughing, and whilst mumbling out an apology, which she gracefully accepted, he surprised himself by asking her if she wanted her if he could make amends by taking her for a drink after school.

He was even more surprised when she said yes, and he took lunch at a more sedate pace that day, amazed by the fact that he'd asked for and got a date and he didn't bother with the computer lab that lunchtime after all. The drink that evening was a success, and it was quickly followed by several further dates, and before he even had the chance to realise, they were an item. He couldn't believe his luck, he was dating a girl who was probably the best-looking girl in school, and who seemed to really like him.

That first year of high school rushed past, and left him wondering just where the time went. His studies were going well, and if he continued to get the kind of marks he had got during the first year then he would have no problems getting into any university he wanted to.

The job at Trebling was also progressing nicely, and with what he had picked up in experience there, and with what he'd been taught on his course at high school, he had been allowed to do some test coding for one of their new games, and was making some decent money for a part time job, and he was going to have the opportunity to get some serious work done during the vacation.

His relationship with Keera was also going well, and they spent nearly all their spare time together, which was a lot better than the planned long hours he was going to have had with his home-made computer. The only problem on the horizon for their relationship was that Keera was finishing high school that year, and in the fall, she would be off to university at Duke.

The summer vacation was the most difficult of his young life. In some ways it was a good time, with full time employment at Trebling. He was hardly doing any of the clerical work that he had originally been taken on to do the summer before, but spent time alternating between doing some coding for one of next year's releases, testing for this year's releases, and writing documentation. He really couldn't believe that he was getting paid to spend a large part of his time playing games.

Despite how well this was going, he found that his relationship with Keera was somewhat strained. Keera having been accepted to go to Duke, had got the required grades, and would be leaving in a matter of weeks to move down to North Carolina.

The year's age difference, which should have caused no problem, seemed to loom large over the pair of them. She wanted to spend as much time with him as possible, but when they did spend time together, there was a tension between them that hadn't been there previously.

It was obvious that Keera was apprehensive about the fact that she was going to be away at university. Even though Duke wasn't the other side of the country, it was still a few hours' drive away, and both would be busy, with both work and study. Chances to be with each other at weekends would be few and far between, and they would only really get any time to be with each other during vacations.

The entire summer was spent with increasingly uncommunicative evenings, though at least they didn't argue. As the start of the fall term approached, things had gotten to the point where they agreed to separate, so that they could try and go on and live normal lives as individuals in different cities.

If he was honest, he wasn't happy with the separation, and he thought that he could have done things differently, and been more supportive, as it must have been a difficult time for Keera, but once again there was a level of selfishness to a situation that had shown up, something in his character that made him less inclined to think about how the situation was affecting other people.

They had parted on a reasonably friendly basis, and hadn't managed to have any major rows that may have soured their view of each other. They had decided to keep in touch, and for the first couple of months he wrote to her every week, just inconsequential chat, and was quite pleased to get replies from Keera on a similar frequency.

Thanksgiving arrived before he could even think where the time had gone, and Keera came back to Philadelphia for the holiday. They spent a lot of time together over the Thanksgiving holiday, and the general atmosphere between them was so much better than it had been during the summer, and at the end of the break it was upsetting when Keera had to go back.

As well as writing they now spoke several times a week on the phone and when Keera came home for the Christmas holidays, they rekindled their romance and became an item again. In the new year he took a weekend off from work and study to go down and visit her at least once a month.

Chapter 16

He was shaken awake.
    Again!
    What was it with people shaking him awake today? He wasn't a damn bottle of Orangina that needed the taste awakening inside of him by shaking him every so often.
    He was prepared to let his latest shaker know exactly what he thought of them, and their bedside manner, and he opened his eyes. However, this time there was nobody shaking him, and as he took a few seconds to get his bearings and have a look around, he remembered that he was on board a plane. Not only seated.
    But tied into his seat.
    On a hijacked plane.
    Now bound for Kangerlussuaq.
    In the frozen wastes of Greenland.
    Such was his life today.
    Without someone standing over him, he wondered what had shaken him awake this time, only to realise that the whole plane was shaking. As he came round to be fully awake, he became aware that there were some people somewhere on board screaming, and he looked across the short distance to the cabin door, to see the head honcho of the hijackers leaning into the cabin, and having a heated discussion with one or more of the flight crew. Although there were raised voices, he couldn't manage to make out what was being said due to the rattling noises elsewhere within the plane.
    The discussion came to a halt and the hijacker came out of the cabin door, and looked more concerned than angry, and within seconds, the pilot's voice came over the intercom system.

"Good evening ladies and gentlemen, this is your captain speaking. As you may have noticed, the flight today has encountered some very heavy turbulence. The situation is under control, and there is nothing to unduly worry about."

"The cause of this turbulence is down to the fact that due to the circumstances on board today, and our changed destination and extended flight time, we are not in a normal commercial flight lane, and we are flying somewhat lower than would be normal. Therefore we are flying into air currents that we would normally have avoided, and this is causing the turbulence that is having such an effect on the flight at this time."

"We expect this severe turbulence to last for about another 20 minutes, until we turn in to make our final decent into Kangerlussuaq. For those passengers feeling queasy, it is worth remembering that there are air sickness bags located in the pouches on the back of the seat in front of you. Let me stress again, that there is nothing to be seriously worried about, and I would like to ask all passengers to remain calm. Thank you."

His immediate thought was that at this point just how calm the captain had come across as this time around. The previous time he had spoken, several hours ago now, he had sounded a bit frazzled, but he seemed well under control now. He wondered whether there was a dealing with hijacking course, that the airlines sent their pilots on, to try and train them how not to lose it in pressure situations like this.

Then again, he considered that surely part of a pilot's make up would be the need to remain calm in pressure situations. They wouldn't be much good if they started running around like a headless chicken at the slightest problem, a sudden vision of a bucket of KFC flying the plane flashed into his mind and he smiled to despite himself.

Granted the pilots might be shitting themselves, but they knew how to deal with it, and perhaps even got some kind of adrenaline rush from it, and perhaps having to deal with the additional work that the turbulence was causing them was focusing their minds on that part of the flight, and less so on the hijacking of their plane.

He thought about the message, and realised that if they were going to be starting their descent in about twenty minutes, then they would be on the ground in Greenland in less than an hour.

He still had reservations about how they were going to land this plane anywhere on the godforsaken icicle his envisioned Greenland to be, and the earlier vision of the plane sliding across the ice like a big silver pen, that a kid had put a ruler under the slide on it, still flowed through his mind and made him smile.

There again the hijackers had obviously planned this lunacy, and therefore had probably considered that kind of thing carefully. It also dawned on him that although it was an icebound country, they would still need some contact with the rest of the world, and for this end, supply planes must be able to land somewhere on the massive island, so even if there wasn't a large civilian air strip, it was virtually certain that there would be a military strip big enough.

That only left the question of why on earth would anyone want to go to Greenland, let alone be so desperate to go that they were willing to hijack a plane to get there. He hoped that he would be able to find out why, because he was intrigued by the idea of there being something interesting behind this hijacking, rather than a bog-standard terrorism plot.

Besides that he also hoped that once they were in Greenland, he would get the chance to talk to the two women he had been next to originally on this flight, both the lookalike who had spoken to him, but also the mystery woman, often seen, that he had not spoken to. There was so much that he felt he needed to ask them both.

He suddenly had the chills, as someone had been tap dancing on his grave, and had the notion that he was supposed to be here, and so were the women, and he knew that his part in whatever was going on wouldn't be over when they landed.

He shifted slightly under his binds, and felt the weight of his phone in his trouser pocket. He'd been sat like that for more hours than he should have done, and it had never entered his mind to try for his phone. He couldn't get at it now, being hog-tied as he was, but if they were going to be letting people off the plane when it landed, he could try and use it then.

The more he thought about his phone, the more he wondered why there had been no attempt by the hijackers to come round and collect any communication devices. Phones, tablets, laptops, e-readers, watches, in fact, there were all sorts of equipment that could be used nowadays to contact the outside world.

Yet, despite this, there had been no attempt to stop this, no announcements to warn people not to, nothing, he hadn't noticed the hijackers rushing around taking devices off people. More and more, planes had Wi-Fi and phone connections, and it hadn't seemed to wave any flags with the hijackers, in fact he was sure this flight had advertised Wi-Fi being available in-flight. Had they made some kind of error in what seemed to be a well-executed plan?

Or had they not worried about it because they'd found some way of blocking all the signals that could have been used. If it was the latter, that was a serious piece of kit they had at their disposal, and therefore they had some big money backing whatever they were doing here.

The more he thought about what was going on, the more his head hurt. A single cup of coffee and a miniscule orange juice wasn't enough to drink either for the length of time they'd spent on the plane. After the night before, he was getting a headache, as he felt himself becoming more and more dehydrated.

Chapter 17

It may have been twenty minutes down to the last second for all he knew, but unable to check his watch he couldn't be sure, but suddenly, just as promised by the captain, the plane changed direction and began its descent, and the turbulence stopped almost immediately.

He had spent most of the last twenty minutes with his eyes closed, knowing that if he'd kept them open, the vibration effect on his vision, along with the dehydration inspired headache that he already had, would have made him feel quite ill.

He glanced to his right and saw the head honcho of the hijackers come out of the cockpit, looking decidedly happier than he was before the captain had made his announcement. As if he could feel himself being looked at, he turned and walked over.

"I trust you are well rested, if only I could have had such a relaxing journey as you seem to have had, asleep most of the time, seemingly without a care in the world, a perfect little journey. Well without the bindings, of course."

"Oh no, these ropes are really comfortable, and they help with my tendency to fidget. If only all such journeys were so restrictive, I could save myself the money and travel in the economy seats." He found himself replying, with only the faintest hint of sarcasm.

The hijacker shook his head slightly, with a wry smile on his face, and said,

"I could have made things a lot more uncomfortable for you, and lesser men than myself may well have had you shot."

"In fact, with the exception of one other person on this flight, I would have shot them!"

He surprised himself by laughing again before replying,

"Yeah, my journey could have been more uncomfortable, I could have been stood up for god knows how many thousand miles like you."

"As for shooting me, I'm quite sure you're not an idiot. Mad perhaps, but not an idiot, and although the only help I've seen doesn't appear to be the sharpest tool in the box, I'm quite sure that they're all under strict instructions not to shoot anyone unless it's a real emergency. I mean who knows where the bullet might end up, it could end up puncturing the fuselage, and then we'd all be proper screwed then, wouldn't we? You included."

He continued ranting,

"And furthermore, what does it matter who you shoot? Unless of course, you're not really the one in charge here, and you too, are being told exactly what to do, like the rest of the lackeys round here!"

The head honcho's face didn't crack, and through what seemed to be unmoving lips, hissed,

"I am not mad, or anything close to it! And it is probably a good job for your sake that I'm not, as you continue to try my patience, but rest assured if you continue to do so when we are on the ground then I may not look on you in such a favourable light."

"Do not push me, you are in no position to push me, and continued pushing may well end up being bad for your health. With regards to "my help" as you put it, they are all trained shots, a couple of them, including the one you obviously think so highly of, are of Olympic standard, and therefore they wouldn't miss."

"Furthermore, all the guns are loaded with specially designed ammunition, which will go through simple flesh quite easily, but will disintegrate upon contact with a more solid surface."

"Bully for you",

Came the automatic reply, and he immediately thought that it probably wasn't the greatest idea.

The hijacker lifted his gun and pressed it against the side of his head, and whispered,

"I could pull this trigger and from this range you'd have little chance of survival, so do yourself a favour, and think before you say anything else, as if you push me any further, they could be your last words."

With that the head honcho removed the gun from his head, and walked off to speak to his lackey in the first-class compartment. As he did so, an unseen passenger who sat behind him, leant forward, and in a whisper that was full of undisguised panic, and a pitch so high it suggested his underpants were causing him difficulties, said,

"What is it with you? Why can't you just be quiet and stop antagonising them, do you want to get us all killed? It's all very well for you to have a smart mouth and a death wish, but don't force that death wish on the rest of us as well. I think I speak for everyone else in saying that I'd quite like to survive whatever is going on here, so just shut up"

He realised that he didn't care what anyone else thought of him, and he was too tired to think of any additional witty retort, and somewhat wearily replied,

"Shut up and mind your own business, and unless you've spoken to the rest of the passengers then you don't speak for anyone except your whiny little self!"

Some huffing came from the seat behind him, but there were no further whispered words.

Without any further voices to think about, he spent his time on the rest of the descent considering the head honcho. Although his face didn't give anything away, he seemed overly defensive in his response about not being in ultimate control.

If that was the case, it really did beg the question, what the hell was going on?

Chapter 18

As the plane descended, he spent his time leaning over as far to his left as his binds would let him, so that he could get his head into the best angle to look out of the window as best as he could. At first all he could really see was the ocean, which was a lot darker than he would have expected it to be, but then it was probably getting on in the day, and the sun was probably lower in the sky this far north, so there wasn't enough light to bring out the full colour of the ocean below him.

As they descended some more, the seascape he could see turned from a dark grey and as he started to make out the beginning of the land, all he could see in that direction was white. God alone knew why they called this land mass Greenland, much as he tried, he was certain that he couldn't see even the slightest bit of green anywhere. Perhaps with Iceland already have been snapped up as a name, and Whiteland sounding quite unappealing, they went for something that might attract people to come here.

That had failed miserably, and apart from some indigenous tribes, no one wanted to move there, and he could see why, in fact all he could see was masses of white, with the occasional bit of grey, where rock jutted out from beneath the cover of the snow and ice. It looked totally inhospitable and if someone went missing out here; they were never getting found, were they? Was this the reason for diverting here, they didn't want any chance of escape?

In time he thought he saw some buildings, only discernible by the uniform shapes, and the shadows that they cast, but even they seemed white, and as he watched the land coming to meet the descending plane, the whiteness of what he could see out there made him involuntarily shiver, and his mind was cast back to five years before.

Chapter 19

His mind had flicked back to him being in that all white room, with no discernible size or shape, bright whiteness everywhere, and no shadow cast, even by himself, no matter which direction he looked round in.

He could see the same mystery woman on the bed or table or whatever it was next to him, and when he looked past her, there were four more people on the same standard piece of furniture further along in the room. He couldn't judge properly how far away they were, depth perception in that room was virtually impossible.

He also tried to picture their faces, but he couldn't seem to be able to pick out any recognisable features about them, and wondered whether that was because of the time elapsed since then, the distance they were away from them, or was it something else?

He also thought about the fact that he had never seen any of them since, if they were all under the same programme, and he had seen his bed neighbour so many times, why had he not seen anyone else in that room.

Or was it because they all seemed so non-descript in his head, from the distance he had seen them, that they wouldn't be remembered, even if they had been standing on his toes.

Something about that thought set alarm bells ringing in his mind, and he wondered why.

What was it about being non-descript that caused him to shudder, triggering something in his head.

He had another thought as well, in the time he was conscious in that room, he was able to look in any direction, but overall, he always seemed to be looking to his right, down the length of the room, as did everyone else he could remember seeing, they had looked in his direction occasionally, but almost without seeing him. He wondered therefore whether the woman on the next table had seen him properly at all in the same way he saw her, and therefore that was why there never appeared to be a glimmer of recognition. Would she only be able to recognise the person to her right on the way down the room, and did she see them with the same kind of regularity he saw her, and did it freak her out so much if she did? There were just so many questions about that room.

It dawned on him, that the room might not have just had the six of them in, it could have carried on in the same way to his left-hand side, where he really had no memory of seeing anything or anyone, but had that been deliberate, and could there have been another six, or another sixty people to his left?

Was there someone from that room who kept just missing him, who had the same questions to ask him, as he had to ask the woman? Something told him some of these questions may get answered in what was unfolding here.

Chapter 20

He brought himself back to the here and now, and as he looked out of the window, he could see what appeared to be an airport, or at the very least an airstrip.

He strained to get a good view, and he could see a long strip of tarmac, with its blackness contrasting boldly with the surrounding landscape of almost blinding white, and in it there were a variety of different coloured lights. They wouldn't be in the air very much longer; the airstrip was expecting them. As he got closer to the ground, he could see that the area around the airport wasn't all white, there were patches of dark rock, interspersed with some green mossy or grassy areas, and he found himself surprised that there were some patches of green on Greenland.

He looked around the cabin, and saw that everyone was belted in for landing, except for the head honcho, who was stood in the doorway of the entrance to the cockpit, with his back to him, but seemingly alert, moving his head from side to side on a regular basis, so that he could see the pilots at work, and watch the mood of the passengers.

As he looked around, he couldn't see the other hijacker that had been in the first-class cabin, but that wasn't to say that he wasn't there. For all he knew the hijacker could have been sat in the seat right behind him, and he'd never have been able to have seen him, with being tied up like he was, and his view of the cabin limited to the other passengers on the front row.

He looked out of the window again, and was surprised that the plane was almost on the runway. Within seconds there was the bump of the rear wheels hitting the tarmac, and then the secondary bump of the front wheels touching down.

He felt himself leaning forward slightly as the braking effect took hold, and within about thirty seconds they had slowed down to a crawl, and then veered off to the right slightly, before coming to a complete halt. He looked out of the window, and was surprised to see that the tarmac seemed to stretch on for a good distance in front of them, and was a lot wider than most runway strips he had seen on his travels. There were lots of small, prefabricated buildings either side of the runway, giving him the impression that this must have been an air force base at some point, probably judging by the unimaginative state of the buildings, an American one.

So much for sliding off into the icy wastes!

He watched in some surprise as no sooner had the plane come to a complete halt, and then two sets of steps were driven across the airstrip to the plane. It would appear that the whole of the ground crew was dressed in very similar clothes to the ones the hijackers were wearing, jeans and polo shirts, with the only difference being that they all wore hooded parkas and sunglasses. He shivered involuntary again, not from the cold he knew was outside, as that hadn't had the chance to get on board yet, and wouldn't until the doors were opened, but from the creepy effectiveness of the operation he was witnessing here. He wondered what was waiting for him; and anyone else once they got off the plane, always assuming that they ever did.

The intercom clicked on, and the head hijacker came on the air.

"Ladies and gentlemen, and any children on board, I will take this opportunity to welcome you all to the beautiful island they call Greenland. I realise for most of you this is the first time you will have been here, though unfortunately this isn't going to be a sight-seeing tour, which really is a shame, as it is the most beautiful place to be at one with nature."

The hijacker seemed to be smiling and enjoying himself with the microphone.

"On the journey in we have identified those passengers that can leave the aircraft here in Kangerlussuaq, and one of my happy band of new attendants will be around presently to escort those of you lucky enough to be chosen to the exit, where one of our helpful ground staff will escort you to the very humble private airport hangar lounge in the freight part of the airport. Unfortunately we will not be using the main terminal, or the very nice hotel that is attached to it."

"In about twenty minutes a Boeing 727 that we have borrowed from Air Canada will be landing, whereas the passengers we want from that particular flight shall be transferred to this plane, those that we are taking from this plane will be moved from the lounge to that Air Canada 727, and then this plane will be flown on to Philadelphia as originally planned, but obviously with a slight delay to your original planned arrival time."

"However I regret to inform those changing planes that your luggage will not be joining you for some time yet, if at all, and I would like to apologise for the obvious inconvenience that this causes, but the Air Canada 727 just doesn't have the same sized luggage hold we have on this plane, and we have no staff available to sort out the luggage we would need to remove from this plane."

"For the rest of you that are not escorted from the plane in the next couple of minutes, you are going nowhere for the moment, and further instructions will be issued once we have filled back up with the rest of our guests from the Air Canada flight. I will take this opportunity to remind everyone that if you haven't been picked for the connecting flight, do not attempt to force the issue. Any attempts to do so will meet with death. Do not be fooled by the fact that there has been no violence so far. The gentlemen with guns will have no problems terminating you, and the person next to you for that matter. If you haven't been chosen to be moved, then you are not important, and therefore have no value, let that sink in for a few minutes before considering being a hero. There are a lot more bullets on board this plane than there are passengers!"

"Thank you for listening."

And the intercom cut off. The immediate silence on the plane was deafening.

Chapter 21

He sat bound in his seat and thought to himself just how many times the head hijacker had watched Under Siege and whether he based himself on Tommy Lee Jones, or whether it was just that little speech that he seemed to like. Despite himself he sat there laughing to himself again. He heard the passenger behind him theatrically tutting at him, and he sat there shaking his head whilst still laughing.

His mind started kicking in again, and more questions formed. The fact that there was another hijacked plane inbound, and that the head hijacker had said that there were people from that flight they wanted, made him think. Just how many people on this flight were "wanted", and why?

This was obviously a very slick operation, to hijack two flights within a couple of hours and take them to the same destination, and when they get the planes there, to have more men on the ground meant that it was well planned, well manned, and well-funded. He also wondered who was in charge overall. Was it the head honcho on this plane? Was there a similar person on the other plane? Or was there an overall boss man pulling the strings behind the scenes for both hijackings?

Furthermore he began to ponder, what were the chances of these two flights having the exact people that this group wanted on them? How many people booked far enough in advance that they would appear on the passenger lists in enough time for them to pull all this together?

Certainly in his case he normally bought single journey tickets, mainly because the way his job was, there was no set time limit on when a job or client presentation would end, or even when new jobs would come up. For this flight he hadn't booked on until the previous evening, and in speaking to people over the years found that a fair few of the people on these flights did the same, or at least in the first-class section they did. He often travelled at less than twenty-four hours-notice, and in fact had struggled to get his required flight a few times because of the short notice.

With this in his mind he felt himself relax, as if a great weight had been taken off. His sense of foreboding that he had felt earlier on the flight just before landing seemed to be misplaced. There was no way that this hijacking could have had him as a particular target. He now just hoped that he got the chance to speak to the two women that had so fried his mind earlier in the day. That was of course, if they weren't some of the "wanted" passengers on the hijacker's list, and unseen to him, they were in the process of being led off the plane.

Although he had relaxed a little, there was still that nagging doubt in the back of his mind from his earlier conversation with the head hijacker, and the implication that he was somehow wanted, or needed in this operation, what had the hijacker said? Something about him being an exception to being shot along with a couple of others. However, a glance out of the window put that thought to rest as well.

Some passengers were disembarking, and as he leaned over, he could see them walking over to the airport building, with a few men keeping them under observation. There weren't a lot of them, and he could see the last one in the procession, and with that he knew he wasn't one of them.

He found himself relaxing as he watched those passengers walk all the way into the airport building, and it seemed that they had only just got inside the building when the Air Canada flight taxied in and stopped pretty much next to his plane.

Within moments of that plane coming to a halt the men on the ground had positioned a set of steps up to one of its doors, ready for the required passengers from that plane to alight, ready for them to transfer to this plane, and possibly some to be moved to the airport building.

He strained to look out of his window as some passengers from the other plane made their way down the steps, and at the bottom, they turned in the direction of his plane, and headed across the tarmac to it. They were kept in close formation by a whole host of guards that had seemed to materialise out of thin air.

As those passengers walked across the tarmac, he could see a fuel truck lining up under the 727 and the refuelling process start almost straight away, there certainly wasn't any delay in getting things ready to get the planes back out of there.

Then, as they were about halfway between the planes one of the escorted passengers broke out from the ranks as they walked across and made a run for it. Just what the passenger was making a run for, or where they were planning to go was anyone's guess. There certainly wasn't any cover, or anywhere to run to here. Whatever their plan, it came to an abrupt halt, as one of the accompanying guards turned and let loose a barrage of shots from whatever type of machine gun they had. The running passenger ground to a sudden and somewhat final stop, keeling over face first into the ground.

Two more guards walked over to the prostrate passenger, and one of them pulled out a handgun and shot them at point blank range in the back of their head. Then the shooter and the other guard took an arm each and dragged the dead body off in the direction of the airport building.

They stopped short of the building, and opened the lid of a garbage skip just outside, and dumped the body into it, before walking back to where the no longer moving procession of passengers were. As they got back to the passengers, another guard took out a gun and fired it into the air, and as if someone had poked them with a pitchfork the passengers lurched into sudden motion.

He got the feeling that no one else would be attempting to make a run for it. He looked back over at the skip, and despite himself shuddered. He thought for a moment about his own mortality and hoped that his final resting place would be somewhere a bit more auspicious than a garbage skip outside an airport building in a country that no one wanted to go to.

The shooting outside had also stirred up the atmosphere on the plane. Even if other passengers hadn't seen what had happened, they had heard the gunfire, and there was yet again, screams from somewhere on the plane, and a general murmur of whispers and gasps. This was silenced when the intercom clicked back into life.

"Silence! Yes, you have heard gunshots. Let me again make this crystal clear for you, if you co-operate, and follow our instructions, then no harm will come to you. Someone from the Air Canada flight didn't believe that, and they have paid the price for their lack of belief, do not be the next to suffer a similar fate. Keep quiet and you will soon be on your way back to Philadelphia."

The intercom clicked off again, and he thought about his interactions with the hijackers up until now, and realised that they hadn't been playing, and he could have easily ended up dead and dumped due to his scattergun mouth. He wondered if he could keep it shut from here on out, and he could manage to make it home to Philly without further incident.

Chapter 22

Then the doors to the airport building opened, and those passengers that had been taken off his plane came rushing out of the doors, making their way to the refuelling 727. Although he couldn't pick out their faces at this distance, he was quite sure that they would be scurrying across the tarmac with looks of fear and bewilderment across their faces. It also appeared that the number of passengers coming out of the building seemed to match the number that had been removed from this plane; no one was being kept in the airport.

He glanced back down to where the other plane's passengers should be walking across to his plane, but found that he couldn't see them, and therefore they must already be at the plane's steps or boarding now. Furthermore, there were no other passengers being removed from that plane and taken to the airport building. Was this just a swap of passengers? No one seemed to be kept on the ground apart from the mass of similarly dressed hijackers.

The passengers from the Air Canada flight being boarded on this plane was confirmed when in what seemed a few seconds he could hear voices issuing instructions, and he could just about make out someone's voice, perhaps that of the person in overall control, ordering the new hostages just where they would have to sit.

Glancing back out of the window he saw that the refuelling truck was already retreating from the Air Canada 727, and to his surprise the 727 had shut its door and was already taxi-ing along back towards the runway. It was almost as if those heading on to parts unknown, couldn't get away quick enough. No one from that flight had been left on the ground either – well apart from the poor unfortunate soul in the dumpster – it would appear to be just a transfer between planes.

Despite being in the cabin he could hear the thrust (or at least he imagined he could) of the 727 as it sped along the runway to whatever fate awaiting those poor sods. He briefly wondered whether there would ever be an end of the ordeal for those on that plane or would they remain at the whims of the hijackers on that plane for the rest of time?

He noticed movement to his right again, and found the head hijacker coming past him to go back into the cabin. He hadn't noticed him go the other way whilst he was looking out of the window, and it struck him that despite what had gone on with passenger transfers it seemed as if the head hijacker was still in charge on this plane, which might suggest that he was the one in overall control of the situation.

The intercom clicked on, and he heard the head hijacker's voice come over the air.

"Testing, there is no message at this time."

The intercom clicked off and the head hijacker came out of the cabin.

He tried to look over his shoulder to see behind him, before realising that was a futile gesture, as it appeared that the head hijacker was waiting for someone, and sure enough he heard someone come through to the first class and say "Yes". At that the head hijacker's face set and he quickly turned and went back into the cabin.

From his seat he could hear voices emanating from the cabin, obviously at odds with each other, but try as he might he couldn't quite make out any words. The head hijacker stuck his head out of the door and motioned to another of the hijackers, who hurried up to the door of the cabin, where the head hijacker whispered something to him, before the underling headed off back towards the rear of the first class. Moments later the head hijacker's voice came over the intercom, with the same message as before,

"Testing, there is no message at this time."

This time the head hijacker didn't emerge from the cabin, and after a short while the other hijacker came up and leant into the cabin and muttered something before heading back to his post.

The intercom clicked on again, and yet again the voice of the head hijacker was heard.

"This is not a test. Now that the crew have stopped playing silly games and conformed with my simple request, I am now addressing those of you who happen to reside in the first-class section of this aircraft. Those passengers in the rest of this aircraft cannot hear what I am about to say."

"First of all, if you have a look around you, you will see that there are quite a few more of my colleagues now standing in the first-class compartment of this aircraft."

He heard mutterings, and found himself complying with the request and looking around the best he could. As he did, he could pick out three or four different hijackers to the ones he'd seen before in view, whereas previously he had only ever seen the head hijacker and one other at the most at the same time from his seat. The voice continued.

"If any attempt is made at making any noise to raise a signal to the rest of the aircraft, that person will be shot. This is no idle threat, as you will have noticed with the incident on the tarmac below us; we are perfectly capable of killing and disposing of people if the need arises. I have no wish to kill anyone sat in the first-class compartment of this aircraft. In a few minutes everyone in first class will be leaving the aircraft. No one in the rear of the aircraft will know that you have left the aircraft, and the stewarding crew will not know either, as they are temporarily indisposed. The intercom system will be disabled, and in less than twenty minutes this aircraft will be taking off to head to its original destination, and until it gets there no one will be any the wiser about your exit from this flight."

"If anyone attempts to escape during disembarkation they will be shot in the leg, there will be no escaping, and I really do not want to harm any of you. If you have not guessed you are all required for something special, and my superiors would not be amused if you didn't all make it alive, and trust me you would not want to meet my superiors when they are in a bad mood. However, being alive, but in severe pain is an acceptable delivery criterion."

His sense of dread kicked back in again, he now knew for certain that this flight hijacking was all part of a grander design, and it involved him, he was part of a set of requirements, and he hated that. Another thing he now knew was that the head hijacker wasn't the overall head man of the operation, even he was taking orders from someone higher up, and while that gave him a small sense of satisfaction, it didn't stop him from wondering just what kind of man would oversee an operation of this size and scale?

Chapter 23

Who he had previously thought was the head honcho overall, but who it had turned out was only in charge of this plane and was in fact a lackey to some other twisted mastermind, came over and started talking to him.

"Right then, it is time to untie you so that you can leave the plane with the rest of the actual chosen passengers. It goes without saying that what I said over the intercom stands, if you cause any trouble to me or anyone else, you will be shot, even though you are a chosen one. Tell me, what does it feel like to be a wanted man?"

"All things considered, strangely predictable."

"What do you mean?"

"It's been one of those days when everything has been too coincidental for there to be anything but a greater force than you at work. Granted, there has been a sense of dread in the background all day long, which turned to imposing doom as soon as you came on the scene. However it's all been mixed up with a sense that I'm finally going to find out a great deal that I want and need to know about things that have been happened, going back a number of years."

"And as for being a wanted man, I'm pretty sure that you will know exactly what that feels like, and if you don't, you soon will after today's escapades."

The Hijacker grinned, and then frowned, and as he spoke. The hijacker untied him, whilst speaking

"The first part explains how you've managed to be the calmest person on board, and yet at the same time been the one passenger in the biggest danger of getting themselves killed before their time. As for being a wanted man, there won't be anyone looking for me, or any of my colleagues, our boss will make sure of that."

With that the Hijacker finished untying him, and stepped away.

"Up you get then, and please, for once, just get off the plane with no incident, and no comments, I have no wish to see you hurt or killed."

He got up and turned around to face the exit. He stopped dead in his tracks as he thought he saw Keera. He started to tremble before he realised that it was the woman from the Tube, who was the double of Keera, and he remembered her voice, and wondered again how she could have sounded so much like Keera as well as being a doppelganger for her.

He would have liked to say he was surprised that she was still on the plane, but he knew that he would have only been lying to himself, it would have been a bigger surprise if she hadn't had been one of those people being escorted from the plane.

He quickly glanced to the left, and as expected the mystery woman from that strange white room some five years before was also still on board. Both women looked at him, and it seemed that, if he wasn't deceiving himself, they both wore concerned expressions. There again, as he scanned the other passengers, they all had similar expressions when they looked at him. The concerned look could well be more along the lines that they were concerned he was going to get them all killed. He did think that if he didn't keep his mouth shut, that may well be the case.

Then he was walking again following the other passengers off the plane and down the steps on to the tarmac. As he came out of the door of the plane the cold hit him. It surprised him at first, and he felt glad he'd never got the chance to take his jacket off, before he realised that he should have expected the cold, after all he was in Greenland which wasn't exactly known for its tropical climes. As he shivered a bit – at the cold for a change – he realised it was at times like this that he cursed the strange fact that he had no facial hair to grow since that spell in that mystery white room those five years ago.

Without even realising he had walked down the steps, he found himself on the tarmac and walking across to the hangar building. He looked around at the other passengers walking to the airport building, both those in front and those behind. He noticed that it seemed that all of them wore what, if wasn't a worried look, and then it was certainly a concerned one. He also noticed that there was no noise, except that of shoes slapping on the tarmac, there was no one talking, and it made for an eerie kind of noise. For once today he resisted the urge to stand out and managed to stop himself from whistling.

The journey across to the hangar didn't seem to take any time at all and he felt himself hit by a blast of warm air as he entered the building. He looked around and was surprised to find that the building was modern, bright and spacious, something he wasn't expecting to find here, in a hangar building away from the main terminal in a remote airport in a country no one visited, and he thought that it looked a far better place to be stuck at than some of the random shitholes that he'd had the misfortune to be waiting at for planes over the years in what were supposed to be first world countries.

Chapter 24

The passengers that had been removed from the plane hadn't been in the hangar building for more than about a minute when the silence in the hangar was broken.

"Good evening, Ladies and Gentlemen."

Hidden speakers suddenly came to life in the hangar, and a voice boomed out of them. The sound seemed to come from everywhere at once but there were no obvious loudspeakers showing, they were all hidden very well. He looked around the hangar lounge they were in, scanning the room to see just how many people had disembarked from the plane, and to make sure his earlier assumption that no one had stayed in the building when they did the passenger swap between planes. It appeared that was the case, and that there were somewhere around twenty-five people from the plane. As he scanned the room, he caught sight of a screen out of the corner of his eye as the voice continued.

"I would like to thank you all for co-operating with my plan so well up to this point, I'd have been most disappointed if I had lost any of you good people before we'd even got acquainted."

He moved through the airport lounge to get nearer to the screen so that he could see the face of the man speaking, and as he did so others followed suit, and soon all the passengers were near the screen, as he did so the voice continued,

"I am sorry to have interrupted your normal lives, but if I had invited you all to come for a get together and told you the reasons why, then I'm pretty sure that the majority of you would have declined, and would have written me off as a crank, despite my previous stellar reputation."

"As yet I cannot divulge just why you are all here, but let me state with all earnestness, that I wish no harm to a single one of you, as you all have something very important to offer, and I hope to be able to make the best use of your talents."

"Unfortunately, I am not there to join you, it would have been a waste of my time to come out to a staging point, especially when you will all be joining me at my headquarters in the not-too-distant future. Therefore in a matter of minutes there will be another plane arriving to bring all of you to me. My helpers there in Kangerlussuaq will be joining you on the final part of your journey, and even though I need all of you, they are under instructions to prevent you from escaping, and they are all very efficient men. So please take a seat and relax for a few minutes until your next plane is available, as it would be a shame if any of you arrived to meet with me with bullet holes somewhere on your person."

The voice stopped speaking and the screen went blank. Almost immediately he heard the noise of a plane, and turned to look outside, however it wasn't an incoming plane, it was the one he'd started the journey on, speeding away down the runway to take off for Philadelphia, where he wished he already was.

Most of the other passengers had wandered off in silence to find a seat at the end of the broadcast, but he just stood there still looking at the screen. He was sure that he recognised both the man who was speaking, and what was even more striking was that voice; even more so because of the fact that the man who had been speaking had alluded to the fact that they would know the man by his previous reputation.

On a personal level he was sure that he hadn't just heard that voice several times, but had met the man speaking, but as he stood there staring at the now blank screen, he couldn't dredge up the information needed to place the man or remember his name. It was going to bug the hell out of him until he did, as the more he thought about it, the more he was sure he had met the man at some point.

Perhaps if he spoke to some of the others they could help. He finally looked away from the screen again and turned around, but noticed that talking to the others may be difficult. Everyone else sat and stood around in total silence, and as far away from him as they could get. He really needed to shake off this outcast persona he'd acquired.

Chapter 25

He had a quick scan to see where the hijackers were, and found most of them were stood strategically around where most of the passengers had gone to stand or sit. There didn't appear to be anyone within ten feet of him, so he set himself up to be as out of direct eye-line as he could be, and checked his pockets.

He found his phone in his trouser pocket, exactly where it had been since he'd got through security at Heathrow, and was surprised to realise that the hijackers had still not made any attempt to ask for, or check for any kind of communications device amongst those other passengers they had extracted from the planes.

Was that a mistake on their part? Was it an oversight by the man he had seen on the screen who appeared to be running things? Did it really not matter to him? Did he really not care about it?

He switched his phone on, more in hope than expectation, He wasn't expecting 4g out here in the frozen wastes of Greenland, but was at least hoping for some kind of signal.

Who did he think he was kidding? He would have had more chance of getting a signal on the surface on the dark side of the moon in an electrical storm.

The phone pinged to life, and he cursed to himself at the noise it made; to him the ping sounded louder than the noise the plane had made taking off, and he quickly looked around to see if the noise had attracted any attention, but no one appeared to have noticed, no one appeared to be watching him, and no one moved in his direction.

After breathing a massive sigh of relief he looked at the phone, but there was no signal. The GPS had kicked in, but that seemed to think he was in the middle of the Atlantic Ocean, which to be fair wasn't too far off the mark, but as a communications device, his phone was as about as useful as any of the supposed igloos that he thought would be scattered around the island.

He left the phone on for a couple of minutes to see if by some small chance a signal would appear, as was often the case elsewhere, but the no entry symbol at the top of his phone was still showing. He quickly put the phone on silent before switching the phone off, so that it wouldn't make any noises next time he turned it on to try and get a signal, he might not get so lucky with people overhearing the next time. Once the phone showed it was shutting down, he stuffed the phone back in a jacket pocket for easier access.

Although the phone might be useless now, it might become useful at some point in the future, once they had left Greenland and moved to wherever they were due to go next, there was nothing to be gained in the phone being taken off him by him wandering around with it in his hand in front of the hijackers.

Chapter 26

When the phone was away in his pocket, he looked up and around to see if he could find where either of the women he wanted to talk to were. He finally noticed them, somewhat typically, for the way the day was going, as far away from him as possible, on the other side of the lounge. They were sat on benches opposite each other, and they appeared from where he stood, to be just sat staring at each other in silence.

He walked across the room to where they were sat, and as he did so he could sense that he was the only person in the room moving. People's heads moved to watch him go by, both fellow passengers, and the hijackers, the only difference in those who did is that the fellow passengers tried to avoid making eye contact with him, the hijackers didn't care. Once he had got over to the other side of the lounge, he stood so he was between them but not blocking their view of each other.

He looked from one to the other, and it looked as if they were both in a trance. They were looking in each other's direction, but he didn't think that they were looking at each other. It was as if they were looking through each other to some distant point far behind them.

He took a step forward so that he was stood between them, and still their gaze didn't change focus. It was as if they had both retreated into their own little worlds, deep down within themselves, and nothing around them mattered.

He stepped back to come out of their direct sight line, and took the opportunity to look around at everyone else.

As he scanned the room, he could see that nearly everyone was now in the same kind of state, just being still, and staring through space. In fact as he looked around, he could see that there was a little bit of movement now from the hijacker's team, as they slowly circulated the room, and exchanged the odd word, almost as if they had been waiting for him to move before settling into their pre-planned routine.

He focused back on the two women and cleared his throat, and spoke

"Excuse me."

Neither of the two women even so much as blinked. Somewhat disconcerted, he wondered if he'd only imagined speaking, and so he tried again, only this time both a little louder and in a sterner tone,

"Excuse me!"

This time, the woman who was the double of Keera blinked, and as if she was a robot just being switched on, automatically responded.

"Sorry, I was miles away."

She then moved her head and looked up at him, and recognition spread over her face.

"Oh, it's you!" She managed to get out before being interrupted,

"YOU!" Someone from behind him shouted,

"Be quiet, there is to be no conversing between the hostages until we reach our final destination. There will be plenty of time for talking once you are there."

Recognising the voice he looked over his shoulder and wasn't surprised to see that it was the hijacker that had been in control on his plane. The word hostages had suddenly resonated, although he had been called that by the hijacker on the plane, and thinking it before, it really sank in this time. He shook his head to clear the thought, and moved to sit down next to the Keera lookalike. Just as he sat down, he heard the voice again.

"Actually dear chap, it's probably not a good idea for you to sit there. I wouldn't want you to have the temptation of talking so close to you, especially with your track record today."

Again the reference to him as a chap from the hijacker brought a smile to his lips, but he shook his head and the smile off his face and made a show of very slowly and very wearily getting to his feet, sighing loudly, before asking,

"Of course old boy, Is there somewhere you'd prefer me to sit or stand? Perhaps you've got a blind-deaf mute, with a poor sense of smell and no fingers stashed somewhere in the building that you would like to put me next to just in case I moved from my normal chatty self into someone that can use non-verbal communication methods?"

The hijacker let out a small laugh, before replying,

"No, as far as I am aware, there are no deaf mutes here, no blind people, and everyone still has all of their fingers, well, for the time being at least. So bearing that in mind, I think that the best place for you, all things considered, is sat just here in front of me, seeing as there seems to be a lack of your fellow hostages over here by me. Overall they appear to not want anything to do with me, or, unless I am much mistaken, with you for that matter, you don't appear to have bonded with your fellow travellers very well today. Most of them don't even want to make eye contact with you. If I am public enemy number one here today, you have probably made yourself number two."

"No, I definitely think that you would be a number two, without a doubt in most people's minds."

There was a flicker of anger on the hijacker's face before he barked,

"Just sit there public enemy number two."

He couldn't really disagree with what the hijacker had initially said, but he hadn't been able to resist a little jibe. He slowly walked over to the seat indicated by the hijacker, and wondered just what had got into him today. He had always been sarcastic, but had normally kept this to himself when the time was right to do so, and yet all he'd done all day today was be sarcastic to people with guns, that were threatening both himself and everyone else here.

Most of what the hijacker had said was spot on. He wasn't surprised that none of the other passengers wanted anything to do with him. He was being a mouthy liability, and there was a real danger that if he kept it up, he would manage to get himself killed, and it wasn't too far outside the realms of possibility that he might just take a few other poor unfortunate bystanders down with him.

For some reason, despite the circumstances, he found that he just couldn't help himself, and that the words were out of his mouth and off and running into the ether before he could stop them. Perhaps he would be better off asking for the gag that his hijackers had threatened him with earlier on the plane, at least of he was gagged then his mouth couldn't get him or anyone else in any more trouble today.

Once again, he felt the urge to start whistling in the silence in the airport longue. He had his lips pursed ready to start blowing before thinking better off it and remaining silent himself. Enough already for now he thought.

Chapter 27

He sat down on the seat, and within seconds found himself doing what he had noticed every other one of the hostages doing. He was just sat there in his seat staring off into the distance in front of him as if in a trance. There was an uneasy silence all around, and he drifted away focused intensely on a flight departure board. It was empty, their flight out wasn't even listed, it would be the flight to nowhere, then again, he supposed that this was a freight hangar, there may not be any scheduled flights showing over here normally, and he wondered if there was anyone over in the normal departure lounge, waiting for flights off the island, or short hop trips somewhere else within Greenland.

The staring lasted a long time, and he felt himself drifting off again, however he stopped himself, and he shook his head and focused his vision off the departure board, and through the windows out into the dark airport. Night had fallen without anyone noticing or caring, and he looked at his watch and was surprised that it was tomorrow already.

He tried to think whether that was in real terms, or whether he had already put his watch forward the five hours to Eastern Standard Time ready for his arrival back in Philly. He normally did this as soon as he got on the plane, but really couldn't remember if he had or not this morning. He really needed one of the GPS watches that changed to the local time wherever he was in the world, and he made the decision to do so once he got home. Well he would if he ever got back home that was.

As he peered into the darkness outside, he found he could see several people moving around on the tarmac outside, and it looked as if they were preparing the refuelling lorries, and a set of the steps that they had used for disembarking from the planes earlier in the day.

Pretty soon he could see the reason for the activity. At first it was some distant lights flashing in the sky, and then as it got closer, he could see it coming in to land. It was a strange looking plane, which although he recognised it from films, he couldn't think what it was called. It just looked like a long cardboard box with some wings stuck on as an afterthought, and then sanded down to take off the harsh edges. It did however make a lot of noise; he could hear the engines from a long way away, even inside.

It took a few minutes for the thing to land and taxi up to virtually outside the hangar lobby, the noise emanating from the plane was almost deafening, even inside the hangar. Wherever they were going on that thing, he hoped it wasn't going to be a long journey, otherwise by the time they landed, all of them would have ringing in their ears for the following week.

Once the plane had ground to a halt, and the engines were shut off the men outside sprang into action, and the refuelling rig was hooked up in double quick time. The steps were rolled up to the side door of the plane, but someone from the plane opened the door, and gesticulated for a few seconds, before closing the door again. The steps were towed away out of sight.

Then a voice broke through his viewing pleasure, and he was focused back inside again.

"Ladies and Gentlemen, could you all please stand and move to the external doors. You are about to embark on the last part of your unusual journey. Yet again, let me stress that if anyone tries anything then we will shoot you. It will hurt you, and you will bleed, which will stain the nice seats on the plane you are about to get on, so please be considerate."

As if to emphasise the point, one of the other hijackers drew his gun and fired once, and the television screen that had earlier shown the big boss man giving his introduction to them at the far end of the lounge, disintegrated in a pop of shattering glass, plastic, and metal.

The man continued talking through the number of screams and whimpers following the gunshot, totally ignoring the fact that the latest little display had managed to scare the hostages more than they had been scared before.

"Again as previously pointed out, all of the men are extremely accurate with their firearms, so it is best not to try their patience. Just walk out to the rear of the plane parked in front of this building, and then up the ramp, and the men on board will show you to where you are to be seated. Once seated we will be airborne in approximately five minutes. Now, get moving!"

With that the doors from the building out onto the tarmac were opened and cold air rushed in, and the hostages began their walk out to the back of the plane. They acted like they were the quietest bunch of sheep ever, being herded by several irritable sheepdogs that had automatic weapons, nobody tried to venture off course, and not one of them said a word. They all just trailed across the airstrip in line, just concentrating on putting one foot in front of the other to get to the plane, and once they were there, they got on to the plane and followed their sheep dogs to their indicated seats.

Chapter 28

As he approached the ramp of the plane, and started to walk up it, he momentarily froze, as he had seen many of the other hostages do, he suddenly had a numb sensation from the moment he turned to walk up the cargo ramp into the plane. Everything within the plane was pure brilliant blinding white. The only items that took away from the pure white vision in front of him were the other people already on the ramp or already in the massive belly of the waiting plane.

With each leaden step he took into the belly of the plane, his sense of dread increased, until in a space of time that seemed like minutes, but was probably in reality little more than a couple of seconds, he felt himself coming to a complete grinding halt.

His mind was cast back to that room he had spent so much time in over five years ago, and that until moments ago, seemed like another lifetime and very often a dream. Now, as it had been back then, there was no perception of size or depth amongst the whiteness. Although it was almost blindingly bright, there were no obvious light sources, and no shadows of any sort to give a depth to the space he was in. He knew what the size of the space must be, as he had walked down the outside of the plane to get to the ramp he was walking up, but without that as a guide, the inside of the plane could have been absolutely any size at all.

Whatever had happened all those years ago seemed to be starting up again and as he remembered back to that time, he felt the world around him start to disappear. There was absolutely no coincidence possible here; this was connected to his past, and to the past of the others on this plane.

He was however, jolted from this with a shove from one of his "controllers" as he suddenly thought of them now in this bright white space, this was a controlling atmosphere, and he felt it oppressing him, pushing him down.

"Keep moving, over to that seat there."

The controller said, pointing to what at first look appeared to be nothing, but some more whiteness, but he imagined that he could vaguely make out the rough shape of a seat.

He looked around and the looks of distress, the fear and panic on the other passenger's faces, and in their eyes, told him that most of them, if not all of them had been in a white place like this before, and that it wasn't a good experience for any of them.

He got the sense that they had all been in a place exactly like the one he'd been in before, he looked around, and he thought about the passengers in the lounge at the airport, were the other four men he'd seen in that white place years ago here on this plane, and if they were would he be able recognise them?

He got to his seat, and he felt his way into it. Even close to it, it was difficult to get a reasonable view of the seat below him, without it blurring into the general whiteness all around him. When he had sat all the way down, he found that the seat was very comfortable, much more so than any he had encountered on a plane before.

From his seat he looked around, and found that from where he sat, he could see other people, but wasn't directly next to, or face to face with anyone. it appeared that the seats weren't arranged in a regular pattern, as would normally be the case, or that they were arranged at all, they seemed to be set up so that no one was really sat near to anyone else, or sat in a way that they were not facing anyone else, as if they were making it difficult to join in with any of the other passengers.

He could see some of the other passengers looking around too, but again, they all seemed unwilling to make eye contact with him and after a brief period, they stopped looking around, and just stared into the whiteness, alone with their thoughts.

It was a disconcerting feeling.

He thought to himself, that they must have set the seats up in such a way as to discourage eye contact and interaction, and therefore to leave everyone with their own thoughts, alone in the whiteness. Though he also thought that eye contact would become impossible as any sane person would have their eyes shut to try and block out the ultra-bright lights that were installed within the plane.

Chapter 29

As soon as everyone was on the plane, the rear door of the plane started moving and slowly raised until it closed snugly into the gap that was there for it. Once shut he felt the loudest silence he had ever come across in his life. His initial thought was that he'd gone deaf, and a brief panic took over him.

He breathed out and thought he could vaguely hear his own breathing, and he tilted his head to see if he could pick up any sounds from inside the plane. However, it appeared that there were no sounds coming from anywhere inside the plane, or for that matter outside of it, so he clapped just to make sure he hadn't gone deaf.

The ringing sound that he heard upon clapping was reassuring to him, though his peripheral vision had picked up that a couple of fellow passengers flinched at the sound, and as he looked around, he could see a couple of the controllers looked in his direction, though definitely not with their normal air of composure.

He thought about it and smiled to himself as he realised just how much like a gunshot his clap might have sounded to those of nervous disposition, especially in such an overwhelmingly quiet environment as the one they were all in, and doubly so with armed controllers walking around having been threatened with being shot, in the last words that had been said to them.

He realised that what he called them had changed, and that they had gone from being hijackers to controllers on the way into this plane. This wasn't anything remotely like a simple hijacking anymore, it was a small part of a bigger plot, and he was a part in that plot. Whether he was a player, being played, or the fly in the ointment still had to be decided.

He felt the motion of the plane and took a couple of seconds to realise that they were moving, and someone wasn't shaking him again. Whatever had been used to soundproof the interior of this plane was doing a frankly unbelievable job.

The fact that the plane was moving had taken him by surprise, because from where he was sat, there had been no indication that the engines had even started. He strained to listen to see if he could hear the engines, but although he thought that he could, but he couldn't be sure, it could just be his sub-conscious knowledge of what he should be hearing playing tricks on him.

He knew how loud these planes sounded from the outside, as he'd heard this one coming in from inside the hangar, and wondered how much it cost to get this quality of soundproofing, and where he could get it from? He could do with some of this in his apartment so he could blast out his stereo without the neighbours complaining for a change. It wasn't just soundproofing though, there must be some high-end sound dampening going on here, there had to be, it would explain why the silence was so heavy on board the plane. Just soundproofing would work with most outside noise, but the lack of noise coming from inside the plane was just too low to be natural, even in a situation like this, where there was little incidental chatter.

With the thought of the sound dampening, it struck him again just how much money must be involved in this whole operation. He quickly scanned the cabin and from that and his recollection of the hangar where he had already made a calculation, there appeared to be between twenty and thirty people that were, like himself, captives.

The planning to get all these people, where it appeared none of them knew each other on two flights on the same day at the same time was astronomically complex. He wondered how much his life, and the life of all the others on this plane, must have been manipulated in recent months to get him here today.

Then there was the hired help, of which, by the time they had taken those from both original planes, and all the ground crew, and those already on this plane, must have totalled up to at least double the number of captives.

With this specially fitted out plane, the satellite feed into the terminal at the airport, and the fact that the whole freight side of the airport seemed to have been commandeered for the duration, what had happened those five years ago to him and probably most of the others, this was an operation that wasn't going to be anywhere near cheap. In fact he didn't think there could be that many individuals on the planet that could plan, let alone shell out the necessary cash for a project like this.

His thoughts were interrupted by a break in the silence.

"Good afternoon, Ladies and Gentlemen, this is your captain speaking. Let me welcome you aboard this special charter flight."

He wasn't sure exactly where the sounds were coming from, he couldn't see anything but white, and as he moved his head there was no change in the volume or direction of the voice, it was as if the voice was all around him in the ether, breaking through the sound dampening, feeling like the voice was right there by his ear, he had to get a sound system like this. It continued,

"For the most part of this trip today we shall be cruising at approximately one hundred feet above sea level, and shall be travelling at approximately four hundred and fifty knots."

"The expected flight time for the journey is a little over fourteen hours. Your location will be explained upon arrival. Your gracious hosts will be around later with in-flight meals and refreshments to help the journey go as smoothly and as comfortably as possible. If you have any special dietary requirements, please don't worry about them, as your hosts have been made fully aware of these during briefing, and your meals have been tailored as per your tastes. Unfortunately there is no in-flight movie today, due to the special refitting of the cabin area on this aircraft, but please feel free to relax and sleep during the journey, as we are aware it has already been a much longer day than you had originally planned for."

The voice stopped and the oppressive silence kicked back in. The voice and the message had been jovial enough, though there was a creepy undertone to it. He tried to piece the details of the message together in his head.

He calculated the possible distance that the flight could go, and at just over six thousand miles, it gave no real indication of where they were headed. With being so near to the North Pole that put them within range of pretty much anywhere in the northern hemisphere.

He thought about possible destinations, and ruled out the Eastern Seaboard and Western Europe due to the saturation of flight paths, and satellite surveillance in those areas. Travelling at such a low altitude and high speed over land would probably be a no go; it was going to be difficult enough to do that over open sea, so they were probably going to be flying over water for most of the journey.

Unless the captain was lying, fourteen hours could put them anywhere in the South Atlantic, plenty of deserted coasts in South America or West Africa to aim for, not forgetting all the islands available, Flying over the North Pole could put them in the North Pacific, plenty of island archipelagos to aim for there as well. Apart from Australia, and most of Eurasia, the rest of the world could be a target. Nowhere would be a surprise anymore, even finding that they flew about for fourteen hours and ended up back in Greenland, he wouldn't put anything past the person in charge.

Chapter 30

It didn't take very long for the bright light of the inside of the plane to send shooting pains to his brain, he doubted he'd ever have any night vision again if he spent the next fourteen hours submitted to this. He was sure that it was brighter and more intense than he remembered from five years before, though perhaps he felt it more because he was older, and it brought back bad memories. He closed his eyes, but even then, there wasn't really any respite, it didn't go black like he had hoped, it went to a lurid shade of orange, and he couldn't help but think of oompa loompas.

He looked up and glanced around to see what the controllers were doing about the light, and saw that they were all wearing sunglasses. Of course they were, they had been briefed, and they had come prepared for this madness.

Then it suddenly dawned on him that he had brought his sunglasses with him when he had left the hotel that morning, or as it probably was by now, yesterday morning. Although it felt like that was a different lifetime, he was certain that he hadn't lost or abandoned the sunglasses anywhere along the way.

He felt around in the pockets of his jacket and, sure enough, he found them in the left inside pocket, exactly where he'd put them before going through airport security. He took out the Ray Ban wrap rounds, and put them on, and felt the relief almost immediately. The light was dimmed to an acceptable level, of an early evening twilight glow, and his eyes – and brain – began to relax from the sensory overload that he had been subjected to.

The throbbing in his head started to decrease and he strained to have a good look around to try and see where the two women he wanted to speak to were in relation to himself, and although he nearly tied himself in knots turning to try and see them, there was no sign of them anywhere in his immediate vicinity. However the vastness of the inside of the plane and the positioning of the chairs were almost certainly to blame for that. He would try and find their position later when he went to the toilet, always assuming that they were allowed to go.

As he was straightening himself out, he caught a glance of the head controller. It looked like he was looking at him, watching over him, but with him wearing sunglasses as well it was difficult to tell exactly where he was looking. With the same kind of clothes on, sunglasses and similar appearances, the whole of the group of controllers looked even more like clones than before. He hadn't heard many of them speak, but the ones that he had all spoke with that posh English accent, it could well be they were all out of a single production line.

Once back in a comfortable position he closed his eyes and felt himself relax all the way through his body. Although he had been asleep a couple of times during the day, he had never actually felt relaxed, and yet here he was on the strangest plane journey of his life, and there had been a fair few odd journeys, and yet he felt at ease with everything.

His mind wandered from thoughts of Keera, his parents, his school life, to his work, from its outset at Trebling, on to how he became freelance and then a specialist in computer-based security systems. Everything that was going through his mind happened to be memories of people, places and times that were good, and events where he was happy.

These thoughts were a stark contrast to those that had been clouding his consciousness earlier during the day, and then, with what he felt sure would be a silly contented smile on his face, he drifted off to sleep yet again.

Chapter 31

He was born three hours after the Flyers last Stanley Cup triumph, and it has been said by various people that knew or had known him, that it was his birth that was single-handedly preventing the Flyers from ever getting their hands on the Stanley Cup again during his lifetime. Six finals appearances, and countless other playoff runs have all been for nothing. When it came down to winning the big one, they had fallen short for forty years now.

In fact, some people had taken that a bit further and it had been suggested that he was a jinx on all the city's sports teams, with only three championships in any of the big four leagues since his birth, and two of them had happened before he was ten.

In response he always asked the question, who was to blame for the seventy odd years before? As there were no great dynastic successes for Philadelphia teams before he was born either, unlike most other major cities - Except Cleveland of course, the city where Championships refused to go.

Being Philadelphia born and raised – not West Philadelphia though, much as he may have wished it to be the case when the Fresh Prince was in full flow – he wanted his city's sports teams to do well, but just had a string of disappointments. In fact during his life, the most famous sporting icon to come out of Philadelphia was Rocky Balboa, and he was just a fictional character, which pretty much summed up the local sporting life.

Although he followed the other big four sports, Hockey was the one for him, he'd played until his teens, and he enjoyed the cold, the speed, the regular fights, and the general all-round feeling that anything could happen in the next twenty seconds. It had been the only real bonding between him and his father.

He had wanted to be Bobby Clarke when growing up, he was sure that there wasn't a long list of other people who could have said that, or certainly who would own up to it now, and although it never happened from a playing perspective, he could say that he channelled that into a video game design – Bobby Clarke's Flyers' Hockey.

Although it was a vanity project on his part, Trebling had got one of his better designs; He got a small fee and 10 years' worth of season tickets. He thought that they'd come out even. The licensing fees they got out of the game's motion engine would set them all up for life, but they weren't to know that then.

Later, as he moved out of game design, and into computerised security systems, he'd even got to install one of his own systems in Bobby Clarke's house, a job he had gone and done personally, instead of getting one of the normal installation team in his company to do. Again he had agreed on a reduced fee and more years' worth of season tickets for the Flyers.

When this batch ran out, he'd have to start paying for his tickets to watch them again!

Which he would, he was a sucker for punishment where the Flyers were concerned. He wanted to be there when they eventually ended their drought. Even if it was his ninety fourth birthday and he died three hours afterwards, which would be fine with him, it would have a certain symmetry about it.

Chapter 32

He awoke from his latest snooze to find that the controllers were serving food. He had no idea of what time it really was, or where in the world he was. He wasn't sure what had woken him, he couldn't hear very much, despite there being seemingly an army of controllers walking about with trays. He could however smell an array of different foods, and it must have been that which had brought him around this time.

He started to take off his sunglasses, wondering why on earth he had them on in the first place. He only got them a couple of inches before he stopped trying to take them off, changing direction to quickly replace them back over his eyes. The sleep had made him forget just how bright it was on the plane. His mouth had that dry, stale taste that always seemed to follow sleep, and he would be glad of any drink that came with the food.

When a controller brought his food to him, he looked at it in a state of amazement. This was no ordinary airline meal, but then he remembered that this was no ordinary flight.

The first thing he noticed was the tray. It was no miniscule plastic effort that you normally got on flights, it was a full-sized metal tray, with large handles, like the kind of tray you saw in movies when kids struggled to bring breakfast in bed to their mothers on mother's day, or when someone's snooty butler was bringing them cucumber sandwiches. Not only that, but it was the perfect fit across the arms of his seat, and when he put it down, he felt a slight pull on it, as some magnetic force was holding it firmly in place.

What was on the tray was even more amazing. If he had felt disappointed at having his first-class meal replaced by a bog-standard airline food tray, this more than made up for it. To the left sat a large plate, with what looked to be a large well done T-bone steak, thick fries, and onion rings, and all fresh from whatever they had been cooked in, as he could see the steam rising from the food. Alongside were several sachets of various condiments, all of which would complement the meal.

On the right side of the tray sat a plate with a large piece of apple pie, and again, steam was rising from it, and next to it sat a jug of custard, with a lid on it. Then, in the corner of the tray sat two twenty-ounce bottles of Pepsi. He doubted whether he could have come up with a better selection if he had taken the time to choose what he wanted beforehand. In fact he may well have selected this as his favourite foods on one of those online questionnaires that did the rounds a few years ago.

A brief look around told him that people he could see all had different meals, and therefore told him that it looked like each passenger had been catered for separately.

The individual menus were probably based on information that had been extracted from them some five years before, or even from being observed over time by unseen watchers. The strange thing was that he wasn't surprised or even alarmed by that at this point. To his mind this was just another part of the awesome planning that had gone into this operation, and the no expense spared mentality behind it.

His mind came back to the present and he started on the food and drink, which was just as good as it looked, and far superior to anything he had ever had on a plane before. In what seemed like just a couple of minutes he polished off the meal and sat back sipping from one of his bottles of Pepsi.

He noticed a couple of controllers, sat on fold down chairs, that appeared to have come from nowhere and were just floating in the air, and eating what seemed to be regulation airplane food, off grey plastic trays that they struggled to balance on their laps, and he managed to suppress a laugh. It made him feel strangely good, that even though they were the controllers, and they were in charge, they weren't being treated as well as the passengers in some areas.

    He sat there not really doing anything, just letting himself relax. Time slipped by, and what seemed quite soon, the controllers were coming round and collecting up the mainly empty trays. He finished off the bottle of Pepsi he was drinking, and kept the other bottle, as it was full, and from previously being dehydrated because there was no telling when there would be anything else to drink.

Chapter 33

He sat there absent-mindedly playing with his Pepsi bottle, tipping it one way, then another, not really focusing on anything around him, or thinking about anything. He just sat in a semi fugue state on the edge of the void of nothingness, an odd sense of calm surrounding him, as if he was cocooned away from the rest of the world. But it seemed that nothing was going to let him be at rest today for too long, as he was jolted from his safe calm little world by a scream.

As he came back to reality it took a couple of seconds to figure out where the scream had come from. He couldn't see who had screamed, though he had just about got the bearings of it away to his left somewhere, when another scream arose, this time from behind him, somewhere to his right. The screaming noise was strangely muted, as if the sound was coming through water instead of air.

He went to stand to see what was happening, completely forgetting about the tray sat across the arms of his seat. He managed to wrench the tray off the arms, struggling against the magnetic pull, and leant over placing the tray by the side of his seat. Once done he stood and quickly scanned the plane. It was not immediately obvious what had caused the screams, but the one thing he was expecting was to see the controllers rushing to deal with it. The only thing being, there were no controllers to be seen moving anywhere. In fact the only one he had seen was sat slumped in a fold down seat.

He carried on moving over to where the second scream had come from, bumping into the back and sides of seats that were still difficult to see in the white-on-white background, and as he did so he passed several of the other hostages, who looked to see who it was moving among them, and then looking away when they realised that it was him.

He felt a slight rush of anger that the other hostages felt uncomfortable about him, and that they were reluctant to make eye contact with him. Did they feel that he was a troublemaker, and that by being associated with him, he might cause them additional problems? Why were none of them even trying to see what was causing the screams, why were they all so unwilling to be involved, were they so frightened that they lost any empathy that they should feel?

He reached the location of the scream, and saw the reason for the screaming and he felt his blood turn to ice. He could plainly see why there were such screams. On the floor in front of him lay two of the controllers, both obviously dead, with pools of blood and tissue emanating from their noses and mouths.

It looked as if one, or maybe all their major organs had exploded and expelled themselves out of their noses and mouths. The bloody tissue sat in what looked like a black pool, starkly contrasting with the brilliant white carpet, but was probably dark red, made darker by the contrast and him wearing sunglasses. It was the kind of grisly scene that would often be portrayed on television, in films, and in books in graphic detail, but those previous fictional encounters had nothing on the spectacle in front of him. As grisly as it looked, the smell was far worse, a fetid smell that he normally associated with the aftermath of drinking too much on an empty head. It was one of those smells that you could taste almost as much as you could smell it; stopping breathing through his nose didn't quite stop it invading his body.

Even in the short time he had spent walking over to, and taking in the scene, more screams had been raised, and now he quickly moved around the plane, bouncing from seat to seat and taking in the devastation lying all around him in a surprisingly calm manner.

It seemed that everywhere he looked, there was a controller, dead, and in most cases with the same pool of blood and tissue coming from their mouths, noses, eyes, and ears. If there was a hole, internal bodily tissue was coming out of it, he was glad that all the controllers were dressed, who knew what might be trying to escape from elsewhere on their bodies.

The screams that had started out as a fearful reaction, had now turned hysterical, and those that weren't screaming like demented banshees, were sat motionless, stunned, as if unable to take in the scenes around them. He noticed that no one else had even left their seats, or even appeared to be trying to do so, and he felt a strange sense of detachment from the rest of his fellow captives, as if he was the only sane person in a world gone totally mad.

In the few seconds he stood there in the midst of the mayhem, he jumped to the conclusion that the controllers must have been drugged or poisoned, and he thought back to their uniform grey plastic trays of food that had amused him at the time. They had all had the same thing, in stark contrast to the individually tailored meals the captives had had, and all of them having the same thing would have made their food an easy target.

If they had been poisoned by their standard issue meals, then it was a scary proposition. The controllers had all been working for the mastermind that was behind this whole operation, and having got himself and the other captives on board this plane, they had obviously reached the end of their usefulness, and therefore had been terminated. If this is what happened to the hired help, what on earth was going to happen to him, and the rest of the captives before this nightmare was over for all of them?

His musings were disturbed by a sudden jolt by the plane, and there was a tilting of the plane slightly to one side, as if it was changing course. With the peace and quiet, the blindingly bright light, and the smoothness of the journey so far, it had been almost possible to forget that he was even on a plane. He wondered what caused the jolt, and a small degree of panic kicked in when he jumped to a possible conclusion, that even the pilots had been poisoned and there was now no one in control of the plane.

He stood for a moment taking in the dimensions of the insides of the plane, trying to work out the direction to the front of the plane, and therefore the cockpit. He found it impossible to tell without a reference point, and headed back to his seat to get his bearings. He knew the direction his seat had been facing in context to the rear loading doors, and therefore from that he knew which direction the cockpit must be. He headed off in that direction and when he got to the front of the passenger section, he started the search for the door to the cockpit. With everything being white on white, it took a couple of minutes searching along the soft wall lining at what he hoped was the front of the plane before he finally found the carefully disguised handle.

He pulled out the part that allowed the handle to move; he took a deep breath, turned the handle, and pushed the door.

It moved, and he relaxed, as it wasn't locked, but it only opened a little way and then stopped. He could see a line, a darkness in the bright white, and he checked it for some kind of latch or chain on the inside, but there didn't appear to be one. He pushed it again and it gave a little bit more before stopping. He then shoulder barged the door, and it opened a little bit more, the top of the door moved freely, but there was something behind the door on the floor preventing it from opening properly. He tried another two shoulder charges at the door and finally there was a gap large enough for him to get through.

Once he had squeezed through the door, he found the reason for the difficulties in opening the door. Just inside the door was the slumped over dead body of the co-pilot, covered in his own internal organs.

The pilot was dead at the controls in just as bad a state, and several of the controls and dials had the same blood and tissue on them. The fact that the pilot and co-pilot were dead didn't appear to be the issue with the previous lurch in the plane's trajectory; the plane itself seemed to be on some kind of automatic pilot. Although he couldn't be certain of that, it appeared to be continuing on a steady course now, and it appeared that it was the pre-suggested one hundred feet above the surface of the sea. There was no sign of any land in sight out of the cockpit windows

He turned and closed the door behind him, if any of the other hostages saw the carnage in here, there would be full scale panic on board, he had already had more than enough of random screaming for one day, well, a lifetime in fact, and he could do without adding to it. The cockpit sounded as if it was the loudest place on earth, the unnatural silence of the main body of the plane, even with the muted screaming had lulled him into a false sense of security. In the cockpit there was none of the sound proofing or dampening there was on the rest of the plane, and the noise from the engines, and the rush of the passing air the plane was cutting a path through was louder than any concert he had ever been to.

Whilst his ears were being bombarded, he was trying to avoid stepping in anything unpleasant, as he looked around the cockpit for a radio, or any other communication device that he could use to try and contact the outside world. This also made him think about his phone as well. He got that out of his pocket and turned it on. After a few seconds it vibrated to let him know it was on, at least turning it on silent had worked. The signal bar still had the no entry sign on it, and even the GPS didn't want to make any attempt to tell him where he might be.

He left the phone on, hoping it would kick in after warming up a bit, and carried on looking for a radio and after a brief search he found it. The radio was turned on, and he grabbed the microphone and spoke into it, well shouting into it would have been a more accurate description, trying to make himself heard over the roar of the engines.

"Mayday, Mayday, is there anybody out there listening?"
He certainly wasn't expecting the reply he received.

Chapter 34

The voice seemed to come from all around him, much as the pilot's voice had done when addressing all the passengers on the plane earlier on,

"Mayday indeed! Don't you find it strange that a traditional English Holiday is used for a term that indicates that there may be trouble ahead, and help is needed?"

He opened his mouth to speak, but was cut off before he could get anything out.

"Please don't answer that, it was a rhetorical question, allow me to continue. You see after all, it's not really that strange. May Day was taken from a pagan ceremony that involved singing and dancing as an offering so that their crops would grow without trouble that year hence avoiding trouble and possible starvation during the following winter. Yet it was then taken by Christian farmers to celebrate the end of the planting season, in the way that Christians took most of the pagan holidays and used them so they could attract and convert the pagans to their new religion. Then, here we are, centuries later, using it as word to get help so that trouble may be avoided. It is all fascinating stuff if you have the time to read up on it."

"Anyway enough of me pontificating on random subjects for now, as you may be able to guess; there will be no white knights on steeds coming to the aid of the damsel in distress, or even international crime fighting agencies coming to rescue you for that matter. You see, it just so happens, that when refitting this wondrous flying machine you are in, I made sure that all frequencies to and from this craft are directed to myself only. With all the money and time I've spent on these plans to get you and all your fellow recruits together, I wasn't going to chance that one of you would do what you've just managed to do once all my poor unfortunate crew had kicked the bucket."

He blanched from the casual manner the gruesome dispatch of the controllers on the plane had been mentioned in passing, it must have shown as the voice continued.

"I can see that you are a little disturbed by the dismissal of my staff in such a manner, but for what I've planned, no one else must be allowed to know the whole plan, and certainly no one group of people should be allowed to piece all the little parts of my master plan together. The only ones that will know everything will be yourselves when it is all over, and by that time it won't matter who knows the master plan. It will only matter who is in control of it."

Whilst the voice had been droning on, he had been looking around the cockpit for where any camera may be, though with this much electrical equipment, dials, lights and the such around, there could be any amount anywhere. He glanced anxiously at the controls in the cockpit, and yet again the voice picked up on what he was looking at.

"Yes, I can see exactly where you are looking, but don't worry yourself about the controls, this is the most sophisticated and largest radio-controlled plane ever built, though satellite controlled would be a much more accurate phrase. I have a team here that will bring your flight in to land under greater control than if the pilots were still alive."

"So, why kill all the staff in the air?" He finally managed to get out.

"Surely there would have been better opportunities, with less shock and gore."

The voice laughed softly before starting again,

"You really are always the one with the questions, aren't you? I really do wonder what it is that is different with you. There really is no logical reason why all the effort and work didn't take the same way in you, as it did in the rest of your fellow passengers."

He was suddenly rigid, and he found himself listening more intently to what was being said than anything he had ever heard in his life before. The voice continued,

"Do you realise just what happened to you when I hosted you just over five years ago? You, along with everyone else still alive on this plane were taken to rooms the same as the one you obviously remember."

"You all had, what was then, the most advanced silicone implants placed into the base of your skulls. Along with this came an intense course of subliminal impressioning to mould the way you would act in the future. You were effectually programmed to do certain items of work in your respective fields and to be in certain places at certain times."

"There were several safety measures put into the implants. They were designed to keep your features the same. Although the programming was said to be infallible, especially set alongside the implants, I had to safeguard against the slightest chance that one of you would find out that you'd been programmed, and did something to escape the fate laid out for you."

"Therefore part of the implant helped to control such items as hair growth and metabolism rate. If anyone tried to change their hair to alter their appearance, or lost or put on weight, then the implant would kick in. In your case, and the rest of the males, the need to shave stopped, so that you couldn't grow beards or moustaches as easy disguises."

He managed to get another quick sentence in, "If you marketed that, you could have put Gillette out of business."

Yet the voice ignored his interruption and carried on without pausing.

"If one of the subjects had a shift in weight then the implant would kick in and alter their metabolism rate to combat the change. It also stopped hair growth, and made the hair grow in a particular way. If it was changed, then the implant would kick in, and in less than 24 hours the appearance would be back to how it was before the change. Not only that, but the programming stressed happiness to all of you about the way you look and was set up to stop you from changing your appearance."

As the voice paused for breath, he took the opportunity to get some words out,

"It would appear that you are certifiably nuts, with that kind of technology, you could remove so much suffering from people worried about the way they look, what they eat, put therapists out of work, and what do you do? Use it to play a big game of chess with twenty-odd people"

His outburst did nothing to ruffle the voice in the ether, which just carried on as before.

"In the five years since we implanted and programmed you, only one person out of the twenty-four subjects we worked on has attempted to change the way they look at all. Obviously, I don't need to add that that person was you, and your attempts to change your hairstyle, almost as if you were experimenting with it, the silly colours you dyed it, shaving parts of it off, having extensions, all to no avail, but failing to stop you trying to get to the root of it. You have been just like that single jigsaw piece that doesn't fit properly. There is no one that has been involved in this project that understands just what it is about you that allows the level of deviation from the programming that we have seen in you. It really shouldn't be possible"

The voice was triggering memories in him, he knew this person, but he still couldn't quite place where from, and nevertheless the voice continued,

"Not one of the other subjects has ever done anything that could be considered as being out of sync with their programming. You are the only one out of the twenty-four subjects who has ever been late for anything, by now, you should have met Maria Gonzalez over twenty times all over the world, but every single time you have been late to arrive for your transport, and you have missed the designated opportunity to start what should have been a beautiful friendship."

"You have been to places you never should have gone to, and you've done business with some of my direct competitors, which really really should have been impossible, and is most annoying. There should have been no margin for you to go gallivanting around doing whatever the hell you felt like, whenever you felt like doing it. You being able to do so has cost me an inordinate amount of time and money, yet of all the subjects, you are the one I need the most to complete everything that needs to be done."

"As you and the rest of the twenty-four subjects were, all the staff were programmed in a similar way, to the extent that it was certain that they would all have their meals on this flight as planned. I knew they would all die, and in a place where I have complete control of the situation."

"So, in answer to your initial question, no there wasn't a better opportunity to decommission my staff. It may have been messy, but that was necessary to make sure of death, and as every master chef knows, you have to break a few eggs to make an omelette."

He shuddered at the casual way the voice referred to the deaths, as if they were batteries that had ran out, but the voice just continued regardless.

"And to address a point in one of your rather rudely raised questions, trying to interrupt me as I was speaking, all will become apparent when you are with me at the end of your, and the rest of your fellow subjects' journey."

Chapter 35

There was a brief pause as the voice seemed to stop to let him take it all in, and as he did so he looked around, and wondered to himself what he would do now, and if he could tell any of this lunacy to the rest of the passengers when he went back outside the cockpit.

Whilst he was still contemplating this the voice started again, "According to the constant analysis of the people who helped in the programming of my subjects, the conclusion was that none of the subjects would attempt to find the cockpit, let alone try to get in, however after watching you being the exception to the rule so many times, I really felt it would be unwise not to take some additional precautions, and prevent you from contact with the outside world at this point."

"It has to be said that you gave me quite a scare yesterday morning when you dived off the Tube like that. It seemed that once again, all my meticulous planning would have gone to waste, and I would have to postpone the operation for the third time."

"And before you ask, yes, it was you who has caused the previous attempts to be cancelled. Mainly due to your ability of just deciding to change plans at the last moment; something that all my programming should have prevented; something that should have been impossible to do."

"It was quite a wild reaction on the Tube, and it did come as a surprise that Sonia knew who you were when she spoke to you on the Tube yesterday morning. Granted, you're somewhat of a minor celebrity in Philadelphia, a lot more so than you give yourself credit for, and you are now becoming well known in security circles worldwide."

"In fact you may not realise it, but the only reason you are not a household name all over the world is the way I've been able to manipulate the press in to not writing about you. As it is, stories still come through, and you are far more famous than I want you to be. I need the time of you and your colleagues to have my operation come to fruition, but being famous means that people will be missed, and that causes more scrutiny to come on why you are missing. If we had missed getting you on this flight, we may never have got you on the operation as your profile continues to grow despite our best efforts."

"Even with your growing fame it should not have been to the extent that Sonia should know who you were. You have been kept as far away from any subjects in the other three groups as possible, and certain parts of what you all do has been kept out of the limelight as much as possible, despite you all excelling in your fields. I felt that I needed to dig a little more into the background of both you and Sonia to find some reason for her knowing you, and do you know what I found?"

He just stood there frozen. The name Sonia rang bells louder than Quasimodo ever could. His mind raced trying to remember why, but it seemed that the answer was blocked off, and he heard himself meekly saying,

"No, although the name rings bells deep inside, I can't recall the reason why it does, just tell me."

The voice answered, with what sounded almost like an element of glee in it,

"Going back to when we did all our original profiles on potential subjects, well before we took all of you in for implanting and programming, we tried to ensure that no one knew, or had any knowledge of any of the other subjects. If there was any knowledge then we would have to exclude one or both of those subjects, we couldn't have them coming together by accident and relating to each other certain memories. It would seem in yours and Sonia's case there was a slight oversight."

"Whilst it was true to say that you'd never been married, and all your immediate family were dead, and your lack of social circle, you were easily ring-fenced. However we hadn't really considered your prior engagement to Keera Fallenfant, we had felt that dealing with this was unnecessary, seeing as she had died some years before we started this project, and you had no on-going contact with her family, since her death, and you only knew a few before then."

"If the research had been even more extensive then the surname should surely have jumped out at us, as how many people have the surname of Fallenfant in this world? We overlooked this fact with you, and meanwhile it turns out that Sonia Baumgartner, the lady you sat next to on the Tube and that gave you such a start, and who is another of the subjects on your wonderful aircraft, is married, and her name at birth was Sonia Fallenfant."

It hit him like a hammer, well actually a series of hammers. The resemblance was plain to see, and that was why the name Sonia had rung bells. He'd never actually met Keera's sister, she had moved to Europe long before the two of them had met, and although he'd seen photos of Keera's sister, it was of her as a teenager with the rest of the family, long before she had moved away. Even in the photos, the resemblance was uncanny; no wonder it had freaked him out so much on the tube.

The voice continued,

"Of course, you had never met her, had you? She would have been living in Europe, and had already married, well before the first time you ever met Keera, and Sonia was somewhat estranged from the rest of the family because of the marriage, her parents never approved of it, they had refused to go, and didn't remain in contact with her. What we didn't realise at the time was that it would however, seem that she wasn't so estranged from Keera as the rest of the family, and that Keera and Sonia had been in regular contact, and Sonia knew quite a lot more about you than you did about her."

"If we had picked up on this during the initial vetting, as we really should have done, then Sonia would not have made the final twenty-four subjects. We would have found another subject from the long list in her field; we could easily have replaced her special expertise. Finding a replacement for you and your skills wouldn't have been so easy."

Chapter 36

He stood there in a kind of shock, not quite believing what he was hearing. In the space of about five minutes his world, which had got a damn site worse since the hijacking, had really been turned inside out.

The major problem to him was why was he so important to this madman's plan? Were there really twenty-three other people wandering around under the impression they were happily succeeding at life, whilst all the time they were being manipulated into doing someone else's bidding? How much of what he had done and accomplished in the last five years had been him, and how much had been set up to follow someone else's master plan?

He had been used as a puppet by an unknown maniac for going on five years now, and he took very little satisfaction from the fact that he's not been the model of consistency that all the other puppets that had been rounded up onto this plane had been, he may have cost the maniac a lot of money, but that was of little satisfaction compared to being controlled from afar.

Then to top it all off he had found out that the woman who so reminded him of Keera was in fact her sister, Sonia; that he'd never met, or even spoken to, and had only been vaguely aware of. This meant there would now be a constant reminder of Keera with him here on the plane, and wherever they ended up once the plane landed.

Whereas earlier in what appeared to be yesterday, though he could no longer be sure of what time or day it was wherever they were, the thought of Keera had caused him to freak out and black out, this time it spurred him on.

He was vaguely aware of the maniac's voice starting up again, but he managed to shut it off from penetrating his brain, as he turned and looked around the cockpit. How could he stop this lunatic from doing whatever he had planned for all of them?

A crazy impulse took over and he dived over the pilot on to the controls of the plane and pulled at them wildly. He was expecting the plane to lurch suddenly, one way or another, but there was nothing, no matter what he did with the steering column, the plane was serenely carrying on flying exactly as it had been before. He was then aware that he could hear laughter. Then he found himself tuning back into the voice, now speaking with an amused tone.

"Now then, you surely don't seriously think that I would leave any of the controls on the plane active, now that we're guiding it into my location, do you?"

"Especially not given your track record for unpredictable behaviour!"

"I'm intrigued, just what did you think you were going to accomplish if you had managed to get the controls to respond to you? Were you going to ditch the aircraft into the ocean, and condemn everyone on board to an icy, watery grave? What about trying to change course and land somewhere else? I know you haven't got any flying experience, just how were you planning to avoid killing everyone when trying to land the craft on dry land?"

Angrily he responded with a little outburst

"What makes you think that I had any kind of plan? I acted on impulse, just seeing if anything could be done, as I have a tendency to do. As I'm sure you must remember, seeing what you have just told me, I'm not exactly your model programmed unit am I?"

As he said it, a small smile of satisfaction appeared on his face.

An unchanged tone of voice carried on in response

"Part of that behaviour was exactly why you were originally chosen for this project. You were regarded as someone who could come up with solutions to problems, because you don't think or act, like anyone else. However if I'd have known for a single minute just how much trouble you would end up being, I might not have approved your choice after all, though having had met you, I would probably still have taken the chance."

The sarcasm kicked back in, and dripped through his reply.

"I'm so sorry to have been so much trouble to you old chap, if only you had sent me the memo or something, then I really might have been able to go the extra mile and help you out."

For the first time the tone of the voice changed, and it was a very icy tone that came through the ether this time.

"As you have reverted to your childish sarcasm, just go, and join your fellow subjects back in the main cabin. I have no more time or patience to try and speak to you any more right now. You can tell the other subjects whatever you feel like, it will change nothing. Plus I'm not convinced the rest of your fellow subjects would believe you. You have proven to be someone to stay away from for most of them, and they view you with deep suspicion."

Chapter 37

There was an audible click as the voice signed off from the maniac's end. He stood there for a moment and considered just what if anything he would tell the rest of the people on the plane when he left the cockpit, he thought about their attitude towards him, and realised the voice was probably correct, most of them wouldn't even give him the time of day, let alone want to speak to him, most of them wouldn't even look at him. He was probably best not saying anything; they would need to find out what was in store for them on their own when they arrived at their destination.

He looked down and realised that he was stood in the pilot's blood, and quickly shifted side wards, and wiped his feet on a clean part of the cockpit carpet, he also checked the clothes he was wearing, he hadn't thought about the gore lying around the cockpit when he made his mad leap for the controls. As far as he could tell there was nothing on his clothes, how he'd managed to avoid getting anything on himself was one of those little mysteries, and in this case lucky for him. He dragged the co-pilot's body further away from the cockpit door to make it easier for him to get out; he opened the door and squeezed through back into the main cabin.

It felt like he had been in the cockpit for some considerable time, but if it seemed like a couple of hours in the cockpit, it seemed like no time had passed at all outside of it. The air of hysteria that he'd left to go into the cockpit hadn't reduced any in the time he'd been in there. Various people were still screaming, others were crying, but there was no one speaking and everyone else remained in their seats.

He slowly made his way back down through the plane to his seat, with a multitude of thoughts swimming through his mind. On the walk back, no one stopped him to speak to him, or to ask about his time in the cockpit, in fact most of the other passengers looked away as he passed them as if he was part of all this madness that was going on. Most of them didn't even know he'd been in the cockpit, let alone how long it was since he'd walked past them on his way there. None of them cared, he thought all of them just wished they were anywhere else but here, and were quite happy to be left alone in their own little worlds to try and cope with the horrors around them.

He got back to his seat and sat down, and went to rub his eyes, not even realising he was still wearing his sunglasses. He sat with his eyes closed trying to clear his head of all the multiple strands of internal conversations going on, and to focus them into a single train of thought, from which he might pull a plan together. He had been doing this for a few minutes when he suddenly felt someone stood over him. He opened his eyes and looked up and said,

"Hello Sonia."

"So you do know my name then." Sonia replied, somewhat tartly.

"Yes, I do now, but only since I spent some time in the cockpit talking to a lunatic." He replied,

"It's amazing what some people will tell you when you act like a massive pain in the arse, and they happen to be a raving egomaniac."

Sonia's voice softened a bit in her reply,

"I had noticed that you were gone for some time. You also looked drained when you came out, but I didn't say anything immediately as I was expecting you to say something to everyone, or at least try to say something."

He made a kind of scoffing noise before replying,

"What would have been the point of that? Most of the passengers fear any form of contact with me, to the extent that they won't even make eye contact with me. They all act as if I'm in some way responsible for what's going on here. Well, that and the fact that I appear to be having problems keeping my mouth shut. They wouldn't want to speak to me, even if I had started saying anything, and they certainly wouldn't want to listen to anything I had to say."

"Besides, not only would they not believe what I've just heard, the majority wouldn't want to believe it, and those that did would be freaking out more than any of the serial screamers we've got going at the moment."

"Furthermore, I would have needed to stop and have conversations with almost every person separately, have you not felt the abnormal silence on this plane; they have some serious sound dampening technology running on full force. I could stand at the front of the plane screaming at the top of my voice, and people two seats away wouldn't be able to hear me properly. Just look at how far you are leaning in to talk to me, and to hear me."

"Not only that, but there are far too many fully loaded firearms lying about all over this place on this plane to start people off with tales of woe."

A new thought entered his mind, and he continued,

"Actually, I wouldn't mind one or two of those fully loaded firearms for myself before we eventually get off this plane. They would be easy to pick up, but I need to do it subtly, to prevent anyone else realising what I'm doing. If they see me picking up guns, it might really tip them over the edge given their high opinion of me that they currently have."

Sonia shifted from leaning over him, and knelt so that she could speak to him at the same level and so they could talk without really being overheard, something he believed they didn't need to worry about. As soon as she did so, that smell hit him again, bringing back buried memories.

He smiled despite himself and looked at Sonia. She looked so much like Keera it was untrue, it was all he could do not to lean over the few inches and kiss her. He closed his eyes briefly and shook his head in an attempt to clear those thoughts from his head, and by the time he opened them again Sonia had already started speaking again.

"As it stands now, I'm not sure which conversation I want to have with you first. I'd like to know what the hell is going on here, which I think you now have a fairly good idea of now after your cockpit visit. At the same time, I also want to talk to you about you. You looked like you'd seen the devil himself when you dived off the Tube this morning, or yesterday morning, or whenever it was? I've no idea what day or time it is."

"I think you would have been more accurate if you had said the devil herself, rather than himself!"

"Why do you say that?"

"I'd never actually seen you in the flesh until I sat next to you on the Tube yesterday morning. I had seen a couple of photos of you as a teenager that Keera had, but hadn't really taken a lot of notice, and you've changed a bit since then. I thought that in the photos you looked similar to Keera, but had forgotten all about those pictures and on the whole about you. I must admit that when I sat down next to you on the Tube, I couldn't help checking you out, but the resemblance to Keera didn't really click whilst I was doing so. Then I smelt the Eternity on you, and that set me off."

"Ever since your sister died, I can't smell Eternity without thinking of Keera, and after I had briefly drifted off upon smelling it, once I reopened my eyes and I looked at you again, the resemblance to Keera was so obvious. Then you called me by my name in a voice that was so similar to hers and I lost it completely. It was like I was meeting a ghost of her. It freaked me out big time and I had to get out of there and bolted as fast as I could. The fact you were on the same plane set me off again, it had already been one of those freaky mornings before "our meeting" on the Tube."

"The strange thing is that when the hijacking of the plane happened, it focused my mind, and I've been sharper and more prepared to deal with anything since then."

Sonia smiled, and responded,

"I had seen photos of you from all the time you were with Keera, she kept in regular contact with me, sending letters, and exchanging phone calls, you haven't changed that much at all over the years, and very little since I last saw you at the funeral."

He was a little taken aback at this, he couldn't remember that happening at all, and whispered,

"You were at the funeral?"

"Yes, I was."

She paused, looking intently at him, before continuing,

"Not that I think you would have seen me, I was there in the distance, watching, but never really getting near enough to the service that any of the other mourners would have noticed me."

After another pause Sonia continued,

"Apart from Keera, I haven't spoken to any of the rest of my family in nearly twenty-five years. My parents disowned me after I came to Europe as a teenager and got married. They didn't approve of my living in Europe to start with, and not of me marrying Thorsten. Their general dislike of Germans would have been bad enough, but the twenty-eight-year age gap between him and me kind of sealed it. The rest of the family fell in line quite quickly, all except Keera of course."

"Being a young teenager herself, she thought it was all so wonderfully free and romantic, and she was always so happy for me. All the way through, she wrote to me, and then in later days e-mailed. I'm quite sure that our parents didn't know about it, as they would have given her such a hard time over it. Rachel rang me to let me know about the funeral details, and I came to say goodbye to Keera, even if it was at a distance."

He questioned the name used,

"Rachel??"

Sonia smiled and continued,

"Of course, you wouldn't have known Rachel, you may have met or seen her, but not have spoken to her. She was my father's secretary for many years. Besides Keera, she was the only person that kept in touch that had anything to do with the family. Though I never really knew whether it was because she felt what the family had done was wrong, she had used to babysit me at one point, or whether it was a way for my father to keep tabs on me and my life, without having to appear to sully his hands in the eyes of the rest of the family by being in open communication with me."

He thought about Keera's parents, and he remembered he always thought that her mother was the head of that family, that she was the one that laid down the law. Even so, her father had seemed a hard-nosed man as well, which was probably required for him to be a success in business. He very much doubted either of them would have gone back on a decision purely based on sentiment.

Chapter 38

His mind stopped wandering as Sonia continued to speak,
"You do realise that you're becoming quite well known now?"
"No, I hadn't really, the maniac in control of all this was suggesting as much when he was speaking to me in the cockpit; he was bemoaning the fact that I was better known than he needed me to be."
"Well you are, I still get news from Philadelphia occasionally, and I have seen you mentioned a quite a few times now in despatches. I've even seen your name mentioned in Europe a few times as well, but I don't think I've ever seen an accompanying photo to the details, so I've never been certain that it is actually you, and not just someone else with the same name, even though it isn't exactly the most common name in the world. It must be said that you never seem to change. You don't look to have aged, and your hair is always the same."
He took that information in and replied.
"That unchanging looks and lack of aging is all part of what's going on here."
She looked at him, with a slightly puzzled look on her face. He continued
"Haven't you noticed it in yourself at all? I lay good odds that you look exactly the same as you did five years ago in every way, clothes sizes, shoe size, weight, face, teeth, everything including your hairstyle."
"I can't do. No one stays the same in all those ways over that period of time; something will have to have changed."
"Seriously, I would normally agree with you, but I've been playing with this hair for five years, and with what I've just been told, if you got a picture from five years ago, you would see it's true for you. In fact it would be true for anyone left alive on this plane. Let me ask you

a simple question. When was the last time you went to a hair salon and got your hair cut?"

There was a silence that seemed to last for ages, before a confused looking Sonia replied,

"You know what, I don't know. I tried to think when I last went, but I can't seem to remember getting my hair cut any time recently."

"OK," He continued, "And how long have you had it styled the way you have it now?"

Again there was a long pause before a stuttering reply,

"I don't know, quite a while I think, I can't remember changing it recently. I like it in this style; it's nice and easy to manage."

Sonia paused before asking, "Why?"

"It's all to do with what was done to us five years ago, and what I've learnt today whilst I was in the cockpit, speaking to the lunatic in charge of this operation. Seeing as you can't remember, I'll tell you that it's probably just over five years since you last had it cut, and in all that time it will have been in exactly the same style."

"Look around the plane. This bright white light everywhere you look, emanating out from every surface, but seemingly without any single source. It hurts to look at anything without wearing sunglasses or squinting. Doesn't that seem familiar in any way to you? Haven't you been somewhere like this before?"

There was another long pause as she appeared to be thinking about that. Eventually she responded,

"I think I have, there is a hazy recollection of something that may have been like this, but I can't be sure whether that's because it happened, or because I want to have that memory for you."

She paused again for a while before continuing,

"When we got on the plane, I did feel a chill come over me, but couldn't place the reason why. Now that you mention it, the bright light does remind me of something, but everything is all too vague and hazy for me to remember exactly what it was. Are you saying that this is all related to what is happening now?"

He sighed, wasn't that exactly what he had just said to her? Everything that was going on here was related. He could see it clearly now, and he had accepted it quite quickly, but in this moment, he realised just how much of a problem it could be to get anyone else to accept even the possibility of what was happening here, it was all so far-fetched.

He felt that he needed Sonia to understand what was going on, and to believe him about all of this. He really needed someone he felt he could trust. If he was ever to get back to his old life alive, then he needed help, and there wasn't anyone better suited to being an ally here and now, that he felt he could trust better, than Sonia.

He just needed to tell her everything he could about what was going on here, and make her believe it. If he couldn't convince her, then he wouldn't be able to convince anyone else. And he needed to do it fast, get it all out of his head whilst it was still fresh, so he didn't miss anything.

He looked at her, took a deep breath, and started to tell her everything he could remember from his conversation with the lunatic in chief.

Chapter 39

It took just over five minutes to get everything out before he stopped talking, and during that time he had been looking at Sonia to see what kind of response there was. In all the time he been speaking to her, telling her all the improbable details, her eyes had never left him, and she hadn't stopped him at any stage to ask any questions. She hadn't even gasped at some of the stranger things included in the telling, let alone said anything.

Even over the backdrop of the noise dampening that filled the plane, there were still screams and whimpers that he could hear, but at his seat there was nothing but a strong silence between Sonia and him. After what seemed an age, Sonia eventually spoke,

"Well, that is certainly a story and a half. I really don't know what to think about it all. There is so much of what you've just said that seems so improbable it's laughable, and certainly if you'd have told me any of this when we were on the Tube, I would have laughed in your face, and written you off as a crazy man."

"However, even though that may still be the case, that view is now somewhat tempered by what has gone on since then. Some of what you have said now seems to make some kind of sense, but it is a lot to take in. The main problem I think I have with all of this is trying to come to terms with the fact that I've been living a life controlled by someone else for the last five years. It makes me feel kind of worthless."

She got up off her knees and stood up before leaning back over and continuing,

"I think I need a little more time to let all of this sink in, I'm going to go back to my seat and think it all through and try and get things a little more aligned in my own head before I can talk about any of this anymore."

"In the meantime, what are you going to do now?"

Without hesitation he replied,

"Get a gun. Discreetly obviously! I don't want or need anyone else seeing me getting a gun for a variety of reasons."

"Well, you don't want to give them ideas, do you?"

"Not really that, I'm not sure they could really get that kind of idea, but there is a level of fear on the plane that would get worse if someone saw me getting a gun. I don't think anyone would be shy in shouting it from the rooftops on arrival that the crazy man who was tied up has a gun. It's not only that though, it really wouldn't surprise me to find that there is someone planted amongst us on this plane, who isn't here as a hostage or a subject or whatever we want to call ourselves, but as a plant."

"If there is someone on board that would report back to the maniac when we got to our planned destination. It would make sense to me, seeing as he's killed all the armed hired help, and the level of planning and contingency that he has already built into the on-going operation."

He looked at her and she was thinking before speaking

"Isn't that being a bit paranoid, sure I can understand why you might feel like that, but if you were going to trust someone to do that role, wouldn't it have been easier to leave a single hijacker in charge? On top of that surely they would expect someone to be able get a gun with so many lying around, and therefore they would have sensors or something to detect that when we all got off the plane when it lands?"

They were valid questions, and he had been thinking about some of those things himself.

"They wouldn't expect anyone to pick up a gun, as I'm sure that their programming would eliminate the chance of that thought coming through, but I'll lay odds again that they will have something anyway, mainly because of the random factor that I seem to bring to proceedings.

I've not exactly been following all their programming recently, and yes there is more than a touch of paranoia about me now."

"Anyway I have been thinking about the possibility of having sensors, and that gave me an idea about the guns. The hijackers on the original planes managed to get their guns on board without any problem, and they were passengers on our plane originally, and therefore they should have gone through all kinds of sensors just to get onto those planes in the first place. I'm going to carry on laying odds about what is going on here and bet that the original hijackers must have had some kind of porcelain gun, such as a Glock, one which wouldn't have shown up on metal detectors, and with the right kind of packaging or wrapping, one which wouldn't even show up as being gun shaped on the baggage scanners."

"That's exactly the type of gun that I'm going go and have a look for now. Having one of them should enable me to get through any kind of sensor they may have got set up as we exit the plane, or go into any building once we get there."

Sonia stood there as if thinking about what he had said carefully, before leaning back in and replying

"If you are sure, and you can do it without being found out, then do what you feel you need to, just be careful though, if there is someone planted on this plane to watch us, you can pretty much guarantee that they would have you firmly in their sights with how you have been all along."

"Yes, I know that, and now that you've been seen having a nice long chat with me, I'd bet that they will probably be watching out for you now as well, so be careful yourself."

"I will."

Sonia smiled, stood up straight, and headed back to her seat. He watched her as she walked away, leaving a faint trace of her smell behind, making him think of Keera again.

That was going to take some getting used to.

Chapter 40

He sat for a while before looking around leaning out of his seat trying to place any of the controllers from one of the original flights, as opposed to those on the ground. He found that he couldn't really differentiate between any of the controllers, they were all dressed the same, and they all had that similar non-descript look, which was being ruined by the fact all of them were covered in their own gore.

Whilst he was looking for controllers, he also spent the time checking out what the other passengers he could see were doing, trying to work out if any of them were being as watchful as he, but none of them appeared to be watching anything, some of them were still whimpering, and some were sat stock still, either with their eyes closed against the brilliant whiteness all around them, or looking straight ahead in worlds of their own. He could dance naked in front of them, and they wouldn't even notice him doing it.

He got up out of his seat again, and spent a few moments getting his bearings before wandering slowly around the cabin, only just managing to avoid bumping into the haphazardly laid out seating arrangement, all whilst making sure he didn't trip over any of the dead bodies strewn randomly on the floor around the cabin. He was trying to look as if he was just wandering around randomly, just in case anyone was watching him, whilst looking for the best place for him to be able to procure a gun without being noticed by any of the other passengers.

As he wandered about, stepping around bloody bodies and random tissue samples, he was amazed that there were no putrefaction smells emanating from the bodies. The ways their innards had virtually exploded out of their mouths, and the fact that they had been lying there for what was getting on for well over an hour now, he had expected the initial foul odour that he had smelt when he first walked past them to have gotten worse, but it hadn't, in fact the smell had disappeared. There must be an air purification system on this plane that was just as, if not even more impressive than the sound dampening on the plane was.

As he had that thought bouncing around inside his head, he saw what he wanted. There were two controllers that he was sure he had seen before, they had been sat together near the rear of the cabin, and they were now slumped over, virtually on top of each other in a pile on the floor. He made his way slowly over to where they lay taking as circular route as he possibly could, checking out the rest of the passengers that he walked past as he did so, none of them seemed to be watching him, and they still didn't want to make eye contact with him. In a small way that was beginning to freak him out as weird behaviour.

There were no other passengers very close to the two controllers at rear of the plane, and he stood for a few more moments working out the angles of sight from where passengers sat to where the two men lay, and he was fairly sure that none of the passengers would have a direct line of sight to them, and therefore wouldn't be able to see him if he was next to them. Well not unless someone snapped out of their reverie and stopped staring straight ahead and turned around in their seats.

When he arrived at the two men and looked down on them, he was quite thankful there wasn't as much mess from these two as there was from some of the other bodies lying around. He bent down towards them, and placed a couple of fingers on their necks, so that if anyone did glance over it would look as if he was looking to see if there were signs of life. As he was doing this, he was checking around the men for their guns and he smiled to himself as he saw what he wanted.

In fact there was more than he expected as next to each other sat two handguns. The two men must have had them on different sides of their persons, as they sat in clear sight almost touching each other between the two men. One was sticking out of a jeans pocket, the other hanging from an old western style holster.

He leant in, carefully removing them from their positions on the bodies and picked them both up with his left hand, putting them both quickly into his inside right jacket pocket one after the other. He made a show of touching their necks again and stood back up. He could feel the bulk of the guns pulling the jacket down out of its normal fit with their weight, and he realised that it would be obvious to anyone who looked at him that he had got something inside his jacket that hadn't been there before. He got his bearings again, and keeping the right side of his body out of people's eyesight as much as he could, and headed for where he had worked out the toilet should be.

He was only a few feet out in his calculation, and in a similar manner to finding the door for the cockpit, he managed to find the handle and open the door. He went through the door and closed and locked it behind him. Once the door was locked, he took the guns out and put them on the side of the sink. Even the toilet on the plane was special. It was three times the size of a normal passenger plane toilet, and there was room to turn around without having to resort to being a contortionist.

When he had the guns on the edge of the sink, he was able to examine them properly. They were Glocks; they looked like other handguns he had used before, but the weight, feel and sound of them told him they were exactly what he wanted, as they weren't made of metal.

Although he didn't own any guns himself, he had been to one of the local gun clubs in Philly, and had target shot quite a few times. He knew how to check the action of a gun, and how to fire them, and although he was no marksman, he was a reasonable shot.

He checked for the safety switches on both guns, and after making sure the safety was on, he checked out the cartridge and magazine to both guns. Both were fully loaded, and would be ready to shoot as soon as the safety had been switched off.

Happy that he had what he wanted, he thought about where he would put them on his person. He already knew they made his jacket bulge in the wrong place, so he'd skip that, so he slipped one into the small of his back, where it felt slightly uncomfortable, but it sat without moving, and was easily covered by his jacket. He then put his left foot up onto the edge of the toilet bowl and started to put the other gun into his sock, but stopped, as that was stupid.

It may work in films, but it felt uncomfortable, there was an obvious bulge when he pulled his trouser leg down over it, and he took one step and felt it moving around. It wasn't really going stay in place there and would affect the way he walked, and would probably fall out onto the floor as he got off the plane. He lifted his leg back onto the toilet bowl and removed the gun from his sock. He then tried his trouser pocket, where he found with some surprise it fitted in there quite nicely and didn't really show. He moved all the items from his right trouser pocket into his left so he could accommodate the gun in his right pocket without it clanging off any of the change in there. Once in his pocket and with his jacket properly in place he looked in the mirror for any telltale signs, and couldn't see any. He sat on the toilet seat, and the gun in his pocket didn't move, and didn't stick out abnormally. Happy with this he got back up flushed the toilet, ran the faucet, unlocked, and opened the door.

He was surprised to see one of the other passengers stood outside the door, but in the now traditional style, she avoided eye contact with him, and went into the toilet, closing the door behind her. Someone had obviously needed to go but hadn't any idea where it was, and had no one to ask. When he found it, they must have seen it and headed there to use it. Or at least he hoped that was the case, he wondered if it was possible he was being watched and that the other passenger hadn't been listening at the door. Either way there was nothing he could do about it, and he made his way back to his seat.

He sat in his seat and contemplated just what he was going to do now that he had guns. He had no idea of just what would be facing him once he and the rest of the passengers arrived at the final destination that had been decided for them all. Would a gun be any use to him, would two, would a million? Was there going to be any way out of this situation for him?

He shifted around in his seat as he struggled to get used to having the concealed gun in the small of his back. It felt uncomfortable pressed against his spine, and it took him several minutes to get into a position where the gun didn't dig into him, and he was able to sit and forget about it. The one in his pocket didn't cause him any issues at all.

He opened the other bottle of Pepsi from the earlier meal and as he sipped from it, he took a bit of time to think about the other woman he'd seen so many times before, and of all the questions he had wanted to ask her. He now knew that her name was Maria Gonzalez, and that he should have already met her by now on numerous occasions, if of course, what the maniac in charge had said was true, and he realised now, that none of those questions mattered any more, he would have different questions for their host, and he knew why he had seen her, and knew about that white room and the tables. The fact he had never actually met her meant he didn't know her, and he didn't have to try and get a level of trust with her.

Every time he would have seen her previously, they had been programmed to be near each other, their paths had been pre-destined by a maniac to cross paths in those places, but despite all that planning from afar it had never actually happened.

He found that now he had the chance to speak to the mystery woman, now that he could get up from his seat, seek her out on this plane and talk to her, that he no longer had the desire to speak to her. All it would do is make the current situation worse, and he would have to explain to another person what he had found out. This Maria might not take it in the same way that Sonia had done, she didn't know him from Adam, and any reaction was possible. He decided that he would stay away from Maria if he could. If she came and talked to him, he would deal with that at the time. There was no need to go hunting out additional issues. He had Sonia if he needed to talk anything through, and that would have to do for now.

Chapter 41

As he sat there contemplating everything that was happening, the hidden speaker system suddenly crackled back into life and the newly familiar voice started speaking to the whole plane from everywhere at once. The voice certainly wasn't having issues cutting through the sound dampening to speak to them all. He could see a couple of the other passengers shift in their seats as the voice started, as if being awaken from a dream, or more likely, a nightmare.

"Ladies and Gentlemen, as I'm quite sure you will have noticed by now, my staff and the crew on your flight today have all had unfortunate accidents – they have become expendable, and therefore their services were ended as quickly as they could be. I understand that their method of termination may have caused a few issues aboard, and may have upset several of you, but unfortunately there is little that could have been done to prevent this without further delaying the operation we are all involved in."

"Nevertheless let me assure you all that you are in no danger whatsoever, as you are definitely not expendable, and I am looking forward to meeting each and every one of you again, and having the opportunity to work with you all."

"The automated controls on this aircraft are the finest ever constructed within the airplane industry, even if I do say so myself, and you will be safely at the destination for your flight, here with me and my staff, within the next ninety minutes. Once you have landed, you will be escorted to your rooms for the night, after all you have been travelling for some considerable time now. Then tomorrow morning, after you have been fed and had time to acclimatise to your new surroundings, you will all be told the reason for you being here on this aircraft this evening, and, as long as you all behave yourselves, you will find the very comfortable lodgings you will be placed in tonight will remain your home for the next couple of weeks."

The speaker clicked off, and once again he was stunned by the silence on the plane. For the first time since the guards had started dropping like flies with blood exploding from their internal organs, no one appeared to be screaming, and there were no sounds to be heard at all.

He noted the comment about the delay to the operation, realising it was probably a pointed barb at him, but one that no one else would know about.

He also now knew how much longer they were going to be on this plane, and looked at his watch and was shocked that it was early evening already, he had completely lost track of time, and they had already been flying around for longer than the previously advised fourteen hours.

He had approximately ninety minutes before he would be at the final destination for this plane, and he needed to come up with some kind of plan of action for what he was going to do when they landed. He would have to assume that they would be keeping a close eye on him; as he had had it spelt out to him that he was the perennial thorn in the side to the maniac in chief, and the fact that he wasn't acting as he had been programmed to do was causing the operation problems. He took a bizarre source of pride in this; at least he was making a difference.

Normally when faced with problems, he would have gone straight to the source of it and tackle it head on, trying to remove whatever the root causes or blockage was. In this case this would lead him to try and shoot the lunatic in charge of the operation. As a root cause there couldn't be a more obvious one, but in the current circumstances, going straight down that root and trying that would probably get him killed before he got anywhere near the target.

He was going to have to be patient, and probably subtle as well, which would be entertaining, he wasn't well known for either his patience or subtlety. Smashing the nut with a sledgehammer as soon as possible was his usual style, and to hell with the consequences. He thought that he could do with finding out exactly what was going on first, and then seeing if he could sabotage everything at the same time as taking care of the maniac in charge.

The identity of that maniac was niggling at his brain as well. That calm, almost monotone voice was certainly familiar to him, and so was the face that they had all saw briefly when he had addressed them through the television screens back in the airport terminal at Kangerlussuaq. The voice had also just alluded to the fact that he had met them all before, which in the circumstances made sense to him, perhaps he was there when they were being implanted and indoctrinated.

He knew who this person was, he was certain of it, and it was driving him round the bend trying to think about getting the man's name to pop up in his head. He would kick himself when it did eventually pop up, and if he could manage it, he would kick the maniac as well, just for good measure.

Eventually he got up out of his seat again, and slowly headed over to where Sonia was sat. The time to have a plan was drawing ever closer, and perhaps Sonia had some idea as to who the lunatic in charge of the operation was. If he had met everyone before, that would include Sonia, and maybe she would remember his name.

Chapter 42

The main reason he was making his way slowly over was that he hadn't really seen where Sonia had been seated before, and he realised that he hadn't noticed which way she had come from when she'd approached him earlier, or which direction she had gone when she had headed back to her seat, he just remembered watching her behind whilst thinking of Keera.

He had been a little preoccupied, and therefore was having a bit of difficulty locating her. The way the chairs had all been set out facing different directions didn't help much either, but he didn't want it to seem that he didn't know where he was going. He had wandered around most of the plane so far, and tried visualising where he had walked past previously.

It wasn't like walking down the aisle of a normal plane, and some seats faced him, some were side on or at an angle and some had their back to him. It took him a couple of casual wandering minutes to find her, in typically the last area of the passenger cabin that he got to, and the only area he hadn't passed before. He approached her seat from her right, and stood over her looking down, and as he did, he noticed what he already knew but hadn't expressly thought before now, that he cast no shadow in this unrelenting light.

Sonia squinted up at him, before leaning over and reaching into her bag, from which she retrieved and put her sunglasses on. He wondered why she had ever taken the sunglasses off in the first place in this hellhole of bright light. As he asked himself that question, he thought back to when she was over at his seat earlier, and as he did, he realised couldn't even recall if she'd been wearing her sunglasses when she had come over.

"Sonia,"

He had almost shouted trying to make sure he would be heard against the dampening, and she flinched a little. He knelt to be at her level, and with a little less volume continued,

"Were you watching the television when the maniac in charge spoke to us all back in the airport lounge in Greenland?"

After a short pause, Sonia responded with an unsteady "Yes, we all were, weren't we? Why?"

"Well, it's been bugging me ever since then. I know I recognise that face from the screen, and having heard him speak to me numerous times since, the voice seems familiar to me. Then he has just alluded to the fact that he will be meeting us again, as if he has met us all before. I get the feeling that we should all know who this man is, but I can't put my finger on just who he is and where it is that I recognise him from."

Sonia paused again, and frowned before speaking,

"Are you sure? You may well have said the very same thing about me no more than an hour ago!"

He hadn't thought of it like that, if Keera hadn't been dead then Sonia would have been easy to mistake for her, so much so that as he looked at Sonia now, it was all he could do not to address her as Keera. He mumbled out a response,

"I suppose so," Before weakly adding, "But it's not really the same, is it?"

Sonia nodded, before adding softly, "It's alright, I understand."

There was another brief uneasy silence as they looked at each other, before she added,

"I don't think I know him; if I have ever met him then I certainly don't remember doing so. The voice doesn't ring any bells either, he sounds like any number of people could. I'm sorry, but there isn't anything else I can help you with on who he is."

His face dropped a bit, and he wondered if part of the programming was to keep this man's identity a mystery to everyone.

Sonia must have noticed his change in expression as she continued speaking.

"Don't worry about that, I do have some help for you in another matter. I've got something for you, but you'll need to in further towards me for me to be able to give it to you safely."

He knelt wondering for a moment before moving in closer to her, catching himself glancing at her cleavage as he did so, and feeling himself flush as he did so. Once he had stopped moving in, he looked directly at Sonia's face and wondered if she could have noticed where he had been looking from behind his sunglasses. He doubted it, but it didn't stop the feeling of embarrassment he had, and even if she had seen him looking, she didn't let on. He found himself asking,

"Well, that sounded promising, go on and surprise me then, what have you got for me then?"

He was grinning, but also finding it difficult to reconcile the fact he was trying to flirt with his dead fiancée's sister in the middle of a kidnapping.

She looked around surreptitiously before picking up her bag, delving back into it, and like a magician pulling a rabbit from a hat, producing a gun from its depths, which she quickly thrust into his hand.

He knelt there looking gormlessly at it for a few seconds before realising he really needed to put it out of sight and he quickly put it in to one of his jacket pockets, whilst he quickly scanned the surroundings to see if there was anyone else watching the pair of them.

Sonia then added in the way of an explanation.

"I just saw that lying on the floor slightly away from one of the dead bodies, as I was walking back over to my seat from speaking with you, and so I picked it up as no one was looking and put it in my bag. I was going to bring it over to you later."

Chapter 43

He found that he was surprised that Sonia had picked up a gun, let alone stashed it away ready to hand it over to him, she had seemed quite squeamish, if not outright afraid at his mention of guns when they had spoken earlier, and she seemed that she would be one of the last people he would have expected to have had picked one up for him.

Regardless of that though, he was quite glad of the extra gun, though his brief look at it had told him it was different from the other ones. He still didn't know whether he needed to check whether it was made of metal before getting off this plane, and he certainly wasn't sure about the size of the arsenal he was now carrying around with him. The new gun felt heavy inside his jacket pocket, and he thought about where he could move it to.

Regaining his composure he started,

"I've been thinking about what to do when we get off the plane."

He didn't know when he had decided that they were going to be a "we" in this situation, but it just came out naturally. He continued

"I've decided not to go for the all-out attack method, it's too risky, and although that is my normal life strategy, I think for once it would be better to try and see what's going on first. In fact the longer I leave it without acting, within reason obviously, the bigger surprise it will be when I do actually do something, and I think that that would make it more likely for there to be any chance of success in pulling it off."

He paused and then asked Sonia,

"Sonia, I've made the assumption there when I said we, do you think that you would be able to stay calm until we can see what unfolds, and more importantly are you sure that you even want to get involved in whatever goes down?"

Sonia sat there for a second and calmly replied,

"Yes, I'm sure that I can stay relatively calm, and yes, of course I want to help you. Us. All of us. You just need to let me know when it's the right time, what you need me to do, and I will back you all the way to the best of my abilities."

He smiled, feeling relieved and glad at the calm and confident reply that Sonia had given him, and he was glad that there was going to be at least one other person there to help him when he got round to doing whatever he ended up doing.

"Thank you very much Sonia," he said,

"I don't know when it will be, or even how I will know the right time yet, but I will come and seek you out when it does come, but I suppose for now it's just going to be a case of see you later, as we should all be seated for the landing, it can't be too much longer now, and I need to sort out where I'm going to put the gun you have given me so it doesn't cause any unsightly bulges that might give me away."

He wasn't planning on waiting for a reply, and started to move so he could get to his feet. Before he could stand, Sonia said "OK", and she leant over and kissed him. He felt himself melt in that moment, as it felt good and there was that smell of Eternity that carried him away. He looked at her and smiled stupidly, overcome by the moment.

After what seemed like an eternity, Sonia said,

"I'm sorry, I couldn't help it! I hope I didn't startle you."

He struggled to speak, his head still swimming from the kiss before managing to push out a simple,

"No."

Another seemingly endless pause followed before he managed to string a coherent sentence together.

"I have wanted to kiss you since I first saw you, though I'm fairly sure that it's not really for the right reasons."

"Do I remind you that much of Keera?"

"Yes, yes you do, and it's not fair on either of us. I mean, it's not your fault you look like you do, after all it's only natural for sisters to look alike. It's a struggle for me to separate you from her, and for your part you deserve to be treated as an individual, and not as a reflex memory on my half."

Sonia smiled at him, and he could see Keera again, his face twitching as his emotions threatened to overwhelm him. Sonia spoke again,

"I can see why Keera loved you, there is something different about you that intrigues people, and that would have been right up her street. It may well be a Fallenfant children family trait; it certainly was with me and my husband. I don't feel bad about kissing you, it felt the right thing to do, and I'm not going to worry about it, as long as you don't."

This certainly wasn't a direction he had expected this conversation to take, and he really didn't want to disappear down this rabbit hole now, he just needed to get back to his seat and compose himself the best he could. With this in mind he replied.

"I don't know, this is all just really strange, it will take some time for me to be able get my head around any of it."

Sonia smiled again and said softly to him,

"That's fine with me; it's not as if either of us is exactly going to different places in the near future, is it now? All I ask is that you just think about it please."

He smiled himself and replied,

"I will."

"Good. Now then, off to your seat, before anything else happens to delay you."

Sonia replied with a wink.

He managed to get out an "OK," as a somewhat dazed response as he clambered back up to his feet. He touched her on the shoulder as he turned, and he half walked, half floated back down the plane to his seat.

Things just kept on getting weirder.

Chapter 44

He made it back to his seat without managing to bounce off some other poor unfortunate passenger's seat or without accidently tap dancing over one of the now expired controllers lying on the ground. He sat back down in his own seat in a daze wondering whether he was just dreaming this. All of this! There was just far too much going on for him to take in at once. Could he even contemplate being with Sonia? Although it looked right to him, it didn't feel quite so right. He couldn't imagine that he would manage to get through more than a day without calling her Keera by mistake at some point, and that wouldn't help anything except causing issues. More issues were something he didn't need right now.

Would it even matter what he thought or did though? At the moment there were other, probably more important things to consider. He suddenly remembered that before he started floating back to his seat that Sonia had given him a gun, he could feel it weighing the inside of his jacket down. He got back up and headed back to the toilet to check out how it looked, and to sort out the best place for it.

Although he knew where the toilet was having been there before, he still had difficulties finding the door the second time around. When he did feel the handle and tried turning it the door didn't move. It was locked. He briefly had a mini panic attack before common-sense kicked in and told him that there must be someone in there.

He leant against the side of the cabin and waited. A couple of minutes later, the door opened and a short woman with long blond hair and a worried look came out. She looked at him, and as if she was hit with a cattle prod, she flinched across her whole body, as she recognised him compared to the rest of the passengers on board; she turned her head away from him and scuttled as quickly as she could back in the direction of her seat.

He was getting used to this by now, and he was now resigned to it; with a small, tired smile, entered the toilet and locked the door behind him. He stood in front of the mirror looking at himself and his attire. Although he could feel the pull of the gun on the inside of the jacket, there wasn't any sign of a pull or a bulge on the outside. Happy that there were no visible signs of gun carrying, he unlocked the toilet door, walked out, and went back to his seat.

He sat back down and looked at his watch, and saw that there shouldn't be long left on this flight now, they would soon be landing and off out to whatever awaited them. He picked up his drink, undid the lid and started sipping again, waiting for the descent to start.

And as if on cue, a reminder came, as the speakers clicked into life and that same voice of a maniac came floating through the ether.

"Ladies and Gentlemen,"

"If you could all please return to your seats and strap yourselves back in, we shall start the landing process. Due to your low cruising altitude, there won't be much of a descent, and you will be on the ground within the next five minutes. Once the plane has stopped, please remain in your seats, and await further instructions."

Sure enough, about three minutes later the plane had come to a halt, and the passengers sat silently awaiting what was coming. The voice sprang back into life and continued.

"As you may be able to tell, there has been a successful landing. At any moment now the rear door to the aircraft should be opening and then, a few of my finest representatives will be on hand to show you your way to your accommodation for the night."

"It is advised that once you have been shown in your accommodation, you take the opportunity to shower and then get some sleep. The local time here is 9.57pm, and for most of you it will have been a very long and somewhat confusing forty odd hours."

"It is also advised that you all make yourselves familiar with the layout of the complex you are staying in, as you will need to make your own way down to the dining room for Breakfast at 7.30am in the morning. There are maps that are attached to the back of each of your room doors that should help you in this matter."

"While you are staying with me here, it is mandatory for you all to attend all meals, and any other gatherings that you are instructed to join. There will be a head count made at every gathering, and any person that is missing WILL be found and they will be punished accordingly. Punishment is something that all of you would be best advised to try and avoid."

"However, if all you wonderful people obey all instructions whilst here, then everything here should be completed within two weeks, and after that then you can go back to your normal everyday lives, your family and friends. Anything else apart from total co-operation on your part will lead to a much longer and possibly even a permanent stay. It is important to remember that all of you are important to the success of my operation, but at the end of the day none of you are indispensable."

With that the voice stopped speaking and as if by magic the rear door started to open, the oppressive silence having stopped with the last announcement that had been made.

The dark night that crept in from outside was a welcome contrast to the excessively bright light within the plane. A man and woman, dressed in the now familiar jeans and polo shirt combination, walked up the ramp and onto the plane as the passengers started to get up and head for the exit.

He undid his own safety harness, and slowly got up from his seat ensuring that he didn't dislodge any of his arsenal, and that his clothing outline looked as normal as possible. He then found himself joining the rest of the departing passengers. Yet again they tried to keep as far away from him as they could given the small space they were in. He looked around to the rear of him on the other side of the cabin trying to make out Sonia and finally spotted her making her way to the exit, and he looked for a way to get over to the other side to join her before getting off the plane.

He found the way blocked and then saw that the short queue of people on his side of the plane were filtering across to the other side anyway, and all the passengers were getting off through the same gap. Without pushing through and past people he realised that he wasn't going to get across to the exit before the others had let Sonia through.

Chapter 45

He might only have been about three people behind Sonia as they got off the plane, but that was as close as he got to her as no sooner had they stepped on to the runway then they were led off individually by a member of staff.

Although the passengers had been filtered through a small part of the rear of the plane, they hadn't been put through any scanner that he could see, and there certainly hadn't been any alarms blaring out or flashing lights suddenly springing into life as he had got off the plane.

A stern-faced man, again with no distinguishing features, nothing to make him stand out, led him to a nearby building without a word. The darkness and the fresh air had seemed wonderful to him as he got off the plane, and once they had walked for about a minute his normal sight returned, and the darkness relented, and he realised it wasn't as dark as he had thought, it still looked as if night hadn't quite finished it fall.

They didn't take much longer to reach the building, and once they entered the building, through what appeared to be a normal simple wooden door, they immediately turned left and walked along a plush carpeted, picture lined corridor, which was all bathed in that bright light again.

His relief at getting through another door without sirens going off was tempered by that blasted light. It hurt his eyes again, seeing as he had only just got used to the twilight on the runway after coming off the plane, and he found himself scrambling in his pocket for his sunglasses that he had only just taken off again.

His escort turned right suddenly, and he followed suit, and then they turned quickly right again into a stairwell, and fairly trotted up four flights of stairs that he had difficulty seeing. He almost stumbled on the steps a couple of times, but his escort didn't seem to have any such issues.

At the top of the stairs they came out of the stairwell and turned right and then left again before his escort stopped suddenly. He almost trotted straight into the back of him as the stop was so sudden. The escort pushed a button on the wall that he'd not previously seen, and a door swung open inwards, before the escort said his first words on the way to the room.

"This is your room,"

The voice was that same upper class English tone that had come from the controllers on the planes, again he wasn't surprised, and the escort carried on.

"Everything you need to live normally for the next couple of weeks will be found in this room. The bathroom has been furnished with your usual brands of toiletries; if you run out of anything it will be replaced. You will then find a selection of clothes and shoes in your sizes in the wardrobes and drawers. You should find the brands and styles acceptable to your tastes."

"There are hot drink making facilities, and a mini fridge with a selection of drinks in. You will also find some snack foods in the cupboard above the fridge. All of these will be replenished when required. Guidelines for your stay here in this accommodation and a map of the complex are on the back of this door as previously advised."

"The doors to all rooms are locked automatically from eleven pm to six-thirty am, and you really don't want to be found outside your own room during these times. The locks that kick in automatically during these times can only be overridden by one person, and as he is in charge of matters here, he would not take kindly to being disturbed."

With that the escort turned and walked away leaving him at the door to the room. He stepped inside, and closed the door behind him. The light inside the room wasn't the same as in the corridors, and he was thankful that he could take his sunglasses off without being blinded. He looked at the back of the door and sure enough on the back of it; there was a quite detailed A3 map of the building he was in, and several A4 instruction sheets. He really couldn't be bothered reading all of that now, he just felt he didn't have the required concentration to do so.

To his left was a small area, that couldn't quite be considered a kitchenette, but contained, the items described. He wandered over, and found a selection of coffees, teas, and malted drinks, along with sugar, milk, and cream.

He opened the fridge, and was pleasantly surprised to find it stocked with numerous bottles of Pepsi, cans of Stella, a bottle of Smirnoff, and a bottle of Bacardi. However he also shuddered as he thought just how much was known about him. He also wondered why if they could stock the fridge to his tastes, why they had bothered with the hot drinks' variety? He opened the cupboard door above the mini fridge, and there were a selection of candy bars, chips, and other snacks. He was pleasantly surprised to find it was fruit free – another bonus.

To his right there was a door, which led into the bathroom, and he had a quick look to find it well stocked with any toiletries he could think of using, and a few that he wouldn't have. There was a pile of towels to put a linen store to shame.

The rest of the room had a large wardrobe in the corner and a chest of drawers next to it, and then next to that a desk, with a great array of stationery and what looked to be a comfy chair. He went over to the wardrobe and opened it to find a few shirts, jackets, trousers, and jeans hanging up, and shoes and trainers on the floor of it. The chest of drawers had t-shirts, socks, underwear, and a couple of jerseys in it. A quick glance told him they were all in his sizes.

Then there was a big, probably king-size, freshly made bed, with a small beside cabinet next to it, on top of which a digital alarm clock sat.

The alarm clock made him think and he could see an electrical lead coming out of the back of it, and disappearing behind the cabinet. He looked around the room again, and noticed that it was the only piece of electrical equipment in there apart from the fridge. He looked behind the cabinet, and the alarm clock's lead went straight into the wall, there was no socket it was plugged into.

There was no television in the room and no telephone for that matter either. He looked around the room and found that there were no power points anywhere in the room, but that there was a network port in the wall above the desk, but there was no telephone port.

He went over to the curtains beside the wardrobe and pulled them back, only to find that there weren't any windows behind them, there was just the plain cream wall that went around the rest of the room, yet the map on the back of the door had suggested he was on the outside of the building

He took his phone out of his trouser pocket, and switched it on, and then removed the various guns he had acquired from their places on his person and went around the room finding hiding places for them all whilst the phone booted up.

Once the phone came to life, yet again, the phone showed no signal, and again he wasn't surprised at that fact at all, and the GPS was working this time, but it suggested he was still somewhere in the middle of the Atlantic, not more than a thousand miles away from Greenland.

Things like that were making his head hurt, as either the GPS was acting up, or they been flying around in circles for more hours than he could remember to waste time and put people off balance, pursuers off their trail, all before ending up here – wherever here was.

With no way of charging his phone without his luggage – which if he was honest, he seriously doubted that he would ever see again – he turned his phone back off, hoping that down the line there would be a chance to use it, and therefore he wanted to conserve as much of its power as possible.

He went back to the alarm clock, and spent a couple of minutes figuring out its features before setting himself an alarm for the morning. He undressed, putting his clothes over the back of the chair next to the desk and he turned the light off.

There was nothing else for him to do, he could have wandered out into the corridor, but it was already getting towards the eleven pm curfew, and he could really do without another session in the blinding white light, plus he really didn't want to be outside of his room when the automatic locks were activated tonight. He could really do without raising his profile any further and getting himself into more trouble tonight, which would need to wait until he was more alert.

Now that he was by himself within a room with a big bed calling him, he was aware that he was feeling properly tired, and that he felt a bit disorientated. He would be far better off sleeping, recuperating, and trying to see what he could do tomorrow in the fresh light of day, when he was properly rested and raring to go, or at least able to go!

He laid down on the bed and as he closed his eyes to get to sleep, he heard a click as the automatic locks kicked in, and it wasn't long before sleep found him again.

He would be able to check everything else out in the morning.

Chapter 46

Norbert sat and thought about the security expert he had brought into the program. Of all his subjects, this one, number nineteen, was the only one that showed any deviation from what had been programmed into them, the only one that showed any resistance to on-going subliminal programming that he was sending to the subjects in what they read, what they watched, and what they listened to.

He had been back over the records of the indoctrination regime that had been used all those years ago, and there was absolutely nothing to suggest that the implant hadn't taken in the same way as all the others, or that the brainwashing sessions had been any different for number nineteen. There was just no way to explain the level of performance outside of the expected results for number nineteen.

It was obvious that the implant worked in some ways, all of the bodily functions the implant set out to control, around the look of the subjects worked just as well on number nineteen as they did on all the other male and female subjects, number nineteen looked the same, his hair was the same length, there was no change to facial hair, and his weight was as it had always been. He didn't look the slightest bit different to how he had five years ago when he had undergone the indoctrination.

Additionally, number nineteen was always in the general vicinity of where he was supposed to be within the plan, but there always seemed to be little wrinkles to the plan for him. He would always be a few seconds later than he should have been, a few yards away from where he would be expected to be, as if he was always pushing the outer limits of what he was supposed to be doing. As if he was chipping away at the boundaries that he shouldn't even know were there.

Norbert considered whether it was possible for number nineteen to break out from the invisible confines that had been woven around him. Everything he had seen from all the other subjects told him that it wasn't possible; there was no way this one subject would be able to defy everything that had been instilled into him. Yet number nineteen seemed to be testing Norbert at every possible turn.

He had spoken to the head of the behavioural programming team employed to do the initial indoctrination of the subjects at great length about number nineteen. In the two batches of beta test subjects they had run for a year each, and in this live subject run, none of the other forty subjects had shown any deviation at all. The behavioural scientist had expressed some reservations about continuing with number nineteen compared to the other subjects, but had also said that there was always room for a little deviation in the initial plan. Yes, it added a small element of risk, but from a scientific discovery point of view, it made this live trial more worthwhile.

Norbert had had to agree with that, this all-important group that he had managed to call back to him, here at his headquarters, were all leading-edge experts in fields that he needed to use; they were only going to be the tip of the iceberg of what he had planned. When it really took off, no computer model simulation showed that he could expect a hundred per cent success rate. He had the opportunity here on hand to see what could be done with that small fraction of a per cent that could resist his machinations, and to see what they could do to oppose him.

Norbert wasn't overly worried about number nineteen now; he was excited to see just what the subject could come up with. Number nineteen's own security measures were set up all over the complex, so he didn't need to worry about keeping track of him. He had his own private security force on site to manage any unfortunate incidents, plus he'd already put in back up measures to help prevent any further deviations from his script.

He watched the footage of the subjects leaving the plane again, paying particular interest to number nineteen, the man didn't walk off the plane in quite the same sheep like manner the rest of the subjects had, but he hadn't been going round butting up against things like an out-of-control ram either. Norbert was happy that where number nineteen was concerned, everything was going to be just fine thank you very much.

He turned the screen off, finished his little glass of single malt whisky, before pushing himself out of his chair and heading off to his bedroom, whistling a little tune to himself as he went. Yes, he thought, everything will work out as planned.

He got into bed, and was asleep within seconds.

Chapter 47

The plan had been for him to complete high school and then head off to university, but in that final year of high school, and with how the part-time work at Trebling was going, he had come to the conclusion that he wasn't going to go to university after all, and he would get out of education and start full time work instead.

He had spoken to Dave and Andy about it, and they were more than happy to take him on as a permanent employee.

His mother wasn't as happy with his decision not to go to university, and she desperately tried to get him to change his mind, with her saying that his long-term prospects would be much better suited having a university education and a degree behind him, rather than just his high school diploma. She also alluded to the fact that she didn't think that the computing craze would last forever, and that when it stopped having that degree would help him find a job in another area.

Despite his mother's protestations, his mind was set, he wanted to work, he disagreed with his mother around the long-term prospects in computing, and he also believed that working would give him better opportunities to see Keera more often, not that he used that as a reason when discussing it with his mother.

In fact it was an argument around going to university that happened to be one of his last conversations with his mother, who died peacefully in her sleep just after the New Year. The small funeral, attended by friends of his mother's and a couple of people he knew, just went to show the lack of family he now had. He was pretty much on his own now – except for Keera.

His work at Trebling over the next three years was of such a high standard that he was given almost total autonomy to design more than just gaming software. With a burgeoning internet, he started to look at online games, and found that he needed some level of security in what he was building online, and took time to learn the about the whole security protocols and layers for internet programming.

He was even given the leeway to develop his own Hockey game – a vanity project by him in reality – and although the game was given a release by Trebling, it hardly made enough in sales to cover the costs of its original development and the small amount of marketing there was for the game. Outside of Philadelphia no one really cared about Bobby Clarke, and the sales figures for the rest of the country were shocking. However, four years later, EA Sports licensed the hockey motion engine he had designed for the game, for their NHL series of games, making him and Trebling software a shit load of money.

However by that point in time, he had already left Trebling to strike out alone, as after the death of Keera, and his self-imposed isolation for the months after her death, with his general shift in manner and demeanour, and even despite the massive amount of support and understanding from Dave and Andy, he felt that he couldn't work in that kind of environment anymore.

He spent a few months after working out his notice period with Trebling not really doing a great deal, he spent days wandering around the city, and with hockey being out of season, he spent most of his evenings just reading or watching television. He dabbled on his computer from time to time, but couldn't really concentrate enough to do any programming.

Then in the spring, whilst he was out aimlessly wandering around the city, there was a burglary at his apartment. The security in his building hadn't done a great deal to stop someone being able to break in, and although there wasn't a lot stolen, the main things were his computer and television, it gave him a jolt that would focus him enough to come back to join the real world again. He was thankful that he had kept backups of all his files, and he went out and got himself another computer and started working almost immediately. The lack of security had given him an idea about what he could do with his computer skills.

For the next year he spent almost every waking hour setting about designing both physical and technical security, and he worked on ways to combine the two in ways that would allow individuals and companies to personalise their security requirements so that no two systems would be the same. Having suffered a personal breach of security, he also tried to design it in a way where the costs of having such personal security systems would be in reach for most people.

Once he had finished building and testing his designs, using his own apartment as a test at first, and then persuading his apartment block management company to test the wider capabilities on their building, he set up his own company SAsec, taking his initials, and shortening the word security. He registered the company, and applied for patents for his designs, and started out to sell his product.

It took a bit of time for his fledgling business to take off, initially he couldn't afford to advertise his products, and there were no other staff working with him at first. He found that he was doing a ridiculous amount of paperwork to cover off all the tax and other regulatory requirements that the company had to do. The early sales and installations came from word-of-mouth recommendations. His first few jobs were installing systems into other buildings that the company that owned his apartment block owned.

After a couple of years his company had grown, and was considered as an industry leader, and he had a team to oversee the day to day running of the company, as he concentrated on building updated versions, and taking on some very high-end specialised work, both for large corporations, and more recently an ever increasingly security conscious celebrity market.

Chapter 48

He had a somewhat fitful sleep, which was unusual for him nowadays, thankfully nightmare free considering the events of the last two days, and when he was woken up by the alarm clock, the bed looked like it had hosted a full-on WWE wrestling match rather than a night's sleep. He struggled to find his bearings and to find the location of the alarm that was waking him, it was very dark in the room, and the digital display from the alarm clock wasn't very bright, and it had been behind him when he woke.

He fumbled for the light switch, scrambling around the wall either side of the bed for it, uncertain of which side it had been when he had used it to turn off the lights the night before, taking longer to find it than he would have liked. When the room lit up it took him a few moments to realise just where he was, and when he did remember he just slumped back down onto the bed struggling to reconcile what the hell was happening to him.

A couple of minutes after he lay back down, he heard his door click, and immediately wondered who was there. But there was no further sound at the door, and he eventually recalled his short brief from the previous evening that the doors to the rooms were on timed locks, and it was opening time at this human zoo.

He glanced at his watch and saw that it was six thirty, and he was surprised that his watch showed the same time as it was at his current location. He had struggled to remember whether he had reset the watch to Philadelphia time when he had viewed it in the last couple of days, he had thought he had done when he looked at it in Kangerlussuaq, but the more he thought about it, the more he was sure that he had forgotten to. He was sure he hadn't changed the time on his watch when he had arrived here last night.

If all that was true then he was somewhere that was time aligned with Greenwich Mean Time, and that narrowed down his list of possible locations he could be in. Granted it only narrowed it down from tens of thousands to just thousands.

He managed to drag himself out of bed, and went into the bathroom. He spent just over thirty seconds in the shower, in water as cold as he dared to have it, before drying off and spraying himself with deodorant, and then went back into the room to dress. He wasn't going to bother shaving, as there was no point in doing so, even after five years; the automatic reaction was still there for him to reach for a razor. The same thought went through his head every single morning. At least this morning wasn't one of those when he did start shaving.

He went through the various drawers in the chest and pulled out the first socks and underwear he laid his hands on, before moving on to the wardrobe, where he pulled out a pair of jeans. He was going to pull out a shirt as well, but changed his mind and went back to the drawers and got himself a polo shirt. He would amuse himself by dressing in what appeared to be the corporate dress around here. Once he had dressed, he went to find his shoes, and then as he went to put his shoes on, he saw a gun sitting on the desktop.

It may have been the one from the small of his back, he couldn't be sure; all he was sure about was that he couldn't believe he'd just left it lying out on the desk in plain sight. Last night when he had been shown into his room, he hadn't even considered the possibility that there might be hidden cameras all around it, but this morning looking at the gun lying there he had difficulties thinking of anything else.

He quickly opened the drawer to the desk and slid the gun along the desk and into the open drawer. He slammed the drawer shut, annoyed with himself for that kind of oversight, and then headed for the door. If there were hidden cameras in the room then he was already done for, not only for the gun he had left sitting on top of the desk, but also for the other two he'd hidden elsewhere in the room the night before, all of it would be on film.

At least if that gun was now in a drawer, if there were any passers-by when he opened the door, they wouldn't see it just lying there. If there weren't hidden cameras, then he could do without advertising the fact he had a gun to anyone who might be able to look into his room as they were passing.

He stopped at the door and studied the map on the back of it, and took thirty seconds to get his bearings so that he knew he could find the route to the dining area from his room, he also looked at all the various instructions and guides on the four other information sheets on the back of the door, taking the time to read all of them. The detail was overwhelming, and so much of it was just petty rubbish, just putting in random controls for the sake of it. He didn't know how much of this rubbish he was willing to put up with before he snapped and found a way out. He took another last look at the map before he left the room to head down for breakfast.

Chapter 49

He had the route to breakfast firmly embedded in his mind, and with one last check that there was nothing showing in his room to raise suspicion he opened his door, stepped into the corridor, and closed the door behind him.

The bright light hit him almost straight away, after the normal lights in his room he had forgotten about this blinding, mind numbing light that all the corridors he'd walked through on the way up to his room last night had.

He was going to walk off and just squint all the way down to breakfast, but thought to check his door before doing so anyway. He turned, and found the little button in the wall that his escort had pushed the night before, pressed it and pushed the door to his room, and found that he could open it easily. He realised that this meant that the only locks on the doors were the time lock ones that came into force at night.

He found this somewhat disconcerting, as it meant that anybody could come along and get into his room and have a look around, and with the guns he had there, it would be better if he could lock his door.

With the door being open, he quickly nipped back into his room, and retrieved his sunglasses from the top of the bedside cabinet he had left them on the night before. It would be so much easier to walk around the corridors if he didn't have to squint and didn't have a headache.

Despite his initial misgivings about the lack of lock on his room, as he made his way to breakfast it dawned on him that it could work in his advantage if all the doors in the complex worked on the same system, and not just those that housed himself and the rest of the hostages.

It took him just over two minutes to make it to the dining area. As he entered the room, he stopped to look around the room to see if he could spot Sonia, but the room was pretty much empty with only a couple of people down there before him. In addition it didn't seem as bright in there, and he took his sunglasses off to find that the dining room was lit normally. He folded his sunglasses up and put one arm in the v of his polo shirt to hang them down his front.

The room he found himself in was huge with rows and rows of small tables, each with two chairs, and one on either side of the table. He quickly made a count and worked out there must be over one hundred and fifty tables in the room. Down the left had side of the room was a long serving area, to the back of the room was what looked like a bar, and in the right-hand corner were some double doors, that he assumed must have been through to the kitchen. On either side of the room were long windows, with a few sets of emergency exit double doors at regular intervals.

He went over and took a seat down on the left-hand side of the room so that he was near to the buffet area, where most of the breakfast food was set out. He went to the end of the serving area and took a plate and worked his way down the serving area piling his plate full of food, trying to get as many different items on as possible. It seemed to him like it had been an age since he had eaten, and was feeling hungry, and he fully intended to take advantage of this buffet.

As he ploughed his way through the food in front of him, he kept one eye on the entrance, looking out for Sonia, and generally watching as other hostages came into the dining area.

The dining area was filling up, but to his amusement, it was mainly filling up on the right-hand side of the room, and as he looked around him as it filled up, he could see that there was no one sat within four tables of him. It was obvious that they were still wary of him, and the trouble he seemed to attract. Additionally he could see that the other subjects were somewhat wary of each other. Most didn't sit on an adjacent table to anyone else, let alone on the same table.

Sonia came in after about half an hour, and he lifted his arm and waved to attract her attention, and as she saw him, she smiled and made her way over to his table. They exchanged greetings and Sonia went to get herself some food, and he went and got himself a second plate of food before joining Sonia back at the table.

Once back at the table they spoke to each other; trying to casually talk about the usual pleasantries, such as talking about their new accommodation, it just didn't seem to be the most naturally flowing conversation ever. He didn't feel quite as comfortable with her this morning, and he couldn't place his finger on why, but assumed it was because of the whole situation. He wondered if she felt the same way, and whether the awkwardness was due to the end of their conversation on the plane the night before. Their stilted conversation was abruptly interrupted.

"Good Morning ladies and gentlemen," Boomed a voice suddenly through speakers,

"This is your generous host speaking. I hope that you all had a comfortable night's sleep and that you found all the facilities in your rooms up to the standard you are used to. By now I can see that you are enjoying your breakfasts, feel free to have as much as you want, it may be good to refuel, as I am aware that your usual timetable for meals has been slightly off kilter for the last two days."

"Now, I am sure that you are all still wondering why you are here and what awaits during your stay, and though I would like to tell you all now, there are a couple of little issues that have popped up that I need to attend to this morning, and therefore my full briefing to you will have to be delayed until this afternoon."

"You can all have the morning free to wander as you like, use the leisure facilities, wander around the grounds, or just relax, before lunch is served at one. If you do decide to wander the grounds then please be aware that the warning signs on the ground's boundaries aren't there for decoration, the fences are electrified, and there really is a minefield out there."

Without even changing tone, the voice continued.

"When lunch is finished then I shall come and fully introduce myself to you all, and I can finally get around to telling you all what is going on here, and what you can do to make this operation a roaring success, so until then, Goodbye."

Sonia looked up at him and asked.

"What are you going to do until the briefing then?"

He responded straight away, knowing what he needed to do this morning.

"I'm going for a tour of the facility and grounds; I feel that a good look around would be most useful. Would you like to accompany me?"

Sonia paused and she hesitated before responding nervously.

"No, I'm still having difficulties adjusting to the time and what has happened, and I'm going to go and try and relax. I noticed on the plan of the site that there is a steam room and Jacuzzi, so I think I'll head there and enjoy."

Her voice changed, and she smiled at him before saying,

"Are you sure you wouldn't like to come and join me instead?"

The way she looked and the way she looked at him when she said it, he was sorely tempted. He would be quite happy to spend some time with Sonia in a Jacuzzi, but he really needed not to be distracted in that way. His primary concern today was to scope out the site as soon as possible.

"Sorry Sonia, but I really need to get this place sussed out a bit first, I won't be able to relax properly until I've got a good handle on the layout, but hopefully that's an open invitation that I can hold you to at a later date?"

"Of course it is." She almost purred as she carried on smiling at him, "Why don't you just come and find me when you want to take me up on it, I'm in room 115. You'll have to drop by, as there doesn't appear to be phone service around here."

"I shall see you later then?" She asked as she got up.

"Count on it", He replied.

With this Sonia smiled again and bent down and kissed him on the cheek, before heading off to the door. He watched her walking all the way to the door they had come in for breakfast, his mind in turmoil, as it was exactly like watching Keera walk away from him.

He finished his cup of coffee and headed for the exit himself, he had some exploring he needed to do.

Chapter 50

He put his sunglasses back on and he went through the building, straight past the stairs back to his room and headed back out of the door that he and everyone else had been brought through to get into the building the night before. Once outside he removed his sunglasses and hung them back in the v of his polo shirt.

Straight in front of him stood the airstrip where they had landed last night. He could see the ugly looking plane that they had been flown in on some two hundred yards to his right; it must have been moved after they had all disembarked. Just behind it stood what looked like it must be a hangar building, with a little tower just above it. Apart from that there was nothing but barren countryside in his view from that side of the building. He thought about walking straight down the runway to see what he could find at the other end, but he decided that he could leave that journey until later.

Instead he turned to his left and made his way around the building he had just come out of. He found that it was laid out in an E shape, just as the map on the back of his door had said, with the dining / assembly area stuck onto the end of the middle prong of the E. From what he could tell, the entire building was for accommodation, and had the look of a down at heel Holiday Inn about it. As he looked at the outside of the building, it looked like there were windows all the way around the building on three levels. They were made up of tinted glass on the top two levels, but thinking back to the wall behind the curtains in his room wondered whether this outer tinted glass just hid the walls behind them to give an impression of the building having windows.

The windows on the ground level were different, had clear glass and he was able to see what was inside. The lower prong of the E shape held a swimming pool, with the jacuzzi and steam room off to the side, and then there was a gymnasium with various machines lined up. There wasn't anyone he could see inside either of those areas.

The upper prong of the E held what appeared to be a series of meeting rooms, and a small games area with a pool table, a billiards table, a couple of pinball and video game machines and a dart board. If he didn't manage to get out of here, he would probably find himself hanging out in that room for something to do, given the lack of other possibilities in his room.

He completed his tour around the outside of the accommodation building, going into the arms of the E shape, and there was nothing that had really caught his eye apart from the fake windows. As he had made his way round that building, he had seen another two buildings, one stood just opposite the assembly hall, and another off to the side of the upper prong of the E.

He made his way back towards that second building first. It had the look of being built out of stone, looked like it was two stories high, and was probably the length of a football pitch. On the side he approached it from there were no windows, just a large double door pretty much in the middle of the building. He decided to have a look around the outside of the rest of the building rather than heading towards the doors, and aimed for the end of the building to his right. He turned the corner, and was surprised that the building wasn't very deep down that side; it could only have been twenty yards at the most. There were no windows or doors at all on this side, and he turned the corner to the far side of the building. Again there were no windows or doors, but on this side of the building, the wall had been painted in a variety of greens and browns, almost in a camouflage pattern. The final side of the building he got to had a large metal shutter opening, the kind that would be used for vehicles to enter and exit the building. There was no man size door cut in it though, and there wasn't any control panel he could see on this side of the shutters.

He went back to the only other door in the building and as he did so he got the nagging feeling that he'd been to this building before.

There was something about the size and makeup of the building as he approached it from this angle that triggered a feeling of Deja-vu, making him shiver.

He got to the doors and looked for a way to open them. There didn't appear to be and handles or locks on them. He looked around the outside of the frame looking for any buttons similar to the one outside of his room here, but saw nothing. With no other way to try the doors, he did the only thing left open to him and he gave the doors a push.

Chapter 51

To his astonishment the left-hand door swung open.

That damned bright white light spilled out of the door and had him reaching for his sunglasses again. He stepped into the building and looked around the edge of the door, there were no locks or catches on it, but on the inside of the door there was a nice big sturdy handle – a novelty around here.

But, with a handle there he felt comfortable in closing the door behind him, confident that he would be able to get back out of this building when the time came around for him to leave it.

There was no way of telling how big the area he was in was with the light around him, all he knew was that if it was as big as the building then he had about a third of a football pitch to feel his way around. He turned to his left and had only taken a few paces when he came across a wall in front of him, he turned right and continued along the wall. As he made his way across the building he found two doorways in the walls, and they had the same buttons outside of them as his room door did.

The room he was in was the width of the building, and he turned right again, and after about twice as many paces as he'd taken when he'd first come in by the double doors, he came up against another wall. Walking along this longer wall he again found two doorways and buttons as he had on the other side of the room. He carried on around until he came back to the door he entered.

Having scoped the current room out as a kind of entrance lobby, he made his way back to the last of the four doorways he had passed on his way around this room, and pushed the button to open the door.

Chapter 52

When that door swung inwards, what was inside the door was a shock to his system, although it wasn't really a surprise to him, part of him had been expecting what lay before him since he had that feeling of Deja-vu walking around the outside of the building.

Inside that room he could just about make out a padded table directly in front of him, he recognised this table all too well from his nightmares, the memories of this room had been real after all, it hadn't all been a dream. It was one of the tables he had spent quite some time on over five years ago, this was the room where they had messed with his body. This was the room where they had really messed with his head. This was the room where they had put a chip into his brain. This was where they had programmed him to be one of their performing monkeys. This was the room where for whatever strange reason it had been, that they hadn't fully succeeded with him.

As if walking through treacle he slowly edged his way to that first table. As he peered through the light, he thought he could make out the outlines of a further five retreating into the distance. He couldn't be sure whether he could see the other tables, or whether his memories were telling him they were there. He shuddered; six tables in a room, all he could remember from that time of his life, and a sight that had been replayed to him through his dreams on countless occasions.

The blood pounded through his ears, rushing, and swirling around his head getting louder and louder. He could feel his heart pounding away, beating far faster than it should be, and he felt like he was being overwhelmed by his senses, as if just being back in this room was giving him a panic attack.

He reached the first table, and put his hands on it to settle himself. He stood there leaning on the table, trying to control his breathing, trying to bring himself back to normal, trying to calm down. He lay on the table before he keeled over, but as soon as he had, he realised that was a mistake and his senses all shut down. He faded into unconsciousness on the table.

Chapter 53

He had been on a business trip to London when it happened; he had been meeting with a large accountancy firm on the outskirts of the square mile with a view to installing one of his firm's security systems. The meeting had gone well, the company seemed serious about the security they needed, something that he was always keen on when agreeing to install one of his systems, and they had seemed impressed by the capabilities of the system they were being shown. It had however been a struggle to suppress the laughter when one of the senior partners had asked about using a walking stick as a sword effect. He spent the next twenty minutes trying to clear his mind of the images of ninja accountants dispatching their numeric foes using samurai swords.

He would be sending the company details of the installation contract, and the final quotes for the work once he made his way back to Philadelphia. He joined the clients for a few drinks at The Williamson's Tavern somewhere off Bow Lane. The few drinks turned into a few more, and upon leaving he struggled to find his bearings enough to find a busy enough road to flag a taxi down. He stumbled over his words, but eventually managed to get out just which Holiday Inn he was staying at, and he was on his way. He spent five minutes trying to get into his room before successfully getting the key card in the right way round for the right amount of time for the light to flash green. He slammed the door behind him, no doubt endearing himself to his hotel neighbours, and slumped on to the bed.

When he woke, he was lying in that bright white light, strapped to a padded table with a sore head that he didn't entirely put down to the previous night's drinking, although he wasn't even sure if it that had been yesterday, or how long he had been here.

People in white coats moved around him, peering at him, poking at him, looking at machines that they had hooked up to him. He tried to move his head, but it felt like it was made of lead, and it wouldn't move. He squinted through the bright light, making out further people on similar tables to the one he was on, he couldn't tell if they were males or females. The light started to hurt his eyes and he closed them again, quickly drifting away.

He lost count of how many times he came round in this room, though each time he did his head hurt a little less, he was able to keep his eyes open for longer, and he could make out more about the other people in the room. The next table to him housed a woman, as time went on, he could clearly make out her features, he would have been able to recognise her easily if required. He finally worked out there were another four tables past the woman's at regular intervals down the room. All the other people on the tables appeared to be men, but he couldn't really tell any of them apart from each other, he wouldn't have recognised any of them if they had walked up to him and stood on his toes.

He had several experiences of having some kind of goggles placed on his head, covering his eyes, and blocking the bright white light out. However they were hooked up to some kind of media player, images brighter than the lights flashed through on the inside of the goggles, searing into his mind, flooding through his eyelids even when he had his eyes tightly shut. He found that he had had earphones placed into his ears as well, loud noises, voices, music of all kinds flooded through his ears at a volume where it would be impossible to hear anything outside of his own little cocoon. During these sessions he felt like he was going mad, he pulled at his restraints with all the strength he could muster, trying to get his arms free so that he could rip the goggles away from his eyes, and pull out the sounds from his ears, but no matter how hard he pulled, he couldn't break away.

There was no way of judging time in that room, the white light was constant, there were no meals, they must have been kept alive by some of the tubes that were attached to them. When he was awake in that room, without enforced sound and vision, he wondered where he was, and how long they were going to keep him here. Would anyone notice he was missing, would anyone care?

Then as suddenly as he appeared in the bright white room, he was back in his own apartment, lying in his own bed, totally unencumbered. He felt himself coming round, and prepared himself for the light as he slowly opened his eyes. As he did, he realised it wasn't that bright. He fully opened his eyes and looked around, he recognised items around the room as his own, he went the rub his eyes, and realised he could move his arms, though they were stiff, and they felt like they weren't quite fully under control.

He pushed himself up to a sitting position, and the change of position made his head spin, he felt lightheaded, and a little dizzy, and he only just about managed to stay sat upright. He sat like that for at least twenty minutes until the light headedness went away, only trying to stand up once he was confident that his head wouldn't spin again and dump him back on the bed, or worse, on the floor. He pushed himself up off the bed slowly, waiting for a sudden dizzy spell that didn't come. His legs felt stiffer than his arms, once he was stood up, he found he could just about shuffle across the floor to the door of his bedroom.

His travelling bag that he used for hand luggage on these business trips was laid carefully on the table. Nothing seemed out of place in the apartment. He gingerly made his way through to the kitchen, heading to the fridge. He opened the door, not quite sure what to expect. A few items had the look of being spoilt, and he picked up the milk carton and shook it. It felt full of sludge rather than liquid, and he decided against opening it to smell it, he wasn't sure his stomach could take up the challenge. He dumped it in the bin, along with any other items that looked past their best and then reassessed what was still in the fridge. He pulled out some orange juice and scuttled over to the cupboard for a glass.

He turned on the TV, and flipped through to a news channel, shocked to see the date as being just over three weeks since his business meeting in London. He went back to his travel bag and pulled out his laptop, opening it up only to find it was dead. He rummaged through and pulled out the charger and plugged it in. He let some power charge the laptop whilst he went into the shower to freshen up. Once dressed he came back to the laptop and logged in.

His e-mail inbox went crazy as it started downloading three weeks' worth of messages started coming through. The tone of the messages changed with the later the date that was on them.

The ones coming through from his employees started off light in tone, moving on to concern, rising to panic the longer the time without a response went. Apparently, they had reported him as a missing person; the local police had called in the FBI when there was no sign of his name on any flight manifests coming out of London or into Philadelphia.

Client e-mails made uncomfortable reading, the London accountancy firm, having had no response from him, had contacted his company, only to find that no one there knew where he was, or anything about the contract he was drawing up for them. After two weeks they had sent details cancelling their potential contract. Other clients that were further along in the process were getting to a similar stage, and even more where there were future leads had already withdrawn their enquiries. It was going to take him a few days to even start to sort this mess out.

He got hold of his director of installations, never hearing a more obviously relieved response from anyone in his life before. He tried to explain what had happened to him to his subordinate, but got the feeling that the more he talked, the less he was believed. He told his director that he would be in the office later in the day, when he would try to sort out some of the issues that had arisen. He had other things he needed to sort out this morning.

He rang the local police department, being bounced around before getting put through to the detective looking after his missing person's report. Detective Sampson didn't even start a conversation over the phone, just telling him to get down to the third precinct as soon as he could.

He put on some more clothes and headed for the door; his keys were hanging on a hook by the door where they usually were when he was at home. Behind the door were a pile of papers, nearly four weeks' worth of the Philadelphia Tribune. He went back to his room and picked up a bag, putting all the papers in them before heading off to the third precinct.

When he got there, he was sent up to a meeting room on the third floor to await Detective Sampson. As he waited, he flicked through the papers, to his dismay he realised he had missed seven Flyers games, all of them losses as they had fallen out of playoff contention, perhaps he wasn't such a jinx after all.

He also found a picture of him on page three of an issue from the week before under the headline of;

"Local Businessman Missing For Two Weeks Now"

With a sub heading of "Police and FBI involved, but no sightings since the beginning of the month." He flicked through previous editions, finding a couple of smaller mentions prior to the page three story, he really wasn't sure that he merited a story that soon in a newspaper, even a local one.

Eventually Detective Sampson turned up, introducing Special Agent Marcos from the FBI. They spent the next couple of hours grilling him over his disappearance, the further the session went on, the less the pair of them looked like they were believing a single word he was saying.

They had a host of paperwork for him to sign, and mentioned they may be in touch to discuss any possible bill for wasting the

Police's and the FBI's time. He would look forward to that amongst whatever other losses his business was going to be hit by due to his disappearance that no one seemed to believe.

He headed to his company offices and was greeted by staff that were grateful to have him back, though he knew that probably wasn't on a personal level, more about the fact that it would mean that they would get paid. It would appear his earlier conversation with his director had made the rounds, and he got some very strange looks.

His afternoon was the first of many over the next week where he spent a lot of time apologising, and making some overly ambitious promises that he hoped he would be able to keep. It was dark when he left the office and slowly walked home, all his muscles aching as he used them properly for the first time in weeks.

The following morning's paper showed just what people had thought of his story, with a page five picture of him with the headline of;

"Local Businessman Found Back In His Apartment After Three Week Bender"

He lost some more business over the next couple of days, and three of his staff. It took a good six months before the business was back on an even keel.

As those months went by, his experience in that white room faded, the longer that went by, helped by a very expensive shrink who only seemed to suggest that the more he thought that it had all been a dream, the more likely it was to have been one, granted one that reoccurred on a regular basis, but much easier to deal with than if it had been real.

Chapter 54

He wasn't sure how long it took him, but eventually he came round again, quickly pushing himself off the table and back on to the floor, felling like he was getting himself back under control, his breathing was returning to normal, and his blood had stopped pounding through his head, and so, he pushed himself away from the table and walked around it.

He walked down the right-hand side of the room, walking past the remaining tables, counting them as he did, it was confirmed; there were six tables in total in this room. Once he reached the last table, he went all the way around it and came back up the room on the other side of the tables. As he walked down and back up the room, he looked around the rest of the space as best as he could, but apart from the six tables there wasn't anything else in the room that he could see except the bright light.

He went back out into the central lobby space of the building, and moved across to the next door on his current side of the room. He pushed the button by the side of the door, and as the door opened, he knew what he was going to see. It was another room, laid out exactly the same, six tables down the middle of the room and again apparently nothing else. He walked down one side of the room and back up the other side checking the tables, and looking around the space for anything, any little sign that something apart from whiteness was in this room, but there was nothing.

He exited that second room and crossed the central space and opened the door opposite the last one. Once again he found a room set out with six tables down the centre and nothing else, but pure bright whiteness, he still walked the length of the room around all the table before exiting back into the central space, where he moved sideways to the last of the four doors, knowing that what was behind the door would be the same, but he felt he had to open the door and look inside and make sure.

When the final door opened, he knew what it all meant. The feelings he had in the first of the four rooms had been overwhelming, but he now knew there was no way of knowing which of these four rooms he had been in, they all looked the same and it could have been any one of them.

He also knew that all of the other passengers or subjects or whatever they were from the plane had been in one of these four rooms at the same time he was, all of them being subjected to the same body and mind alterations, having a chip put insides their heads, being programmed with sets of instructions, instructions that had brought them all back to this place at the same time to continue on doing something that had started five years ago.

He now knew there was no way in hell he was going to go along with anything that the maniac in charge was going to try and get him to do. He was going to get out of this place, and he was going to get out of here as quickly as he could, and he was going to bring others back here to put a stop to all this lunacy.

He had exited the last of the rooms and was going back to the outer door, when he remembered the large, shuttered door he had seen at the left end of the building as he had walked around the outside of it. There must be some way through to it from one of the rooms to his left. He went back across the central space and into the last of the four rooms he'd opened. He walked quickly past the tables and to the end of the room. He looked and felt across the whole of the end wall, but couldn't find anything to suggest there was another way out of this room. He couldn't find a door, or any button to push that might make a door appear.

He made his way back out to the central area and headed into the other room on this side of the building. Once again, he made his way down to the bottom of the room and started searching for a door.

This room did have a door in the middle of the wall at the end of the room, but unlike all the other doors he had encountered in this building and for that matter in the accommodation block and plane, there was no button to either side of the door. He looked around the door, starting at the floor on each side, going around the whole of the frame, eventually finding it above the door. He pushed the button and the door started to swing inwards.

He quickly stepped back out of the way of the opening door, and when it finished moving, he stepped forward and stuck his head out of the door.

It was dark in the space behind the door, and he took his sunglasses off to look around, part of the room was lit up from the room behind him, but it didn't penetrate the gloom in the way he would have expected it to, in fact very little of the light made its way across the threshold.

His eyes adjusted to the gloom, and he looked around the area. Apart from the inside of the shutter, there was very little else to see, just stone walls and some steps up the wall to his right. There was nothing else to suggest that this area had ever been used; though he thought it would have been perfect for driving people in to, before moving them to one of the tables. He walked over to the shutters, his footsteps echoing up from the stone floor, the first time he had been aware of footsteps whilst in this building. To the right of the shutters was a control panel, a small square panel with a circular metal hole in the centre for a control key, the key would be the only way these doors would be able to be opened.

He moved back to the steps and started to walk up them. They stopped at an upper level, a vast dark space heading away from him towards the far end of the building. He moved from the steps into this space, taking a couple of tentative steps out into the void. It felt like board underneath him, and he shuffled carefully sideways testing each potential step first. All he found was boards across the whole space, apart from two metal strips about a foot wide each, one on each side, the metal strips weren't as secure underfoot as the wooden boards had been, and he managed to lift one of the metal pieces. In the gloom he couldn't make out what under them by sight, he carefully felt into the space and found cables. They must have been the cables that provided the strange light to the rooms.

He made his way back to the steps and headed back into the loading bay, had he been brought into this building through here, driven in here in secrecy, or had he willingly walked through the other set of doors, he really couldn't remember, but was determined to find out.

As he got to the bottom of the steps, he put his sunglasses back on and went back into the last of the rooms with the tables. He walked up the side of the room and back into the central space, walking across to the entrance and out of the building. He didn't bother closing any of the doors behind him.

Chapter 55

Once he had gotten outside of the building, he could take his sunglasses back off, they were getting a lot of use of the last couple of days, more than they usually did, and he was glad he had gone for the wraparound shades this time, rather than the aviator style that he had usually bought previously.

There was only one building left that he wanted to check out now, and he headed across to that final building behind the dining area of the E shaped accommodation block. This final building was again different in style from the others. It was all red brick and small tinted windows; the kind of nineteen eighties bog standard office building that was usually a blot on the landscape in town and city centres everywhere. Here it really was a blot on an actual landscape, at stark contrast with the wild countryside he could see behind it. This building was smaller than the other two buildings he had been in, and it showed signs of being weather beaten as well. If he had to hazard a guess, he would have said that this building had been here longer than any of the others.

As he made his way towards this building, he got another Deja-vu style nagging feeling that he'd been to this building before at some point in his past. From the angle of approach, with both of the other buildings out of eye-line, it looked to him as if some of the surrounding countryside seemed familiar, as did the building he was heading for.

Once he had gotten closer to the building, he was certain that he had been here before, and that he'd been here in a work capacity. If he wasn't mistaken, he had done some security work here, but it must have been a long time ago, back in the early days of his company as he still couldn't place it.

When he got to the front of the building that feeling of certainty was confirmed. He had definitely been here before as he had installed one of his own security and entrance systems to this building, the entrance keypad in front of him bore the legend SAsec, the name of his company.

The name was a private joke for him, and although it was named after his initials and the shortening of the word security, he maintained to himself that it stood for Sod All Security, though he would never told anyone else that that was what it meant, that wouldn't be the kind of name that would have inspired confidence in his then fledgling business.

He stood at the entrance and tried to remember where on Earth this could possibly be. He knew that it must have been one of his very early installations, as the entrance pad on this door was a series one business model, and he hadn't used any of them for more than fifteen years. It was a surprise to him that anyone still had that model, he thought that all of them had been upgraded over the years, either that, or had been replaced by a competitor's model, it was good to see that the units had that kind of longevity, something that would never have crossed his mind all that time ago in his business's fledgling years.

It took a couple of minutes of him standing there and racking his brains before it eventually it came to him. He was on some remote Scottish Island, he couldn't remember the actual name of this island, he only knew that it was somewhere in the Outer Hebrides, and that its name was more like a noise that an animal would make, rather than something that could be said be a human. He also remembered that when he came to install the system here, it had been a torturous car and ferry ride to get here; several ferries if he remembered correctly.

Back then, there certainly wasn't an airstrip on the island, if he remembered correctly, there wasn't even a big enough flat area to have landed a helicopter easily, let alone a behemoth like the plane he had arrived on last night. The accommodation block and the windowless stone building hadn't been here then either, all those changes had put him off, and were the reason he had taken so long to realize where he was. To flatten all the required ground to build the other buildings and to get an airstrip installed must have cost millions, let alone trying to get planning permission to do such a thing, especially out here in the Scottish islands where they were fiercely defensive about changes to their landscape. It may have been fifteen years since he had been here first, but it was still impressive what had been done in that time.

As he stood there realising where on the planet he was, it suddenly came to him that that was where he had seen the man behind all this before. No wonder he'd recognized the face and the voice, he had worked for the unconscionable little shit for over a month, setting up all the staff's individual access moves for the entrance pad, and the numerous other pads for various "secure" parts of the building; doing long days here on the island in this building before a ferry ride back to the next island over; to the only bed and breakfast within miles of this godforsaken island.

Setting up an operation here had been no mistake by the man, the likelihood of someone accidentally stumbling across this complex out on this remote island were somewhere between slim and none; and slim had left town.

He knew that the man had been rich and famous in his own right back then, it looked as if he had become more so judging by the complex he had built here, but he still couldn't recall the man's name – it was really bugging him, he was usually so good with names. It would come to him in time.

He looked at the entrance pad to the building and decided that he wanted a look around this building; he was sure that a lot of answers to a lot of questions would be in this building, including the name of the maniac in charge, and so he set about letting himself in.

Chapter 56

Normally in his security access systems, the entrance sequence consisted of three parts. First of all there was the access card, at the time the early systems were set up, they were years ahead of the game, in that it was set up like the modern chip and pin cards that were now standard use by financial institutions. He'd replaced this with a more up to date access card system as chip and pin became old hat, but the remaining two parts stayed the same.

This would then lead on to using a key in pad which was set up in a four-by-four way using the hexadecimal notation of 0 to 9 and A to F. They had to enter a six-digit code, which then brought up the third part, which was unique to his company, a signature move. Based on computer games, each user of the system could set up a move that only they knew and that they could repeat. There was a motion capture devise in the keypad machinery which could tell the distance away a person was, and calculate their relative height to the sensor, against the height of the person with the access code and card, and therefore could work out if the motion used for the signature move had been done in the correct way, regardless of where the person stood, and work out if it was the correct person doing it.

Some of the early adopters of his systems had gone over the top with their signature moves, trying all kinds of lunacy, things like spinning heel kicks, and dance moves. The original set up only required a person to do their move twice the same for the system to log it, future models had upgraded this to five times as a minimum, but they recommended ten. The more repetitions meant there was less chance that they could "fluke" their signature move, and then fail to be able to reproduce it to get in.

For most people the problem they would face now would be the fact that he didn't have an access card to this door, wouldn't know what the access code was, or know the signature move to finalise the entry.

What he did have is the details for the back door entrance that he'd built into the system for emergencies. Normally this information was squirrelled away in a high security vault at his company headquarters, and the client would have access to that in case of death, system failure, or a complete lack of ability to be able to reproduce their signature move. However that method for getting "back door" access to the system hadn't been built into systems, or been the case until version two of his software, giving individual back door codes for individual clients. From that version on the back door entry had been two fifteen-digit codes.

The version one system that was still installed here had the same back door entry details across the fleet, as he had never really expected his systems to do as well as they did, and at the time he was pretty much working by himself, and therefore had built a two step back door that he could execute.

He set about overriding the system in front of him. The first step in version one had been a nine-digit code, and the most memorable thing to him had been Keera's date of birth, and to fit the hexadecimal format, the initial of her surname. The second step had been a motion, and the motion for it was blowing a kiss. Nearly twenty years down the line he had never expected himself to be stood in front of one of his company's keypads, using this information to break into one of his own systems.

Thirty seconds later the code had been entered, and he had blown that kiss; the door swung open towards him, and as it did so, there, just inside the door stood the man.

As soon as the door opened and he saw the man he finally managed to put a name to who it was; Norbert Granville, the somewhat reclusive head of Granco, a multinational conglomeration, with business ventures in every sector that you could think of, and a number that you probably couldn't; stood there in front of him.

Norbert stood there smiling, almost as if he was waiting for him to come through the door, and to be fair he probably was; he was likely to have been seen by various hidden surveillance cameras watching his every move as he had walked around the buildings.

Then Norbert spoke.

Chapter 57

"Good Morning. Welcome to the headquarters of Granco, and my own personal operation bunker. Of course, you have been here before, to install this wonderful security system of yours. I had always wondered whether you built a back door into your early systems, and now I can see that obviously you did. I knew such an emergency feature was built into your later systems, but as I was such an early adopter of your wonderful systems, mine was installed before that feature came online, and it did make me think what redundancy there was for systems like the one I have here."

"I suppose that you realise of course that if you weren't such an honest man, you could make a very good living out of being a thief. With the ability to slip in and out of places like a ghost it could almost be the perfect crime. Your system is excellent of course, still amazingly effective after all these years. That was the main reason why I chose you to be a part of my bigger operation."

He interrupted Norbert before he'd finished his sentence, overlapping the last few words.

"I built the systems to protect people from thieves, and of course after all of this time, it wouldn't be any use to me, I thought all these old series one systems had gone, I was surprised to see one still in use."

"Of course, I was aware why you set up the business, our research into you found out things that aren't in the public domain. I shall probably look at upgrading after this little exercise anyway; perhaps once you've had a chance to have a look around and hear what we are doing here, you might even do the upgrade for free."

"I doubt it; I was mainly looking around to find a way out."

"There isn't one until I say there is, and there will be plenty of time for you to look around the rest of my facility in this building later. Though it has to be said that you won't notice a great deal of difference in the layout here from when you set up the security systems initially, and of course you have been for an inspection around a couple of my other buildings on campus, and I realise that you may have recognised one or two of the other parts of the facility here from when you were here previously to be implanted."

With this Norbert smiled, the smile didn't suit him, and it took everything he had not to lunge across and choke the life out of a very smug looking Norbert. The fact Norbert had two shaved downed, suited, and booted gorillas stood hovering, one over each shoulder, dampened that idea somewhat, he would need to return to that thought of strangulation at some other point.

Norbert carried on speaking,

"However now isn't the time to give you the tour of this building, as I have more pressing matters to speak to you about. You can of course, come back any time you want, as it seems that you have access to this building in a manner that I can't deny you access, and therefore I can't exactly stop you getting in if you want to, can I?"

There was a smirk on his face as he replied, "True, though perhaps if you hadn't been such a skinflint, and upgraded to one of my later models sooner, you wouldn't be having this problem with me now, would you?"

Norbert frowned before continued,

"With all the money I have spent on this operation, I am hardly a skinflint, but I do not see the need in replacing anything that still works correctly, something that it would appear you do not. It is this matter that I need to deal with now, as it is at this precise moment in time, I need to escort you back to your room and have a few serious words with you, as there seems to be a little matter that we need to sort out."

Norbert indicated to walk back in the direction that he had come from.

"Shall we?"

As he turned around, he was half tempted to offer his arm as if they were going to dance, but he got distracted as he realised that there were no bright blinding lights in that building. It appeared that Norbert liked inflicting those lights on everyone else, but didn't seem to care for them much himself. He was just glad he hadn't needed his sunglasses again.

They headed back around the top of the E shaped building, passing close to stone building, with its still open door.

Norbert started talking at him again.

"Were you born in a barn?"

"Eh?"

"Were you born in a barn? I curious to why you felt in necessary to leave all the doors open in my other building?"

"I'm sure you can afford the heating and lighting bill."

"That is not the point, they were closed when you got there, why couldn't you put them back in the way you found them?"

"I could ask you a similar question."

"Really, what would that be then?"

"Why couldn't you leave my brain in the same state you found it when you opened it up and poked around in there?"

He heard a sigh and Norbert's voice changed to the one of ice he had heard before,

"This is not a topic for discussion now, I've already told everyone that this will be covered in the briefing later. If you are going to wander around my facility leave things as you found them, I will not warn you again."

"I wasn't aware you had warned me the first time." He replied with a broad smile on his face.

Chapter 58

The four of them walked around the rest of the side of the building in silence, with Norbert watching him with a half-scowl on his face from a half pace behind him, and then his two meathead bodyguards lumbering along just another pace behind Norbert.

They all went back into the accommodation building through the front doors that he had been escorted through into the building the previous night, and they all headed through the corridors and up the stairs all the way up to his room. He had looked over his shoulder and Norbert and his two goons had all slipped sunglasses on before entering the building. It felt good to know that none of them liked the bright lights either.

The four of them got back to his room, and he pushed the button by the side of his door. Ignoring Norbert and the goons, he went straight to the fridge and got himself a bottle of Pepsi out of it, and went and sat with his feet up on the bed. In a mocking voice he asked.

"So then, Granville old chap, what's so pressing, that it required a conversation all the way back here in this room with Tweedledum and tweedle-dumber here?"

The goons looked less than impressed, but didn't move, and Norbert leant against the side of the desk smiling,

"For someone who doesn't know just what he's up against, you're remarkably calm, and have a very smart mouth on you. What a difference 48 hours make."

"The mouth is only smart because the rest of me is!"

"I wouldn't bet on that, for someone who thinks they are smart you have done some pretty stupid things in the last two days. If I were you, I'd think about being a bit less smart in the couple of weeks ahead if you want to get out the other side of this operation."

Norbert nodded to one of the goons, who turned and went back out of the door before Norbert continued.

"The reason I'm here, in your wonderful little home from home for the next two weeks, is because of the little matter of the gun you brought into my complex with you last night. I am going to need to relieve you of that, as I really can't afford any loose cannons walking around with hand cannons, going off on an ill-informed rampage at this stage of my carefully planned and very expensive operation."

"Would you like to save me the trouble of searching for it, or shall I have my associate here start looking?"

He sat there desperately trying not to show any emotion, and tried to compose himself before he started speaking, as he desperately needed not to give away any more than was entirely necessary.

"How about we play a game? Something in the style of, "colder, warmer, ooh boiling". As I doubt that your "associate" could find his arse with both hands and a map and a five-hour window of opportunity."

Norbert did not seem amused.

"I have warned you about your mouth, now how about we play it in the manner of you tell me where it is, and I won't stuff your mouth full of used socks?"

He paused for as long as he thought was reasonable to push it for, before giving a response.

"The gun is in the drawer of the desk. I'm not sure where you will find the dirty socks though." He managed to get the words out in as even a voice as he possibly could.

Norbert smiled and leaned over and opened the drawer, and pulled out one of the Glocks that he had retrieved on the plane, the one that he had left lying on the desk all night. Norbert waved the gun from side to side, before saying.

"Very impressive, perhaps I should have put sensors in to detect guns for all the subjects when they came in off the plane. Just goes to show that you can never have enough contingency."

Being unable to help himself he chimed in,

"Fat lot of use that would have been, your dispensable hijackers managed to get those on a plane through security for the hijack of my plane."

"Not really, they may not set off metal detectors, but they still show up on scans, I just happened to be able to apply some financial leverage on an airport worker to ignore a particular rucksack full of these."

"You mean bribed, don't you?"

"Such an ugly word, I was able to help him pay off a number of debts he had accumulated for a small favour, financial security for a service rendered, a win-win situation for all involved."

"Except for that poor soul dumped in a trash bin in a cold Greenland airport."

"They were all warned, examples had to be set."

"I'm sure their family will feel pleased to know that they set an example to others."

At that moment the door to his room opened again, and before he could see who it was, he heard a voice he recognised say,

"That's not the gun I gave him."

Chapter 59

He couldn't quite believe what he was hearing and shouted out,
"Sonia! What are you doing?"
Norbert laughed softly before speaking,
"As I have said before, you can never really have enough contingency."
"It's amazing what you can do with a great plastic surgeon, and a good cover story. I'm afraid that once again I've not exactly been straight with you. From the time you were originally implanted my team has seen time after time that you're capable of overcoming the control of the implant and going freestyle on me, a little bit rogue if you will. Therefore I came to the conclusion that I needed to take out a little additional insurance to get you to fall in to line, and to have you here on my own private island, working for me on schedule for a change. Even then it very nearly backfired on me, but here you are."
"It's time to tell you, what I think you may be able to work out. This fine specimen of womanhood isn't Sonia, the sister of your beloved dearly departed Keera. So without further ado let me introduce Michaela O'Riordan to you."
"Top of the morning to you,"
The creature he had thought was Sonia exclaimed in a broad Irish accent as she took a bow. He just glared at her not saying a word, thinking murderous thoughts about what he would do to her and Norbert.
Norbert continued, as if it was nothing,
"I am so sorry to inform you that poor old Sonia passed away a couple of years ago, she was in a devastating car accident alongside her husband when he had a heart attack driving through the Simplon Pass. It was a story that got a bit of press over here in Europe, due to her

husband's standing, but failed to make most of the press in the US, where you are so much more insular in your news reporting."

"So we thought that we could use that unfortunate event as an opportunity to have someone who could get through your personal defences, and we had Michaela transformed, not that she's complaining of course, she's much more beautiful now than before we started. Though that wouldn't have been difficult."

The woman flinched at the last comment and turned to glare at Norbert.

Meanwhile, his mind was swimming a dangerous mixture of anger, confusion, and helplessness, was it really this hopeless? What could he, as one man, do against such organisation, planning and downright evil? He had been set up to confide in a woman he thought he knew. He had been correct on the plane when he had told her that there could be one of the other passengers set up as a watcher. He was just too stupid to realise that the only person who wanted to talk to him would be the one doing the watching. She had drawn him in without any difficulty at all, and he fell for it like the idiot he was. He was so well away with his thoughts they he was in his own little world, and he could only vaguely manage to make out that there were voices continuing around him. He shook his head to clear it, and managed to blurt out,

"Huh, what?"

Norbert had been asking him a question, his blank look prompting Norbert to ask again, "Where is the other gun, the one Michaela gave you."

He now sported a genuinely confused look as he stuttered out a reply, "Eh, who?"

As he said it, he realised he knew exactly who Norbert meant, but left the response there all the same, hoping to buy himself a bit of time, he needed to remember which gun was where, as if he gave them the location of the other Glock he had picked up on the plane then he was finished.

"Sonia, HER!" Norbert shouted, his face turning red, as he pointed at the created likeness of Keera who still stood there still glaring at Norbert, as if trying to bore through the man with laser beams.

After a few seconds of frantically racking his brains, to go through his movements when he got into the room the night before, he finally got some words out.

"It's in the bathroom; it's folded into an unused towel somewhere in the stack,"

He had mumbled the words uneasily, hoping he had got the locations of the guns the right way around. Gaining some solidity to his voice he continued

"Although I am surprised you didn't know this already, with everything I've seen you do to keep tabs on us all, I would have thought it would have been an easy step to put cameras in every room, or at least in this one. You must have known which room you were going to put me well before I arrived, and you would have wanted to keep an eye on this little fly in your ointment."

"Despite whatever else you may think about me, I'm not into being a voyeur, and although there are plenty of security cameras around the buildings, I wouldn't want them in each room, meaning I would need a team of hired monkeys to watch them, too many other people knowing parts of the operation that I would need to dispose of, there is enough of that already. Furthermore, although refitting all the corridors in this building for the unique lighting system was easy, refitting all the guest rooms would have been much harder. Until a couple of months ago, we had been using this site for business conferences. The rooms were repeatedly and routinely swept for bugs, so prior to us stopping hosting conferences, we would never have been able to fit such equipment in the rooms without alarming our customer base. After that we just didn't have the time. Plus, despite everything, I was still hopeful that your programming would fall into place. When it was clear on the hijacked plane that it would not, it was far too late to do anything about it."

Norbert went into the bathroom and came out with the towels, dropped them onto the bed and in the second towel, found what he wanted, and pulled out a gun, he held it up and looked at the woman, asking a question.

"Well?"

The woman wasn't paying attention, and Norbert raised his voice and asked a second time.

"WELL?"

The woman looked up, and looked at the gun in Norbert's hand, before replying.

"Yes, that's the right one,"

She said, her glare turning to a smile at a job well done.

Norbert turned back to him,

"Anything else to declare? One in the fridge? Or in the wardrobe?"

He tried not to let his face move at all and give anything away. He had thought about both of those suggestions as hiding places the night before, especially for some reason the fridge, after having previously left his phone in his at home after a particularly messy bender, and he had not found the phone again for another five days.

He counted to ten slowly in his head before pushing out a reply in as sarcastic a tone as he could muster.

"Well, apart from the two AK47s stashed away under the mattress, and the anti-tank missile launcher hidden in the shower, no, I think that's about it."

"Although seriously, how the hell do you think I was going to be able to deal with more than two guns at the same time? Perhaps hold the third one in my mouth and use my tongue to pull the trigger?"

"So, the smart mouth returns! Yes, I'm sure your tongue could well trigger a great many things."

Norbert was smiling again,

"No, I really don't think that you have any more, I was surprised that you managed to pick up the additional one without being noticed, but we live and learn, you are turning out to be a treasure trove of constant surprises. I am going to leave you now so you can sort yourself out ready for lunch and the afternoon briefing that is going to follow it. I'm sure I have left you with quite a few things to think over. I will look forward to seeing you later, and to working with you over the next two weeks."

With that Norbert moved away from the desk and headed out the door, closely flanked by his goon, and joined outside the door by the other one, who he realised must have been sent to get the woman when he was nodded at earlier.

Norbert had walked past the woman on the way out of the door without even glancing in the woman's direction. She just carried on standing where she was, looking at him, as if she still had something to add to the proceedings.

Chapter 60

He really didn't have the patience to deal with this woman now and snapped at her.

"Just what the hell do you want?"

She went to open her mouth to respond, but he continued and cut her off before she had the chance to start,

"Don't answer that, whatever you have to say, just do us both a favour and save your stinking, lying breath and get the hell out of this room as quickly as you can, before I get off this bed and break the habit of a lifetime and actually hit a woman."

She still stood there, still looking at him, and again she opened her mouth to say something, but before she could get it out, he screamed at her.

"GET OUT!!"

And he started to get up from the bed.

She turned and bolted from the room, he carried on getting of the bed and walked over and slammed the door. It made a satisfying thud as it flew into its frame, and the wall vibrated a little bit. He turned around and walked back over to and flopped back on his bed and he started to cry.

As the tears started to fall, he felt shocked by himself.

The main shock he felt was due to the fact that he was crying, something that he couldn't remember himself ever doing. He had been stone cold in so many previous circumstances, so unemotional, that as the wetness on his cheeks dried, he was surprised that he had chosen this moment to start.

How had it all come down to this?

What, if anything could he have done to have changed his circumstances?

How could he have possibly prevented himself from being here? Why had he fallen for the trick that had been Keera's lookalike?

He suddenly had the image of Stone-Cold Steve Austin and his often-repeated mantra of "don't trust anyone."

As soon as this image came into his head, he stopped crying and felt himself change. He got back up off the bed, and he went into the bathroom to wash his face. He splashed cold water on to his face and he also wet his hair. He picked up the towel he'd left across the side of the sink from his earlier shower and dried off. He looked at his reflection in the mirror, and apart from red eyes he looked the same as every other single time he'd looked in a mirror for the last five years.

Having seen the room that had caused the never changing reflection within the last hour or so, it helped set his mood, and he strode back into the main room with a purpose. He got his jacket that he had arrived here in and shrugged his way into it. He then went and retrieved the third gun he'd acquired on the plane from its hiding place down a sleeve of one of the other jackets that had been supplied to him in the wardrobe.

He double checked the gun to make sure that it was loaded, and that it had a round in the chamber ready to go. He made sure the safety was in place and put it inside his trousers in the small of his back. He then changed his mind, took off his jacket and threw it on the bed and went back to the wardrobe and looked through for a different jacket that would hang loose over where the gun was. He found a leather jacket and tried it on. Unsurprisingly it fitted him perfectly.

Whatever else Norbert was, he was certainly thorough and had an eye for detail he hadn't encountered in anyone he'd ever met before. He checked himself in the mirror with the new jacket on and he could not see any tell-tale signs of the gun, even when the jacket was done up. If he left it loose, it would easily conceal the weapon.

The fact that Norbert hadn't known about any of the guns until that damn woman had told him, gave him some additional hope, perhaps Norbert was a bit over-confident. Additionally, having found that he had had an additional gun, he would have had his room pulled to pieces to search for anything else. For whatever reason Norbert hadn't felt the need to carry out any additional search of his room, and in fact Norbert had left it after being faced with a bit of sarcasm. It seemed at odds with the rest of the planning.

Was Norbert still holding out the hope that his programming was working enough to prevent any further action against him? If so, Norbert was being over optimistic as far as he was concerned.

Maybe there was a hope he could do something to stop Norbert if Norbert was going to have this partial blind spot.

Chapter 61

Norbert slammed his office door behind him, it may well have hit one of his bodyguards in the face as they tried to follow him in, but he didn't care, he didn't need his damn bodyguards in the room with him now.

What a mess, not only had number nineteen come waltzing into his office building without a care in the world, through his own security system that should have been impossible to do, but the damn man had managed to arm himself with a gun from the plane. It was bad enough that his plant Michaela had given him a gun, but the fact that he had picked up another to go with it showed that he was virtually off the reservation.

The unmasking of Sonia as Michaela did seem to throw a spanner into the deviation in number nineteen though, he saw the man visibly deflate at that nugget of information, and as he wandered away from the man's room, he had heard the subject scream at Michaela, and had taken a hit of satisfaction at the sound of raised voices, people who were angry made mistakes.

Michaela may be a different matter though, the way she had also visibly deflated, and then hung around like a lost little puppy outside the man's door after the bombshell showed that her heart may not be in this little game anymore. It may be time to arrange for her to have a little accident on her way back to the mainland tomorrow. That would also save him the rest of the fee that she was due.

Number nineteen had been correct about the room cameras though, it had been an oversight on his part, but he had been sure, along with the behavioural scientists, that there would be no issues with the subjects once they were inside their rooms, and that the cameras in the common areas would suffice in the accommodation block. It was something for him to consider once he started ramping up his plan with the help of the subjects here on his island.

Thinking of the rest of the subjects, he needed to get his thoughts in order ready for the big reveal speech to them after lunch, it was going to be his time to shine, and to have the collective brains trust that the subjects represented on board would be the moment the grand plans became reality. He could almost taste the ultimate glory. All the years of planning, all the money spent, it was all coming to fruition.

Once he had dealt with this afternoon's grand reveal, he was going to have to look at beefing up security in the office block. The fact that number nineteen had a back doorway into the building, and probably into all the restricted access areas of the building that only he normally had access to, meant that if number nineteen did shake off all the effects of the implant, he could do some serious damage if let loose. There was nothing he could do about it today, but it would need to be a priority for tomorrow.

Norbert made himself a list of items to do around the potential security changes, and put it to one side of his desk, and then went back to preparing himself for the afternoon's session.

Chapter 62

Michaela traipsed back to her room slowly. She had been a part of this plan for nearly three years now. She had been a struggling actress, bouncing around from small play to small play, none of them paying very well, as she tried to find stardom. There were a lot of hopefuls in Dublin, most of whom were a lot younger, and a lot prettier than her, in her heart of hearts she knew that she wasn't going to hit the big time, but she just couldn't give up on it altogether, if she gave it all up then that would guarantee she wouldn't hit the big time.

Then one night after a particularly lacklustre performance of JM Synge's "Playboy Of The Western World", a representative of Granco had approached her as she left the cast door out into the dingy side street to the back of the theatre, offering her more money than she could dream of to play a single long-term role. When opportunities like this came up; ones that seemed too good to be true, they usually were too good to be true. It had turned out to be the case here, but the money had been too much for her to think about turning it down. She would never need to work again after this.

She had nearly given it all up at the thought of the plastic surgery required, but part of her was delighted at the prospect, she would be able to challenge for roles against the younger, prettier things on a more equal footing.

The voice coaching had been a long process, she had done generic American accents before, but this needed to be a particular local accent, the kind that would be lost to outsiders, but recognisable to someone from that country, it was the same all over the world. She had now learnt to think in the Philadelphia accent, living with it all the time, making sure that none of her own accent slipped out inadvertently. To the extent when she had just spoken in her usual voice just now, it seemed like a parody of what it should have sounded like.

The rest of the time had been spent learning about the person she was to play, the family history, the personal preferences that needed to become second nature, and to study the man that she was going to targeting. She had been quizzed and tested so many times, being corrected and criticised until she was word perfect. The whole role made the theatre look like a child's game.

She had been very sceptical about the fact that the man would get onto the underground train she would be on, get into the tube through the set of doors opposite where she was sat, and that he would find an empty seat sat next to her. She had been told the station as well, and as they pulled in, she thought they had got it all wrong, there were no spare seats, and lots of people had been standing in the area around the doors. They had all cleared out of the way, and sure enough the man had sat next to her. She had no idea how they could have possibly known all of this, and how they could have planned it, but there the man was, exactly as advertised.

She had been given the man's name, and been told to use it at some point during the journey, but she thought that she had blown it all when she had used his name, the man had bolted from the train at being called by his name and disappeared. She didn't know what to do, she got up to get off at the next stop, she could go back and look for the man, but as she made her way to the door another man had sidled up to her from out of nowhere and told her to just carry on with her tube journey, and then to head for the plane as previously planned.

The seat on the plane which they had told her the man would be sitting in looked like it was going to stay empty. However, the man arrived at the last minute, but instead of bolting from the plane when he saw her, he appeared to black out as soon as he looked in her direction. By the time the man came round the plane was being hijacked and she found herself unable to speak to him. She certainly hadn't been told about that part of the plan, it wasn't until she was sat in the hangar in

Kangerlussuaq that one of the many hijackers in the building had told her to make sure she made contact with the man on the new plane, and that the hijacking was all part of the plan. She supposed she hadn't been told about the hijacking to make sure her reaction to it was genuine, which in hindsight told her a lot about what they must have thought of her acting abilities!

What she had seen on the second plane had rocked her to the core, and she had taken longer to approach the man than planned as she was battling to keep her own emotions under wraps. She had seen what had happened to all those others that had been part of the plan; they had all died with their internal organs trying to escape from their bodies. She had spent half an hour frozen to her seat in fear, wondering if what had happened to all those men was going to be her fate as well, and that she would never manage to make her way to the end of this performance to be in a position to spend all her money from it.

Now she had thoroughly betrayed the man that she had been taught to know, and she now sat here in her room, hating herself for doing it, all the money in the world couldn't make up for what she had just done. The man looked as if he had broken, yet while he could quite happily kill all of them at a moment's notice. Norbert had looked upon her with distain as he passed her to get out of the man's room, as if he could see the weakness she now felt within her. She really was now beginning to fear that she would never make it home to Ireland.

She knew that she would have to try and speak to the man, to beg for his forgiveness, even if he quite rightly waved it away. Why would he ever trust her now, she had taken all the money that Norbert's had offered, and ruined another man's life, in reality she probably deserved all she got.

She lay down on the bed in her room and broke down in tears, what a mess she had made of her life.

Chapter 63

He went to the door and again studied the map of the complex, especially the main hall. There were several exits out of the hall marked on the plan besides the one he'd used previously. One to the right rear of the hall which led into the kitchen, as he had previously seen, and there was a fire exit out of the back of the kitchen, and then there were the various fire exit patio doors he had seen in the hall on both sides of the room at regular intervals.

He could do with a proper look at the fire exits and he would do so when he went down to lunch, which if the alarm clock in his room was to be believed, was only a few minutes away, the morning had flown by, he had obviously spent longer in the white rooms than he thought he had. He checked that the one remaining gun was securely in place in the small of his back, and he retrieved his sunglasses as he would need to shield his eyes on the way down to lunch, plus he could also do without making eye contact with anybody. He put them on and looked in the mirror and laughed despite himself. He hadn't realised it until he put the glasses on, but he was going to look like the ultimate man in black.

He left his room and made his way down to the dining area. None of the other subjects had managed to make it down there for lunch yet, and there were a couple of staff setting up the food on the buffet on the serving area down the left-hand side of the room. He walked down the right-hand side of the room and over to the kitchen doors and walked straight through them. He had got no more than three strides into the kitchen before someone shouted.

"Oi you! It's staff only allowed in the kitchen."

He stopped and looked over at where the voice had come from before replying,

"Sorry mate, I didn't realise this was off limits, there was no sign on the door saying as much."

"I don't care if there is a sign on the door saying please come this way, no one but staff in my kitchen, no exceptions. Now get the hell out my kitchen before I turn you into a future meal."

He turned his head away from the general direction of the voice, having a good look around the kitchen, before shrugging, turning around, and leaving through the doors he had come in through.

A voice followed him out of the door as he left,

"And bleeding well stay out."

Once out of the kitchen he smiled to himself, he had found out what he wanted to know from his brief stay in the kitchen. There was a door out the other side of the kitchen, pretty much opposite where the door in was, and that there were about ten staff working in there. It would be best to avoid using that as a route out to the office block without being spotted, that way would only draw more attention to him.

He wandered back over to the left-hand side of the room to one of the fire escapes there. He went to the one nearest the top of the room, which was sat the other side of the serving area. He checked around the frame of the doors and didn't find any sign of any alarm wiring as he had expected to see, though it could well all be on the other side of the door. There didn't appear to be any sensors on the door either, but there was only one way to make sure of whether these doors were alarmed or not, and it would be best to check now, and therefore he pushed the bar and the door opened.

There was no sudden alarm or flashing lights, but that was no guarantee there wasn't one somewhere else, as the alarm could be triggered somewhere else on the island, probably in the office block. He stood outside and looked at the outsides of the doors, and still saw no tell-tale wires, or any obvious sensors around the doors. He stood outside for a couple of minutes to see if anyone came to look at the doors and why they were open, but no one did.

It was only when one of the serving staff stuck their head out of the doors and moaned at him about the fact that leaving the doors open was making the food cold, that made him go back inside, and he closed the doors behind him. He knew he had additional ways out of the dining room / meeting area apart from the main entrance doors, he didn't know whether he would need them, but it was better to be prepared for eventualities than to find out things couldn't be done later.

He took a seat at the table nearest to the service area, taking a seat that was facing the main doors and went and got some lunch. He watched as others came in and started eating. It was nearly two o'clock when Norbert eventually turned up, followed by his two goons. Up to this point there had been no sign of the Irish woman coming in. The main doors were closed when Norbert came in, as if they weren't expecting anyone else to join them. He couldn't be sure of it, but it did look like Norbert had locked the door behind him on the way in.

He found himself wondering whether the Irish woman was still alive, seeing as she had now probably reached the end of her usefulness to Norbert. If he was honest, he didn't really care, the woman had properly stitched him up, plus she had stirred up memories and emotions that had been buried for a lot of years, but even with all of that, the memory about the method of dispatch for Norbert's employees from the last plane journey was still fresh in his mind and he shuddered involuntarily when thinking of anyone else going that way.

Norbert strolled through the room with the air of a man who knew he was in control, and glanced briefly in his direction with a crooked smile on his face as he made his way to the little stand at the far end of the room. He hadn't really noticed the stand before, but he hadn't been looking for it, and he hadn't walked too close to there. Once Norbert reached the stand and settled himself behind it, he started speaking almost immediately.

"Good afternoon, ladies and gentlemen, thank you for your patience, and thank you all for joining me on this momentous occasion. If you are all done with lunch, it would be appreciated if you would all like to make your way to this end of the room, then I can begin to fill you in on the reason for you all being here, and what I have planned for you all over the next couple of weeks of your stay here. Find a seat and make yourself comfortable, there is a lot that I need to tell you, and it will take a few hours."

With this a most of the others got up from their seats and started to move nearer to where Norbert was holding court behind his little stand, and they headed to seats there in virtual silence, like a flock of sheep about to be sheared.

He got up as well, though he had no intention of going anywhere near Norbert, or getting sheared, and he moved quickly over to the fire exit, keeping an eye on the others moving forward, and on Norbert. He slipped out of the fire exit without seeming to attract anyone else's attention and started to make his way over to the secure office building he'd been in earlier.

Chapter 64

He moved quickly, jogging straight over to the office building. Using his back door code and movement as he had before, he entered the building. He was glad this building wasn't full of the brilliant white light that had been everywhere else to do with this lunatic. He stopped inside the door to try and get some idea of where he was going to go.

He had been here previously, working here for nearly a month setting up the physical entry security, not just on the outside doors, but also inside on pretty much every door going. Inside the general layout had stayed very similar to the original layout, but there seemed to be fewer doors than he remembered. He knew some of the rooms were likely to have been repurposed with the other buildings that had appeared on site, and he walked down the corridor to his left as he came in, as he remembered all the working spaces being down there.

Upstairs had been living quarters for Norbert, which had been done out in total contrast to the drab glass and red brick eighties outside in a grandiose Art Deco / Art Nouveau style. There had also been a few other staff accommodation rooms, of a much more basic functional design. He had been offered one of those to stay in whilst he was working here, but he didn't want to work and live with the client for the length of time that was required to get this job done. He wondered now what might have been done to him if he had have stayed here all those years ago.

As he wandered down the corridor, he could see that the doors were at irregular intervals either side of the corridor, as if some had been removed, and others moved. He was happy to find that the doors all had signs on them as to the use of the rooms, and most of them had glass sections in them.

He was surprised to find that all of them still had his original security pads on them. They may well have moved or got rid of doors, but any they had moved, they had also moved the security with them. No mean feat with the way the keypads were set up for series one systems, he certainly wouldn't have wanted to do the job himself, and he had had enough difficulties with the three doors on his original offices when they had refurbished the floor.

He slowly moved down the corridor, checking the names on the doors, and peering through the windows. Most of the rooms behind the windows were medium sized offices now, each with a department name on the door, inside they had varying amounts of desks, each with computer monitors on, some with two or three monitors on them. There were people in all the rooms that he passed, staring intently at the screens in front of them, doing whatever they needed to do in this kind of corporate environment. None of them moved their heads or appeared to look in his direction as he peered through the windows into their offices. He didn't see anyone moving in any of the rooms as he moved down the corridor. It was as if they were all zombies stuck in front of their monitors unable to do anything else.

He eventually found the room he had wanted to find from the outset, and he again used his back door code and move to get into it. He was really surprised that they hadn't upgraded, he believed that all his series one clients had, as they had ceased all support for any issues with it five years ago. No one had complained about that since, a few had requested upgrades, but no one had said they were staying on the old model.

He felt the sudden temperature drop when he walked into the room; from an IT perspective he felt it was good to see they took looking after their computer services seriously. There was some serious cooling air conditioning being circulated through this room. As he looked around, he understood why. When this room had originally been set up there had only been two server racks, and a small patching hub for the cables. Now there were at least twenty server cabinets with a variety of servers, hubs and routers, and the patching hub stretched across the whole of the back wall.

The banks of servers and control consoles set out around the room. He knew what he needed to find; he needed access to the outside world. With this many servers it might take him some time to find the one he needed. At the first server cabinet, the key was in the door, which got a black mark from him for a start, what was the point of lockable cabinets if you were going to leave the keys lying around.

His second black mark for the server security came when he pressed the space bar on the keyboard. The server rack's monitor sprang to life, and he was looking at a standard Windows XP desktop screen, the machine hadn't been locked, and there obviously wasn't a period of inactivity that caused it to lock. He saw a switch box next to the monitor and turned it to the next position. Another XP desktop came on screen. He worked his way through the other two positions on the switch and found the same thing. It would appear that his own security system wasn't the only thing that Granco hadn't been bothered to update, all these servers would be out of support too.

He went to another cabinet, and this also had the key in the door, and was surprised to find that it appeared that none of the servers had been locked and he didn't need to try and attempt to hack into any of them. If he had had found a single unlocked server like these in any of his offices, he would have fired the person responsible on the spot. He wondered which employees had access to this room besides Norbert.

He started to look through the servers' contents, and found that most of the servers appeared to have no access to the outside world; they were all set up on the internal network only. He attempted to ping a known website, and when the ping timed out tried doing tracert on it. Nothing was getting any further than the same router IP address.

He worked his way through six server cabinets with no success; all the servers within them had lots of files of unspeakably boring corporate documents. None of them had any outside connection. He had found internet explorer installed on one of them, and for a moment had got excited that he might find a way to communicate with the outside world, but it was short lived as upon loading he couldn't get any external site to work, the only site that did work was the company intranet. It looked like it had been designed by a bored two-year-old that was colour blind, and he was glad he was able to quickly shut it down.

He was getting frustrated now, it was taking a lot longer than he had expected, he hadn't realised quite how much Norbert would have expanded operations here, even though he wasn't having to log in to each server, it still took time to check each machine for outside connections. He was sure that at any minute Norbert would arrive at the IT Comms room door and have his goons take him away, where he might find himself locked in a room twenty-four hours a day, seven days a week. He glanced down at his watch and was relieved to see he had only been about forty minutes so far; if what Norbert had said to the assembled group, then he still had at least another couple of hours, and he calmed down somewhat. The other server cabinets had an array of kit in them, but no more computer servers. Phone systems, audio and video recording servers, his security system server, and racks of routers and hubs, half filled with cables.

He could also do with finding a phone line, but until he had access to the internet, he wouldn't be able to get the numbers he wanted anyway. He went back to the router cabinet and inspected the cabling. It didn't take him long in there to find the router he wanted. It only had two cables attached, one coming in and one going out, this had to be the connection to the outside world. He started tracing the two cables, found that one went straight down the side of the cabinet and into the raised floor, the other went at an angle into the neighbouring cabinet, and soon joined several other ones. This was the one he wanted; he needed to trace it to its hub.

The systems engineer who worked here had done an impressive job of cabling, he hadn't seen many tidier server rooms anywhere he had worked, and he wondered how someone who took such pride in the cabling could possibly allow all the servers to be left unlocked.

He looked at the patching wall and realised to himself that this wasn't the time for impressive, the tidy uniformly laid out cables, that were grouped with tightly drawn shut cable ties were a pain in the ass. He really needed free running cables to easily follow. He looked around quickly to see if there was anything he could use to break the cable ties, but he couldn't see anything.

Again it was slower work than he would have hoped. He painstakingly inched his way along the cable he had identified until it finally broke free from the rest of them and led into one of the hubs. There were only two other cables coming out of that hub, and the hub sockets were numbered. Both little green lights under the other cables were on and flashing, there were active connections at the other end of these cables. He walked over to the patching hub against the wall and found the two outputs from the server hub. Sure enough there were two cables coming out of here, relatively lonely compared to the mass of cables elsewhere on this part of the patching hub.

Annoyingly, the systems engineer had also tightly packed all the cables here as well, no loose patchwork of overlapping cables slung over or around the hub. They were drawn sideways and then through the gap to the other side. He worked as much leeway into those two cables as he could and got his wallet out and got a couple of dollar bills to wrap round them so he could see them from the other side. Around the other side he was able to trace them to two quite different areas on that side of the patching hub. On that side there were computers and phones next to each other, all labelled to what must be numbers in the floor patching. One of the two cables he was following went to part of the hub that was well populated, but wasn't choked full. The other went to an area that was pretty much deserted from a cabling perspective.

This told him that they were probably for Norbert's own computers, one would be his office, and the other would be in his private living area. Both also showed there were phone lines plugged in next to those ports.

Even now he was still worrying about the amount of time this had taken so far without any useful results, it had been over an hour now, and he made the decision to go for Norbert's office; that was likely to be on this floor, and shouldn't be too far away from the server room as he hadn't passed it already, and there wasn't much more of the corridor he had been walking down left.

He left the server room and carried on down the corridor, and found Norbert's office right at the end of it. Thinking to himself that third time is a charm, he keyed in his back door code to the keypad and did the kiss signature move again. The door in front of him clicked open, he pushed the door, and he walked through it into Norbert's office.

Chapter 65

Norbert's office could have belonged to anyone else in the building, and looked much as it did fifteen years ago, the only things that were different to what he remembered from then, were the server cabinet in the corner of the room behind the door and the bank of televisions on the wall. There was a computer in the middle of Norbert's desk, and he headed for that.

It was on and he tapped the keyboard, and for the first time today, there was a lock screen there, asking him for a password. He got out of the chair and went to the server cabinet, there was no key, but there was no lock either, just a magnetic connector at the top of the glass door. He pushed the door, and it bounced out and opened. He tapped the space bar and was straight on the desktop. Internet explorer was on the server, and he opened it up. It came up and automatically loaded the Microsoft home page. He had finally found an external connection. Despite of all Norbert's planning, there were areas where he just ignored basic security, what was the point of locking your computer, when you left your server open to all and sundry? Perhaps he thought that no one else could get in this room without him letting them in, and he may well have been right if only he was on the access list for the room.

Now he was on an outside connection he got onto the internet and started to search. It took him longer than he thought to get a telephone number he needed, and then it was so simple. He went back to the desk and picked the phone up. He had a dial tone, and he tapped the number in he wanted. He had only put the first couple of digits in and the phone sounded with the dead tone. He tried again using a preceding nine as often needed for outside lines, but still after a couple of digits he got a dead tone. He tried a few other starting numbers, and then tried dialling a different number entirely, but all of them went to dead tone after a couple of digits. He went to get his mobile out of his jacket to try to see if there was signal from this building, only to realise the phone was still in his original jacket, he hadn't transferred it over when he had switched jackets before lunch.

He went back to the server and instead of phone numbers he went searching for e-mail addresses. The ones he needed seemed far harder to find than they should, it was almost as if agencies upholding the law didn't want to be contacted. He opened his Hotmail account and put in the addresses that he had found for the FBI, Interpol, and Scotland Yard, and started to compose the e-mail to get help. He stopped several times to look up details on the internet to help compose the e-mail, getting flight numbers, the name of this island he was on and the like to get as many facts in there that could be checked as possible.

He really hoped that the e-mail would be picked up quickly and that it would be taken seriously. The whole concept about what was going on here sounded so far-fetched it could easily be written off as a crank, in fact he was sure if he received an e-mail like the one he was sending, he would just delete it. However he hoped that the fact that there had been two hijacked planes and the fact that he would have been on the passenger manifest, but had never turned up at his destination should help matters.

He just wished that he had managed to pick up some of the names of the other passengers, as apart from Maria Gonzalez he was missing anyone else's name. He had given them both possible names for the Keera lookalike, and hoped that she had used one of them for the flight. Having additional passenger names for them to try and validate should add credibility to his story.

He just hoped that whoever picked up the e-mails would take them seriously and get someone out to this island as quickly as possible. He clicked on send and checked that it had gone. From his sent mail he forwarded it on to staff at his company, with a few additional lines to show he wasn't trying to play a hoax on them all. Hopefully they could start making phone calls to the agencies as well. The more people that tried, the more likely that there might be success.

In addition to having the connection to the outside world he had obviously found the server to what was Norbert's private domain. There was no attempt made to try and hide the kind of stuff that showed on the screen when he went into file explorer.

Norbert had a complete drive upon which sat the entire plan for whatever was happening here, in print, and in an obvious moment of egotism had entitled the server, 'The Master plan: - How to rule the world in six years.

He went in the folders, randomly opening documents, and his mind boggled at the level of organisation that this set up had. There were vast dossiers on him and all the other subjects, copies of personal documents, hundreds of pictures, and detailed itineraries, he could recognise people on the flights from those pictures, these were people who were here on this island with him. Full details of the implants and indoctrination were also within the files.

There was no folder for anyone called Sonia or Michaela, and a quick flick through photos for other female names didn't bring her up at all. There were twenty-four files, so she hadn't been a part of the indoctrination, she was something else entirely different, and he wondered if there was a file for her in another folder for a different part of the operation.

There were all the building plans for this complex, along with plans for other Granco facilities around the world, he knew Granco was a multinational corporation, but he hadn't quite realised the scale. Amongst all the overload of information sat a single document that caught his attention; it was simply titled Outline.docx.

He opened the document and started reading. The six years in the title from the server was going to start with all the subjects arriving here at the complex, and as he scanned quickly through the plan he was amazed, shocked, saddened and sickened in equal measure. There really wasn't a law that they wouldn't break, and ethics and morals were so far out of the window they would be in another galaxy away from here. There was too much information in the document for him to be able to read it comfortably or quickly on the small server screen. He glanced around Norbert's office, and there was a printer on a cupboard behind Norbert's desk, he printed the document off so he could read it from print. It would be at least fifty per cent quicker to read a printed version.

The printer whirred into life and rattled through printing the hundred odd pages, he took the finished print off the printer, it still being warm from the finishing process, and decided to sit at Norbert's desk to read it properly.

Chapter 66

The twenty-four of them that Norbert had gathered on this island via his hijacking spree were to be the vanguard, he had specialists who were leaders in their particular fields, all of whom he had picked out more than five years ago. There was no doubt that Norbert had been playing the long game. He wasn't entirely sure he understood all the job titles of the other twenty-three, but there were experts in such diverse fields as mass media marketing and biological engineering. He was slightly amused to see that one of the others selected was an expert in the binding of silicon-based information stores to the cerebral cortex, and wondered if they knew their work had been stolen and used within their own head. He thought of the dining area where he hoped Norbert was still talking to the assembled masses, and wondered just how high the average IQ must be in that room, well as long as they didn't count the goons.

Within the plans there was a timetable to bring many more groups of people to the facilities here and to put implants in their heads, and run the indoctrination on, they had six more batches identified to run this year alone, but some of the names in the file shocked him, there were some seriously connected people in here; CEOs of large corporations, high-level politicians, high ranking military personnel, all from a variety of countries. How on earth were they going to be able to take people like this out of circulation for three weeks? Then he looked closer at the dates, they were looking at doing the whole course in three days! Working around weekends, people would be out of normal working time for a day. If they could pull that off, then the chances of success went up dramatically.

With implantation up and running, Norbert would then be moving on to the drugging of water supplies to major towns and cities in dozens of countries, subliminal messaging embedded into all forms of media, with radio and television the main targets, but also going for social media outlets such as Vine and YouTube, all with the end of subliminally programming entire communities. He thought of how much he viewed and listened to, both through mainstream media and more often now through social media, there wouldn't be many people they would miss covering this spectrum of people.

Then once a community had been programmed in this manner, and then they would move in to recruit the people in them to join their operation, expanding what they were doing all the time, and from there, getting the new recruits to help with the programming of the next area and so on. The timeline was quite aggressive, relying on the programmed recruits to double to output on each cycle.

It continued alongside this with Norbert planning to infiltrate hospitals in new areas ahead of subliminal messaging and water tampering, to enable them to introduce the same kind of silicon chip that was in his head somewhere, or more likely updated ones, to be implanted into any poor unfortunate patient who went under general anaesthetic for any kind of treatment.

Moreover, Norbert was also going to be targeting the governments in various countries, his priorities being his home country of the United Kingdom, the USA, Russia, and China, with programming that would cause government destabilisation, solely with the purpose of causing wars and conflicts both internally in those countries, and externally with each other, and other countries.

At every turn Norbert and his conglomerate of companies would be there with one of his various divisions to pick up the broken pieces he had caused, and turn them to his own advantage to ever expand his empire.

Not content with destabilising governments, the megalomaniac had also built in a whole host of side products into the subliminal programming, ones that would affect people's consumerism in his benefit.

The suggestive messaging would stop people from buying his competitor's products and services, their sales would fall off a cliff, and as those businesses struggled or failed, Norbert would be there to step in and take them over one at a time, growing his empire all the time, until the point where his company would be the only one that existed.

What he was reading was so compelling and terrible at the same time, it was incredibly detailed for an outline document, and had so many outlandish elements to it that it seemed as if Norbert had taken details from every Bond villain over the years and pulled all their schemes together into one fiendish plot.

In fact the document was so horrifyingly enthralling that he had totally lost track of time while he was stood there reading it, and was paying no mind to where he was. He hadn't heard the door open, and he almost jumped out of his skin when suddenly there was a voice from the other side of the desk.

Chapter 67

"Are you sitting comfortably in my chair?"

It was Norbert, standing there looking less impressed than ever, but he was standing there alone.

"So you've managed to break into my private office using your nasty little back door and managed to find my personal server then? I supposed you used my printer and paper to print off whatever you are reading, sat there in my chair like you are supposed to be there. I really should have kept you under lock and key after your wandering about this morning, you are the most troublesome man. Of course if you had had the good manners and patience to stay and listen to my rallying call to the troops, you would have found out a great deal of what you wanted to know."

He looked up at Norbert, trying to keep the rising level of anger he was feeling from jumping out of him.

"Yes, I did come strolling back in here, and I have found your personal server, you really have overlooked computer security around here, not a single server with a password on, I don't understand how you could have an IT person who takes so much pride in their job where being obsessively neat with cabling – yours is the tidiest comms room I've ever seen – would be such an irresponsible slob when it came to basic server security. No passwords and no locked cabinets, it's a hacker's dream scenario. I'd be firing people for that kind of carelessness if they worked for me in an IT capacity, but this kind of sloppiness it seems to be a pillar of how things work around here."

"Yes, my IT expert quit, she constantly berated me for the lack of passwords and leaving keys in the doors, but no one should have been able to get in the doors to the comms room or my office, not even her; I would let her in to work in there, but no one else is authorised to have a code to those doors. You only have because you put a sneaky back door in the system."

"Yet, you brought me back here, knowing there was the possibility of it, with all the times I had done things to upset your planning, why on earth would you leave the keys to the potential kingdom you are planning, lying around?"

"BECAUSE IT SHOULDN'T HAVE BEEN POSSIBLE!!"

Poor Norbert looked like he was going to explode, so he continued to poke at him.

"Although you are an overconfident, arrogant, psychotic megalomaniac with delusions of adequacy, I really kind of wish I hadn't found your personal server, after reading some of this outline of yours, I feel like I need my mind bleached clean. You are, without a shadow of a doubt the biggest lunatic going, and it appears that you want to take over the running of the asylum."

Norbert's icy voice had returned, and the volume was back down to normal,

"The bleaching of the mind can be arranged you know, we could do that, whip out your current silicon chip and put another one into you in the hope that one can actually control you."

"Have you got enough of the chips to go around? It looks like there may be a shortage in supply soon from what I've read in this frankly terrifying document."

"Yes, there are lots available, you don't need to worry about that, as I am sure you can see, planning is not an area that I am lacking in, we have been producing these chips for five years, upgrading as the technology has improved, there are enough for every man, woman and child on the planet."

"It is true Norbert; I don't think that anyone could possibly say that you lack in planning. Morals, ethics, humanity, may be a different matter entirely; as they might just be areas that you do struggle in though."

"I suppose some might see it like that, there are always sceptics to any great plan, however, it has to be said that when I was outlining what we are aiming for here, the rest of your fellow subjects didn't seem to be as judgemental as you are."

"Yes, but I bet your little pep talk this afternoon didn't give too many details of the final outcomes of your plans, did it? It's hard to be too judgemental when you haven't given them the full horrifying story of what you are really doing here, only giving them the sanitised version of the plan that you wanted them to hear."

"I have told them enough for them to be interested and willing to be a part of the way forward."

"I take it that you missed out on telling them about all the people that will be killed? How about the wall-to-wall brainwashing, did that make the sanitised version; what about the general stamping out of freedom of thought and deed, how could they have missed that part of it all? What about the crushing of businesses, some of which these poor unfortunate saps are currently employed by?"

"They don't need to know the full details of all of that at this moment in time, and nor did you for that matter. However even if you do now know, it doesn't matter in my grand scheme of things, you can't get off this island, and there are no unsecured communications off the island that you can use to get help."

He looked at Norbert and tried not to look surprised. Could Norbert seriously not know about the internet connection? He had been stood at Norbert's personal server, and had left the door wide open, he had printed off documents from it, it was the same server to which Norbert's own computer must be attached, and Norbert didn't seem aware that if he could use the internet and send e-mails from his computer, then why wouldn't someone else be able to do that using the server? Did he not understand how the network worked?

Perhaps this was another thing that Norbert was overconfident about? Something that Norbert's arrogance wouldn't let him see was a mistake. It didn't make any sense to him, that with all the meticulous planning, there were these big gaping holes that he was able to jump through with ease. Did Norbert still not really understand how computers talked to each other? And if not, why the hell hadn't his systems engineer not told him? Was that the cause of one of the arguments between them, and part of the reason she had quit on him.

Or was it that Norbert still thought that he was programmed to such an extent as to not be a threat when faced with all that was going on, and that he couldn't work out a way to get messages to the outside world? If so, then Norbert really was on the edge of lunacy.

Oblivious to the thoughts going through his own mind, Norbert continued speaking,

"I am however going to need to find some more secure quarters for you. I have had more than enough of you wandering around this complex willy-nilly, accessing wherever and whatever seems to take your fancy whenever you want to. Sitting in my chair like you own the place instead of me. Once you are in such secure quarters, you will stay put until I've decided what to do with you, and whether you can still be a part of my operation."

He sighed at what he was hearing, he really had had enough of this utter lunatic now, and was going to put him straight on that.

"I think Norbert old chap, that you have completely lost the plot. I don't know what caused you to lose it like this, or whether you ever really had it, but I can assure you that you are not putting me anywhere. In fact, I'm going to put an end to your lunacy here and now."

"And just how do you intend to do that then, bore me to death with a never-ending stream of insults?" Asked an amused Norbert.

Norbert's amusement was to be short-lived.

He reached around into the small of his back and retrieved the gun he had there. He made a show of removing the safety, and pointed it at Norbert.

"With this, you complete fruitcake."

Chapter 68

Norbert could not believe what had just happened in front of his eyes. Subject nineteen had managed to acquire a third gun on the plane after all, it shouldn't have been possible to get one, yet nineteen had picked up two and that silly Irish cow had given him a third. He had been way too over-confident in the implants and brain washing that he had submitted the subjects to. The other twenty-three had fallen in line perfectly, yet despite everything this one subject had managed to override everything that had been put into him, and was sat in his own chair in front of him pointing a gun in his face with a stupid smile on his face.

If subject nineteen shot him, it would be all over, the whole plan would be destroyed, and his dreams of ultimate power and immortality would disappear with a single gunshot. He had no way of raising an alarm, he had felt safe in his own private office, knowing no-one could get in here due to the security features, yet here was the man that had designed the damned security features, he had gotten into his office through a figurative back door, and was now staring at him with a white-hot fury in his eyes. There was no panic button, no way of shouting out through the soundproofed doors, no way of getting to a phone unnoticed. He was trapped by his own arrogance.

There wasn't any doubt that subject nineteen would pull the trigger, Norbert's only hope was to appeal to the man, explain why it would be a mistake to kill him, how killing him would kill so many others if he pulled the trigger.

Even if he told him everything, would nineteen believe a word of what he said, especially now that he knew all the other plans that Norbert had pulled together for the future.

There was only one way to find out, he would have to try.

Chapter 69

To him it seemed that Norbert had lost some of his usual composure briefly, but when Norbert spoke again, it was with his normal conviction that he was the only person on planet that mattered.

"Once again it would appear that I have underestimated you and the lack of control your implant and conditioning have on you, your sarcasm worked quite well on me earlier, I should have had your room thoroughly searched, yet another oversight on my part it would seem where you are concerned, and the last one as far as my dealing with you I am afraid. Despite what you may think, once again, I have control here. You can't kill me."

He looked at Norbert with a growing sense of incredulity,

"Would you like to take bets on that last statement? Granted, I'm not a trained marksman, but I am a reasonable shot, and from this distance I doubt that I could miss putting a bullet through your diseased little brain."

Norbert chuckled as he replied,

"Dear number nineteen, you misunderstand me once again, you could physically kill me, and yes you could put a bullet through my "diseased little brain" as you so eloquently put it, but doing so would only mean your death and the death of everyone on this island."

He rolled his eyes at this, tired of Norbert's rhetoric, and now annoyed at the fact that Norbert had referred to him as a number, depersonalising him even more than he had previously.

"Yeah, yeah, of course it would you arrogant psychopath, a thousand little ninjas would suddenly appear out of thin air and karate chop us all to death I suppose."

The ice voice was back as Norbert replied,

"You may well think you are being a funny man, which despite what you many believe, you most certainly are not, but do you see this little box?"

Norbert indicated a little electronic gizmo that looked like a pager hanging on his belt. Unable to stop the sarcasm in the response, he replied with a broad smile on his face.

"Yes, congratulations, you've got a pager, a quaint little artefact that has died out in most of the world in this century, unless of course you want to deal drugs, is this something that you can use to page your little ninjas as you are dying perhaps? Is it pre-programmed with the ninjas' number? Something like 1-800-NINJASNOW perhaps?"

Norbert's face was now a lovely puce colour, he really did look like he was losing it as he shouted out.

"ENOUGH WITH THE BLOODY NINJAS!!"

He laughed, he was enjoying getting under Norbert's skin, and the volume decreased as Norbert continued speaking.

"This isn't a god damn pager, as I'm quite sure you realise you annoying excuse for a man. This little gizmo is there to monitor my heartbeat. If my heartbeat stops for more than five minutes, this device will trigger the self-destruction mechanism for this island. Once it has been triggered, a series of explosions will destroy every part of this complex. There is enough explosive embedded on this island to register the blast on the Richter scale. What is left will vanish into the Atlantic Ocean never to be seen again."

"However, with me never being one to do things by half, added to this box of tricks is another little transmitter of destruction. When the blasts are going off, there will be a signal dispatched which will send a final deadly burst to all the implants in the subjects, you included, which will at the very least will fry their little brains or, as is more likely the case blow their heads off."

He laughed at this latest little snippet, despite the horrific sound of what was being described, he couldn't help himself and replied,

"You know what, you really are totally mad! Absolutely stark raving bonkers! I think you've been reading far too many Dean Koontz books for your health, and that this is all of this is complete and utter babbling bullshit. We should be calling for the men in the white coats to come and take you away to a nice little padded cell."

Norbert still wore a worried look, but his voice didn't waver,

"I assure you that it certainly is not an idle threat, if you kill me, you kill everyone on this island, the other twenty three subjects, Michaela, all of the staff, there are more than two hundred people on this island, and by shooting me you will kill them all, you will be one of the biggest mass murderers in history, and you will have also committed suicide. You can't win!"

"A nice, impassioned speech, worthy of being the last words of a megalomaniac, in your head you may well believe what you have said, but I don't. Either way though, we'll soon see, won't we?"

He said as he made a show of re-raising the gun and putting his finger on the trigger.

Chapter 70

"Don't pull that trigger, I'm deadly serious, there will be terrible implications."

Though the confidence in Norbert's voice seemed to be on the wane.

"I really don't care, I've had enough, I want to go home, I'm sick of all this shit, I'm sick of you, but most of all, you are a total and utter raving psychopath, and you need to be stopped."

"NOOoooooo,"

Was the last word Norbert would speak, as he was shot right between the eyes. Norbert stood there for a second with the most surprised look on his face, before slumping in a heap on the floor.

There would be no more master plan.

He went back to the server rack to look for the disks the files for the server would be held on. He was again surprised that this server only had a single slot of its available RAID array slots in use. He flicked the catches out at either side of the single drive, and slid the unit out of its slot, unplugging all the connections from the back of it.

He didn't believe Norbert's final desperate pleas for his life, but he couldn't take the chance that Norbert might have been telling the truth. With the drive in his left hand, he headed out of Norbert's office door and into the corridor, and he headed down it, back towards the exit from the building.

As he turned the corner at the end of the corridor into the lobby area, there stood Norbert's two goons. They obviously weren't expecting him, and while they still registered shock, and stood there gormlessly, he lifted his gun that was still in his right hand and shot them both. He didn't have the time to deal with them, they certainly didn't seem the type to have the intelligence to have a logical discussion, and he certainly didn't have the size and strength to get involved with the two of them in any kind of tussle.

He got to the door only to find that he had to enter his 'back door' code and move into the keypad to get out, this must have been one of the few facilities where they had installed the full procedure on the exit as well. As he blew the kiss, the door opened. He strode briskly around the side of the building heading for the runway, and he nearly walked straight into Keera's lookalike.

Before he could fully ignore her and walk past, she stood in front of him and asked,

"Where are you going?"

He definitely wasn't in the mood for a conversation with her.

"What's that to you? Surely your little assignment on me is over now. Haven't you got someone else you need to go and betray?"

The woman got a hurt look upon her face. "There's no need to be like that with me."

He couldn't believe she could be hurt by the truth so easily; did she believe she was the injured party here?

"Yes, there is. There's every need to be like that you little money grabbing, backstabbing, piece of shit. I hope your boss paid you upfront, because you won't be getting any more money off him now."

Still looking hurt she replied sullenly.

"I didn't just do it for the money; it was an opportunity of a lifetime to play an acting part."

As she was talking the look on her face changed from hurt to puzzled, there was a pause before she continued as she registered what he had said,

"Hold on, what do you mean? What have you done?"

She sounded concerned. He wasn't and almost gleefully responded.

"Norbert, I shot him, right between the eyes, he was a total maniac. He's now a totally dead maniac, and his two goons are now two totally dead goons as well. Considering which side you are on, you're lucky that you're not already dead conspirator number four."

There was a panicked look in her eyes,

"You did what? Oh my god, shit, we've got to get out of here right now, this place is going to blow sky high any minute."

He eyed her suspiciously; he still didn't believe a word she said.

"Do you honestly believe that utter crock? Not that it matters to me whether you do or not, I'm getting out of here right now, what you do is no concern of mine."

And he moved around her and started walking again. She shouted to him as he did.

"Please, take me with you."

He stopped and turned saying, "What?" He was amazed, that she would even consider asking such a thing,

"Why on God's green Earth would I want to do something that stupid? Do I look like I'm a mentally retarded monkey and you're my care worker?"

There was desperation in her voice, "Please, you can't leave me here."

He was having none of it, "Not only can I, but I intend to."

Another pleading effort came out of her "Please, only until we get off this island."

He thought briefly, before surprising himself with a response,

"Have you got a pen and paper on you?"

"What?" Came her puzzled reply.

"A pen and paper, do you have them? One for writing and the other for writing on. If you don't have them then you are about as much use to me as a chocolate teapot, and you'll be going absolutely nowhere."

With almost a sense of relief she replied, "Hold on let me have a look."

She opened the bag she was carrying and after a couple of seconds she had found a piece of paper, and passed it over to him.

"Here, I not sure that I have a pen though."

Impatiently he snapped back at her, "Anything else that can be used to write with? Eyeliner possibly? Lipstick even? Paper isn't much use to me without something to write on, is it?"

He was annoyed with himself for forgetting to do what he wanted to do now before leaving Norbert's office where there would have been both pens and paper. She was still hunting around in her bag, before eventually replied

"Erm, Yes,"

And after another couple of seconds she produced an eyeliner pencil. He took it from her and started to write on the paper. He gave her the eyeliner back and put the paper around the handle of the server drive. With that he set off across the airstrip leaving the woman standing.

"Wait for me." She called after him.

"If you want to come, keep up," He shouted back without turning around to look at her.

They'd just about crossed the airstrip towards the hangar building when a noise caught his attention. It was faint at first, but became louder and more defined quite quickly. It was a helicopter. He looked around him, scanning the sky and finally saw where the helicopter was coming in from.

He stopped walking towards the hangar and moved back out into the airstrip and then stood and watched the helicopter coming in. He waited as it landed about a hundred yards away from him. As soon as it landed, he started to walk towards it ignoring the draft from the rotors as they slowed to a stop. Some kind of armed forces person got out of the helicopter, if he had to guess they were British, and probably Royal Navy judging by the uniform and with all the ribbons and regalia on the uniform was someone high up in the command chain. They had hopped out and they started making their way towards him. When he got in range, he held the server up and said,

"This drive will tell you everything you need to know about what has been going on here, and all the lunacy that was planned. Take the drive, and do with it what you will, just get me off this damn island."

The officer took the server drive from him, looked at it, and then back at him and after a couple of seconds there was a flicker of recognition on his face, and he started.

"Hey, I recognise you, aren't you…?"

The officer's words were cut short as the first explosion happened well away from where they were stood. Other explosions in, coming from different locations, and making their way closer to where the men stood and the helicopter was waiting, the rotors were picking up speed again, as if getting ready to get the hell out of Dodge.

The noise from the explosions and helicopter was deafening, and the ground was shaking under their feet.

Was this really the end?

Chapter 71

One day after the hijacking.

Lead story in The Times (London)

There is still no concrete news about the alleged hijacking of British Airways flight BA2729 from London Heathrow to Philadelphia International Airport yesterday morning.

A garbled message was received from the cockpit of the Boeing 757 suggesting that there were hijackers on board, but then all communication with the aircraft stopped, and the transponder stopped broadcasting its whereabouts whilst it was in Irish airspace at approximately 10:47 in the morning. The flight then disappeared from radar after turning sharply to the south over the Atlantic Ocean.

As yet no trace of the aircraft has been found. Search and rescue planes and boats have been searching for the aircraft in the North Atlantic since mid-afternoon. The search was abandoned for the night as darkness fell, and is expected to continue at first light this morning.

If this was indeed a hijacking, then there has not been any indication of who may have carried it out, or how they managed to get on board the aircraft. No organisation has claimed responsibility for the alleged hijacking if indeed that is what this is, and not a tragic accident.

British Airways has opened a special emergency contact number for anyone who may be concerned that their relatives were on board flight BA2729, 0800 800 2729.

Lead story in The Toronto Star

An internal flight from Pearson International airport, Toronto to Vancouver International airport, Air Canada flight AC185 went missing not long after take-off yesterday evening. It veered sharply away from its planned route and seemed to be heading over the Hudson Bay when contact was lost with it.

There have been rumours that the flight was hijacked, but no evidence has been found to support the rumour, and no organisation has claimed responsibility for hijacking the plane.

The Boeing 727 had recently been refurbished, and search teams are due to fly over the Hudson Bay this morning to see if any trace can be found.

This aircraft's disappearance follows hard on the heels of another missing plane, a British Airways flight from London to Philadelphia, also rumoured to have been hijacked.

It is not known at this time whether there is any connection between the two incidents, or whether it is just a coincidence that these aircraft have disappeared within hours of each other.

Air Canada have opened an emergency contact number for anyone who want to check if loved ones were on flight AC185, 1 800 185 0185.

Chapter 72

Two days after the hijacking

News story from the Reuters news service 10:03 GMT

Within minutes of each other, two missing aircraft arrived at their original planned destinations, nearly twenty hours after they had been due to land.

British Airways flight BA2729 landed at Philadelphia International airport at 03:37 Eastern Standard Time, after going missing over the North Atlantic the previous morning.

Air Canada flight AC185 landed safely at Vancouver International airport at 00:53 Pacific Standard Time, after it had gone missing over Hudson Bay the previous afternoon.

It is said that both flights had reappeared on air traffic control radar coming out of Greenland's airspace.

The passengers from both flights are currently being debriefed by local law enforcement agencies to see if there are any details that can be put together on what has happened to these flights whilst they have been missing.

Early rumours emanating from Philadelphia, which the FBI have been unwilling to comment on, are that some of the original passengers from the Air Canada flight were disembarked from the British Airways flight, meaning that the two flights must have been at the same location to enable the switch of those passengers.

More to follow.

News story from the Reuters news service 14:39 GMT

News is emerging that there are still sixty-two passengers missing from the manifests of the two aircraft that reappeared this morning. Thirty-six from the original manifest of the British Airways flight, and twenty-six from the Air Canada flight.

It is said that the two flights both touched down at Kangerlussuaq, a former US air force base on the western coast of Greenland, where some passengers were moved from the Air Canada flight to the British Airways flight.

There are reports that at least one person was shot and killed whilst on the ground at Kangerlussuaq.

US and Canadian investigators are already on site in Kangerlussuaq.

The British airways flight was said to have arrived at Philadelphia without any of its first-class passengers on board. It is not known whether these passengers were removed whilst in Kangerlussuaq.

Additionally it is not confirmed how many of the missing passengers were involved with the hijacking of the two aircraft, and how many may be considered as hostages. On-going analysis into the flight manifests are still being made by law enforcement agencies in several countries.

Chapter 73

Three days after the hijacking.

Lead Story in The Telegraph (London)

A series of massive explosions have rocked the Outer Hebrides yesterday afternoon, leaving a trail of destruction on the island used by the multinational corporation Granco as their head offices. The island of Wiay is a small island to the east of Uist on the inner side of the Outer Hebrides. The island had been bought by Granco for quarter of a million pounds back in the late nineties after being uninhabited for nearly a century. A series of development work had taken place on the island over the years, including adding accommodation, office facilities and an airstrip.

A crew from the Royal Air Force out of the RRH Benbecula base on North Uist which they share with the Ministry of Defence were first on the scene, and reporting the devastation.

Several buildings had collapsed in the wake of at least a dozen explosions at different locations on the island. The new air strip that had been built by the company had been damaged in several places, and makes landing there in anything apart from helicopters impossible at this time.

Upon searching the island the team from the RAF found over one hundred fatalities including the founder of Granco, Norbert Granville, and shares in the company dropped by over twenty per cent upon the news.

In addition to the fatalities, there are approximately another one hundred and fifty casualties with various levels of injuries. Less than a dozen people have been found unscathed, though searches will resume today to finish searching through the rubble of destroyed buildings on the island.

There is no official word on the cause of the explosions on the island. Additional investigation teams from other armed forces branches have been making their way to the island to help with on-going investigations. Offers of help from other country's law enforcement and military agencies have been rejected at this time, despite allegations from both the FBI and Interpol that they had been notified of potential problems on the island yesterday before any of the explosions had taken place.

Chapter 74

One week after the hijacking.

Header story on page five in The Philadelphia Inquirer

A week on from the hijacking of the British Airways flight from London to Philadelphia, that saw the flight arrive a day late after an unexpected stopover in Greenland, and still not all the passengers from that flight, and the Air Canada flight that was hijacked at the same time, have managed to find their way home.

It was established that eighteen passengers on each flight were flying under well-constructed aliases, from which it has been assumed that these were the hijackers of each of the flights. With one confirmed dead body found at the airport in Kangerlussuaq, this means that twenty-five passengers are still unaccounted for. With no one claiming responsibility for the hijacking, and no sign of the passengers at Kangerlussuaq or anywhere else in Greenland, it is unknown at this time what has happened to them all.

One of the missing passengers has been confirmed as being Samuel Asbury, the well-known Philadelphia resident, founder of the state-of-the-art security firm SAsec, one of the leading security firms in the world, he is one of the passengers missing from the British Airways flight from London to Philadelphia.

Samuel, 42, is the only son of the famous former local Methodist preacher and firebrand Calvin Asbury, and is also a direct descendent of Francis Asbury, one of the first Bishops of the Methodist Episcopal Church in the United States.

However, this is not the first time that Samuel has disappeared; he went missing for three weeks in early 2012, which caused a deal of issues for his company at the time, and the reasons for his disappearance then have never been satisfactorily explained. It had been suggested that he had gone on a drinking spree, and that he had received censures from the Philadelphia PD and the FBI over the missing person's reports that were raised at the time, especially as there was no trace of him appearing on custom's records as being back in the country from his trip to London at that point.

Furthermore, prior to setting up SAsec he had become a recluse for several months, leaving his programming job with Trebling Software on the death of his Fiancée, before reappearing a lot later in the year to set up his new company.

Whilst he is missing, the leadership of his company is in flux once again, they are in the middle of several large contracts, and Samuel had been flying back from the UK after finishing a series of negotiations with the BBC for a contract to run their physical and cyber security for a ten-year period. His disappearance may yet scupper that potential contract amongst others.

No one at SAsec has been available for comment in the wake of Samuel's latest disappearance, though at least this time around there is no doubting what has happened, but still mystery abounds over his and the other twenty-four missing passengers' whereabouts sine they left their planes in Kangerlussuaq a week ago.

Chapter 75

Twelve months after the explosion.

<u>Lead Editorial in the Financial Times (London)</u>

It's a year to the day since the terrible murder of Norbert Granville, the enigmatic founder of the multi-national, all-encompassing corporation, Granco, and the bombing and destruction of its head offices in the Outer Hebrides by a competitor's security forces, and what a year it has been for them. It had looked initially as if the company might flounder without the charismatic leadership of its now deceased founder, but as soon as it became known that the former government minister William Duncan would be taking up the CEO role, in what was then a surprise move to the markets, from his post as Home Secretary, the company has gone from strength to strength through the year.

In what has been a historically disastrous year across the board for thousands of well-known companies in most market segments, Granco has not only survived the abrupt drop off in sales felt by those other companies, but it had bucked the trend and it has seen its own sales rocket across all its brands in all markets. It is now undoubtedly the biggest single company in the world, and has been taking over the failed shells of companies that have hit the skids during the year.

Some cynics have suggested the British Government has been involved in the downfall of many of the affected companies here in the UK, in order to help one its former senior ministers. It is true that they haven't done a great deal to help stop the decline of Granco's competitors, but that alone can't explain the similar pattern seen in so many other countries' markets around the globe. The growth of Granco this year really is an unprecedented success story, especially given the situation the company would have found themselves in at this time last year.

They are also now expanding into markets where they had had no business interests prior to the last six months, each of the areas it touches seems to flourish and grow for them, despite other players in the same arena failing to break even in the difficult market conditions that abound. Granco really does seem to have the Midas touch.

In the last few weeks they have announced the take-over of three utility companies in the UK, an electricity distribution network in Wales, and two of the major water companies, Thames Water, and Southern Water, the latter two with the intention of merging them and therefore bringing single billing to an area of the country that had been paying separate bills for supply and waste for years. It is rumoured that they have also been looking into the possibility of taking over United Utilities and Seven Trent Water, though it will be interesting how that would ever manage to get through the Monopolies Commission, without some Government intervention, which really would put the cat amongst the pigeons.

However as it stands at this moment in time, as far as Granco is concerned, there really must be something in the water.

Chapter 76

Fifteen months after the explosion

Official memo from the United Nations Security Council

With the overthrow of its government in the last week, and bitter civil war and infighting across all its provinces, China has now been declared a no-go zone to the outside world, and has now been removed from its seat upon the UN Security Council permanent members. Rumours persist that North Korea has invaded the northeast of the country and that they now control the Heilongjiang province, having set up troops and a governor in Harbin.

This follows on from a similar expansion by the North Koreans in to the Primorsky Krai region of Russia, annexing Vladivostok, and cutting off supply routes from the Pacific Ocean to Western Russia, again taking advantage of the civil war and unrest following the assassination of Vladimir Putin six months ago.

In fact it has been an unprecedented time of global unrest; China is the fourth of the original five permanent members of the Security Council to have been removed in the last six months, following similar worrying incidents in Russia, France, and the United States. As it stands this leaves the UK as the only permanent member of the Security Council, and with so many changes in the non-permanent members of the council with the almost weekly changes in governments in most of the world's countries, it effectively leaves the UK in charge of the UN Security Council.

An emergency meeting of the council has been called for tomorrow to discuss what sanctions can be taken against North Korea, as they continue with their scorched earth drive across the demilitarized zone between itself and its neighbour South Korea, ridding the area of all land mines by deliberately blowing them up. The South Koreans have asked for something to be done in the wake of these events, with the removal of all US troops to help with the issues back at home, they are left feeling vulnerable and open to attack, especially with their northern neighbours expanding into both Russia and China, in moves that would have been unthinkable less than a year ago.

Nominations from both Germany and Japan have been put forward to join the permanent council due to the exceptional circumstances, something that will need putting before the whole United Nations conference later in the month given their status at the set up on the United Nations in the aftermath of the Second World War.

It is felt that of all the member nations they are the only ones currently stable enough to take on the role, and who could not be seen to being influenced by the UK as some of the other countries whose names have been mentioned, with Australia, Canada and New Zealand all felt to be compromised by their membership of the Commonwealth. Brazil withdrew their application after several dams in the Amazon basin were blown up in the last six weeks and skirmishes with Argentina escalated.

It is wondered whether the United Nations security forces can carry on at all, with so many of the nations that supply troops to the UN having civil unrest in their own countries, or minor skirmishes with neighbours, the neutrality of the UN forces is being questioned, and the disbanding of the UN security force may yet find its way onto the agenda for the UN conference.

These are troubling times for the UN.

Chapter 77

Eighteen months after the explosion.

Segregation Unit – HMP Shotts

The man sat in the corner of the canteen. No one came anywhere near him. No one knew his proper name, it wasn't written anywhere on any of the prison records, just the initials SA were on the outside of his cell. The other inmates just referred to him as "Sir American", the only repeatable name that they could put together that went with the initials on his cell. The other prisoners had a whole host of other names for the man that weren't anywhere near as complimentary.

The man didn't look at anyone else in the room; he just stared at the tray of food in front of him, trying to piece together the fragments of his fractured memories. He had very little recollection of his life before being in this prison, any that he did have were blurry, as if someone had tried to wipe them out, but had ended up smudging them, like a painting left out in the rain.

The people in charge here at the prison had told him that he had murdered three men, shooting each of them in the head from close range in cold blood. In addition he had also been found guilty on the involuntary manslaughter of another hundred men and women on the basis of reckless endangerment. He had been given several life sentences for all of that, and that was why he was here in prison. Despite all these charges, he couldn't remember sitting in any courtroom, or having any trial about any of the things that they said he had done, in fact the first clear memory that he could remember properly was waking up in his cell, screaming like a banshee, having had a vivid nightmare.

He had been strapped to a white padded table, with bright white light all around him, flooding the room he was in. There were numerous other people in the room with him, and they all looked like they were strapped to tables as well, giving the impression they were floating in the middle of the air, as if floating in a sea of white. There didn't appear to be any single source for the blinding light that surrounded him, it just seemed to explode out of every surface. It was painfully bright, meaning he spent most of the time with his eyes tightly shut, trying to keep the light out of his head. Stopping the brightness invading his brain like millions of tiny daggers, stabbing persistently away into his consciousness.

He briefly opened his eyes and a small man with glasses was stood over him, looking intently at him, seemingly impervious to the bright light that had been driving him insane. He was sure he recognised this man, but he didn't know where from, and couldn't think of a name for him. The man didn't look happy, he had a gun in his hand, and he was waving it around whilst shouting and gesticulating wildly. The man was blaming him for ruining everything, and saying that he would pay. Then without warning or ceremony, the man had put the gun to his temple and pulled the trigger.

He had woken from the dream, screaming at his fate, and feeling a burning pain in the back of his skull. It had faded away within a couple of minutes, and it felt then like he was missing some part of himself; felt like he was missing the spark that would make him remember who he was again.

He had the dream on a regular basis, numerous times since waking up that first time, but he didn't know how long he had been here in this prison. Every time he woke up from the dream the burning pain returned, and he couldn't do anything to prevent it, the prison doctor had done some tests, but hadn't found anything wrong with him, or nothing they could do anything about; they couldn't explain why he couldn't remember anything properly. On the plus side, he didn't wake up screaming anymore, it was more like a large gasp of air, and a little bit of mewling.

He had received visitors that he didn't know or just didn't recognise on a regular basis, to him it appeared that they were always different people, yet all the visitors asked him the same set of questions. They may well have been the same people, but he couldn't remember them from any previous visit, so he was sure that they were all different. Since he had woken up in this prison, he could remember the things that happened to him. It was just all the stuff in his life from before that point that he struggled with.

Something about the questions he was repeatedly asked seemed a bit strange to him, there was the phrasing of the questions, and some of the unusual words that the visitors used in them, but his mind wouldn't work properly to tell him what he was missing; what it all meant. All his visitors had that air about them; the one in which they knew a great deal more about him than he knew about himself at this point in time. He wondered if the unusual words and strange questions were there to see if they got a reaction, perhaps they were testing to see if he remembered what they were going on about. He didn't know whether it was a good or bad thing that he didn't know, wondering that if it ever did come to him would it lead to him exiting in a nice set of civilian clothes, or a suit and a box.

There had been several points in time where he had felt he almost had a recall of his life before, a single word – Granco – had come to mind several times, but it didn't seem like a real word to him. He had no access to any way of looking for the word either. There appeared to be no communication mediums in this part of the prison available to him, and a severe lack of books. Other prisoners had access to the outside world, televisions, or radios; some even had phones even though they were supposed to be banned. None of the other prisoners would let him near any of that though, everyone kept away from him, and made sure he stayed away from them. He had been on the end of a few beatings, and had given up trying after a few months.

He had thought about asking one of his visitors if the word "Granco" meant anything to them, but every time he was about to say the word, something else inside him had told him that these random visitors couldn't be trusted with the word. He would have to find out a way to get the meaning of it himself. He didn't know how he was going to manage it, but something told him he had beaten odds similar to this before.

The other inmates steered clear of him as much as they could, as did the warders, so he couldn't ask any of them about the outside world. He often tried to sit and listen to conversations between the inmates, hoping that something they would say would cause him to remember, give him a jolt to get his old self back, but nothing did. He had heard snippets of conversations that he didn't understand, things that he couldn't make out properly, conversations about wars, falling governments, civil unrest, and uprisings.

All of this had made it more difficult for him to feel like getting back to normal. These little snippets of information rang bells, he was sure he had read about this, but when and where escaped him. Was it in a book, was it a piece of fiction he had encountered during his life, something that others here may have read, or was it a mixture of news stories he had seen over the years, somehow now all concertinaed together in his head? Everything was so hazy and dark in there; he just couldn't clear the haze.

Another word kept entering his mind – Keera – he didn't know who she was, well he assumed that Keera was a she, and he didn't know why the name kept coming to him, but whenever it did, a smile came to his face anyway, he felt happy at the thought of the name, perhaps she knew him, maybe he had known her before all of this, perhaps one day she would turn up here, turn up and take him away from this grim solitary existence.

To bring back his memories.

To take him back to the lights.

How the book came to be written

Having not considered myself a writer, in 2016 I had a few Drabbles published on a website, and that encouraged me to have a look at some e-mails I'd done back in 2002-2004. I hadn't realised how much I wrote back then when I lived in Manchester, I was in too much of an alcoholic haze at the time to know just how much I had done.

During those early noughties years I sent out a collated e-mail to an ever-increasing number of people. I suppose it would get called an e-zine or something similar nowadays. Initially I was doing a random short story / flash fiction piece (without knowing that's what I was doing) in each issue. Only to start to do one for about the fifth or sixth issue and realise I wasn't going to finish what I was writing in that issue. It turned out to be the first chapter of this book written (which is now chapter three).

I wouldn't do a piece of it every week, but one of my work colleagues would pester me to write the next piece, and when I knew I was going to be stopping doing the e-zine I worked to finish it off.

And then promptly forgot all about it for twelve years. Having a hundred-word story published online made me think about this work I'd done all those years before. I trawled back through all those old e-mails and pulled the 'book' together. It came to just under sixty thousand words, and there were some big holes in there. I filled in the holes and did quite a few iterations of edits, and in 2017 after some beta readers had given feedback, I put it on the Inkitt website. Where it sat for six years getting an occasional read and even more occasional feedback.

At the start of this year I decided to withdraw it from Inkitt and self-publish it, and here it is. A twenty-two-year journey from starting to write the book to it being published.

About the author

Kev Neylon is a writer who lives with his partner Helen in Crawley in West Sussex. When he is not writing fiction, he is writing blog posts about his travels, or on the history of Leicester and Crawley, or match reports on the Crawley Town games he attends as a season ticket holder.

To keep up to date with what else he has published, and access to his blog and other social media channels, follow him on one or more of the below.

Website: - https://www.onetruekev.co.uk/
Twitter: - @onetruekev
Instagram: - @onetruekev
Facebook: - https://www.facebook.com/Onetruekev/
Medium: - https://onetruekev.medium.com/
LinkedIn: - https://www.linkedin.com/in/onetruekev/

Also available is his collection of drabbles;

A Drabble A Day Keeps The Psychoanalyst Away.

Get it as a paperback or eBook available on Amazon.

Printed in Great Britain
by Amazon